KNOW ME WELL

KAIT NOLAN

Know Me Well

Written and published by Kait Nolan

Copyright 2015 Kait Nolan

Cover design by Lori Jackson

AUTHOR'S NOTE: The following is a work of fiction. All people, places, and events are purely products of the author's imagination. Any resemblance to actual people, places, or events is entirely coincidental.

For Erica,
Because you said there weren't enough pharmacists
as sheroes.
P.S. You licked it, so that makes it yours.
Love,
K

Dear Reader,

This book is set in the Deep South. As such, it contains a great deal of colorful, colloquial, and occasionally grammatically incorrect language. This is a deliberate choice on my part as an author to most accurately represent the region where I have lived my entire life. This book also contains swearing and pre-marital sex between the lead couple, as those things are part of the realistic lives of characters of this generation, and of many of my readers.

If any of these things are not your cup of

tea, please consider that you may not be the right audience for this book. There are scores of other books out there that are written with you in mind. In fact, I've got a list of some of my favorite authors who write on the sweeter side on my website at https://kaitnolan.com/on-the-sweeter-side/

If you choose to stick with me, I hope you enjoy!

Happy reading!

Kait

RILEY GOWER HADN'T PLANNED on spending her anniversary surrounded by boxes of stock and empty shelves. From a business standpoint, the empty shelves were a good thing. It meant people were actually buying the products she carried, in addition to the medications kept behind the counter. In the year since she'd bought out her boss's share in Wishful Discount Drugs, that had often meant the difference between keeping the lights on and having to rob Peter to pay Paul. She was in the black—barely—and that merited celebration, albeit more of a chips and queso and margaritas at Los Pantalones variety than champagne and caviar.

Instead of celebrating, she was camped out filling shelves, well after the late summer sun had faded, because Ruby Fellowes, her cashier/stocker/order-taker/general-Jill-of-all-trades, who'd worked at the pharmacy since God was a boy, had taken off all week to help prepare for her niece's wedding. At her current rate, Riley would be lucky to eke out a half-assed celebration with the emergency bar of Toblerone in the vegetable drawer of her refrigerator before she fell into bed and passed out from sheer exhaustion.

"Happy businiversary to me," she muttered.

The butt busting was worth it, even if owning her own business felt a little more like prison than freedom at the moment. It meant she'd succeeded on her own terms, without a handout or a hand up from some man. Her success and its consequent stresses were hers and hers alone, and she couldn't put a price on the value of that.

As her phone rang out with the tones of "Crazy Train", all pleasure in her accomplishment bled away. She could ignore it, let the call go to voice mail. It might be nothing.

But long experience had her instincts tightening with dread. She knew it wasn't nothing. Bracing herself, Riley answered. "Hi Mom."

"Hey, baby." Sharilyn sounded tired, with that forced edge of cheer that made Riley's stomach curdle.

"What's wrong?"

"Wrong? Why should anything be wrong? Can't I call my only child to say hello?" She was talking too fast, too breezy, so Riley said nothing, just waited. At length, Sharilyn hiccuped and burst into tears. "Hal left me."

Riley repressed a curse and tried to find some sympathy. "I'm sorry, Mom."

Sharilyn launched into a diatribe about

everything that had gone wrong on the multi-month cross-country RV trip she'd taken with her most recent beau. By the time her mother finally wound down and got the tears under control, a tension headache had sunk claws deep into Riley's scalp.

"I really am sorry." And some part of her was. Because her mother had truly believed Hal, like all his predecessors, was The One, and she'd given herself whole-heartedly to the relationship.

"It will be all right."

The note of determination creeping into Sharilyn's voice made Riley wonder whether she already had some other guy in mind to save her this time. Or was it to be Riley herself in the role of knight to her mother's damsel in distress? Riley's own armor was pretty damned battered after all these years.

"I need a favor, sweetie."

Wary, she asked, "What?"

"I'm out here all on my own and Hal didn't leave me with *anything*."

Don't say it, Riley thought. *Don't you dare say it.*

"I need you to loan me some money."

She said it.

Riley pinched the bridge of her nose. Why was she even calling it a loan? It wasn't like she'd paid back any of the *other* loans Riley had made her over the years, when the boyfriend or husband *du jour* turned out to be a shit and not interested in dealing long-term with the damsel in distress routine her mom had perfected. Christ, Riley had taken over the bill management in junior high school, started paying the mortgage her freshman year of college.

"Just enough to get me home," Sharilyn continued.

"Mom, did you forget you sold the house?"

"Of course I didn't. But Wishful is still home."

How could it still be home when she had nowhere to live here anymore?

"I thought I could stay with you for a while."

Oh God. Riley could actually feel the blood vessels behind her eyes threatening to burst.

"There's no room at my place, Mom. I don't even have a guest room."

"I could sleep on the couch. It'd just be for a little while. Until I get back on my feet."

Until she found another sugar daddy with a savior complex. A thump sounded from above, pulling her attention.

"Riley?"

"Hang on a sec." Straining, Riley listened harder, expecting scratching or other signs that squirrels or raccoons had taken up residence in the empty second floor of the building. But what she heard were clear footsteps. Person-sized footsteps.

"Mom, I need to go."

"But what about—"

"I'll wire you money for a bus ticket home." Never mind that it was her last $300. She couldn't leave her mother stranded in Timbuktu. "Text me where you are." Riley hung up before Sharilyn could say anything else. Striding across to the light switch, she flipped it off so she could see the street outside. The empty street.

Surely anyone with legitimate business up there would be parked out front. And what legitimate business could there be? The upstairs had been vacant forever.

She dialed 911.

"911, what is your emergency?" Riley blessed the interconnected nature of small towns as she recognized the voice of the dispatcher.

"Janette, it's Riley Gower. I'm at the pharmacy after hours and there's an intruder upstairs."

"Are you alone?"

"Yes. I've been stocking."

"Are the doors locked?"

"Yes."

"Okay you stay put. I'm sending somebody as soon as I can, but it might take a little bit.

There's a pretty big domestic disturbance going on across town."

Assured someone was coming, Riley hung up and called Molly Montgomery. Her old boss still owned the building, so whatever was going on up there affected her. From behind the counter, she listened to the phone ring and watched the front windows, waiting to see one of the police cruisers along Pitts Street or a shadowy figure coming out of the alley. Nobody picked up. Riley opted not to leave a message until there was something more definitive to report. No reason to worry her unless something was really wrong.

In the silence, the ticking of the wall clock sounded almost as loud as the intermittent footsteps over her head. The intruder wasn't making any efforts to be quiet. There were no sounds of stuff being moved. Of course, there might not be any stuff to be moved.

Five minutes dragged into ten that seemed more like weeks. Still no police.

Riley was tired and edgy, and all she really wanted was to head home. But she couldn't just go with somebody up there. Somebody who was evidently in no particular hurry to leave.

Oh, for heaven's sake. This was Wishful, not the big city. Anybody looking for drugs would try to rob the pharmacy directly. It was probably kids, looking for…who knew what. Maybe some kind of love nest or a place to smoke. They'd be more scared of her than she was of them.

Riley swiped the counting spatula from behind the counter. It didn't have an edge and might have had more in common with a pie server than a knife, but in the dark, it sure as hell looked like a blade and it was better than nothing. Taking a deep breath, she stepped outside and circled around to the side of the building. Slipping cautiously through the access door, she noted that no light shone in the stairwell, but a faint glow spilled out from the partially open door at the top.

Hardly daring to breathe, Riley climbed the stairs, thanking God that the treads were concrete, instead of wood or metal that could creak. At the landing she hesitated, peering inside.

In all the years she'd worked for Molly, she'd never been up here. Hadn't ever had reason to. Like many of the buildings downtown, the second floor of the pharmacy was an apartment. Or at least it had been at some point in the distant past. In the narrow entryway, wallpaper peeled off in strips. She couldn't see past the wall to the room beyond. Everything was silent now. No footsteps. No sound of teenagers necking.

Was there another exit? Had whoever broken in managed to get out before she came upstairs?

Ignoring the voice in the back of her mind telling her to turn back around and wait for Wishful PD, Riley clutched her counting spatula tight and eased inside.

No one was in what passed for the living

room, which boasted two of the four street-facing windows. A hall branched off at the rear of the room. The only light shone out from a single open door on the wall opposite the windows. Moving as quietly as possible, Riley sneaked over to the door and looked into the room.

A hand clamped down on her shoulder.

Riley shrieked. The spatula fell to the floor as she reached across her body to grip his wrist, acting on long ago training as she tugged her assailant forward, jamming her elbow back into his ribcage, as she ducked and pivoted to twist his arm behind his back. Except that he countered, moving with her, doing something to shift the balance, until it was her arm twisting, her body crumpling.

Terror whitewashed her mind. She lashed out, no finesse, no technique, striking whatever she could reach. Her assailant let out an *ooph* and wrapped her in a bear hug, pinning her arms. She couldn't suck in enough breath to scream again.

"Hey, hey! It's okay! Riley, stop. It's okay. It's me! It's Liam."

Liam Montgomery. Her one time savior.

Because he meant safety, she let out a sob of relief.

His arms loosened, shifting her to face him, and she couldn't fight because her legs had turned to noodles and every atom in her body wanted to turn into him and hang on.

"It's okay. I've gotcha."

Except he didn't. He hadn't. Not for twelve years.

She stood on her own now.

Straightening, Riley pushed at the wall of his chest. "Let me go."

"Just take a minute to catch your breath."

How the hell was she supposed to catch her breath when he was *right there*, in all of his big, badass Marine glory? Her heart renewed its frenetic thumping for entirely different, wholly unwelcome reasons. She shoved at him again before she could do something *really* stupid, like fist her hands in his shirt and drag his mouth to hers to put all this adrenaline to better use.

"Let me go, Liam."

LIAM COULD STILL FEEL Riley shaking. His instincts shouted to soothe and protect, and he was becoming very aware that the woman in his arms was a long damn way from the girl he remembered. He'd known that, objectively. But seeing with his eyes was a helluva lot different from feeling with his body. Now he knew just how well those exquisite curves of hers fit against all the hard lines of him. And damn him, he liked it.

She shoved again. Liam wasn't sure her legs would hold her yet, but because he wasn't positive she wouldn't try to slug him again, he released her.

She stumbled, throwing up a hand in the universal *stop* gesture, even as he stepped forward, reaching out to steady her. Because, of course, she'd rather struggle than take help from him. And he'd earned that.

Liam curled his hands into fists to keep from touching her.

Riley let out a shaky breath and straightened. Whatever momentary softening had been brought on by fear was gone. "Jesus Christ, you about gave me a heart attack. What are you *doing* here?"

Clearly continuing to fuck things up with you.

He eyed her still clenched hands and tapped the tape clipped to his belt. "Measuring."

"For *what?*"

"Mom's decided she wants to rent out the apartment. She wanted me to look into doing some renovations up here."

"She didn't tell me."

Liam found himself wanting to smooth away the furrow between her dark brows. Instead, he backed up a few paces to give them both some space and kicked back against the kitchen counter. "She only just decided at dinner. I ran out of projects at home, and I think she wants me out from underfoot. I'm making a floor plan."

"At ten-thirty on a weeknight?" Riley demanded.

"It's as good a time as any."

"In the *dark?*"

"Most of the light bulbs are burned out. What are you still doing here? The pharmacy closed hours ago."

"I'm *working.* Or I was, until you scared the bejeezus out of me."

"Doing what?"

"Stocking."

"What happened to Ruby?"

"Are you living under a rock? She's out helping with Vivian Buckley's wedding."

Liam dimly remembered his friend Reuben Blanchard, who owned the local boxing gym, was standing up as best man in that wedding. He knelt to pick up the counting spatula Riley had dropped. "And you were planning on doing what with this?"

She scooped a hand through her dark

brown hair and didn't quite meet his eyes. "Intimidating the intruder."

Liam lifted a brow. She scowled back at him, an expression he'd come to expect whenever he got within ten feet of her—which wasn't often. It was a far cry from how she'd looked at him in high school.

"Good to know you still remember some of the self defense I taught you. That probably would've worked on somebody without combat training." She could do with a refresher course, but now was absolutely not the time to bring that up.

Something flickered in her eyes before she held out her hand for the spatula. "Thankfully, I haven't had cause to use it until tonight."

"Glad to hear it." He'd worried about that after he'd enlisted. Not that she'd have believed it, and not that she'd given him opportunity to say so in the last twelve years.

"I'll go ahead and warn you, the police are on their way."

"Sensible to have called them. Why didn't you wait for them?"

"Good question." This came from the open doorway.

Of course the responding officer would be Judd. Because the best friend who'd had Liam's back since fifth grade was going to walk into this situation and know something was up. *Shit.*

Judd stepped inside, thumbs hooked in his utility belt. He nodded a greeting to Liam before pegging Riley with a gimlet stare. "I know Janette told you to stay put."

"I thought it was just kids," she protested.

"Was that before or after you called 911?"

Her shoulders stiffened. "If he had been a burglar, he could've trashed the place and been gone before you ever got here."

"And you could've been hurt or worse," Liam pointed out. "You know better."

Her blue eyes narrowed to slits. "I'm not a child anymore, Liam, and you are not my keeper. Judd, I'm sorry to have wasted your time. As it's not actually an emergency, I'm going home. It's been an exceptionally long day. If there's nothing further?"

"Just a warning. Next time you have to call on the police, wait for us to do our jobs instead of charging in blind. You might not be so lucky as to have one of the good guys on the other side of the door."

Riley shot a glance at Liam that clearly questioned whether he fit into that category. "Understood. Thanks for coming. Goodnight." She strode by him with an aloof grace worthy of any silver screen diva and slammed the door behind her.

Judd raised a brow.

Liam shook his head. "Sweet. She used to be sweet."

"She still is—to everybody else. What's up with that? I thought you were supposed to be charming with the ladies."

"Obviously not that one." It was exactly his luck that the closest he'd managed to get to Riley Gower since he came home was by nearly scaring her to death. It made repaying his debt damned hard.

Judd radioed the all clear to dispatch. "What was that about you teaching her self defense?"

That was a secret he'd told no one, and Liam didn't plan to start now. Not even with one of his oldest friends.

"There was a time once when she needed it." A time when she'd needed a helluva lot more than that. "It was a long time ago."

Judd waited with that expectant cop stare he was as likely to use on the job as over the poker table, but Liam didn't volunteer anything else.

"I know something about putting your ass on the line for somebody who can't defend themselves. It's hard to let go of the sense of responsibility you feel for that person."

Because that hit uncomfortably close to the truth, Liam shrugged. "As she said, I'm not her keeper."

"You lookin' to be?"

"No." There were a whole lot of reasons Liam wasn't fit to be anybody's keeper. But he couldn't deny that Riley fell under the heading of unfinished business. Business that had consumed far too many of his waking—and sleeping—thoughts since he'd walked back into her world. This apartment renovation right over her head might be just the opportunity he needed to get some much needed resolution.

"Uh huh." One corner of Judd's mouth quirked. "I've got eyes to see you noticing she's not a kid and ears to hear around town that you haven't said yes to any of the assorted offers of female companionship that have come your way the last six months."

Liam wondered how long it would take him to be replaced as one of the hottest topics of local gossip. "I would have to be dead not to notice she grew up to have a rocking body, and why does my rejection of female companionship have to have anything to do with that?"

"Because you're not dead, as you pointed out."

"Man, you were at my welcome home party. My mother fully expects me to find some woman, settle down, and start giving her grandchildren. She gets a whiff of interest in anybody, she'll start pushing china patterns or some shit. This town is too small and too damned nosy—as you've just illustrated—to be anything but very careful in choosing my companionship. I haven't even settled on a permanent *job* yet. I'm sure as hell not in any position to start looking for a permanent woman. And even if I was, Riley Gower is not for me."

So why the hell couldn't he get her off his mind?

"Admittedly, she's not one of the candidates in the pool Omar's running up at Dinner Belles, but that's just because nobody's thought of it."

"And they can just keep on not thinking of it. Everybody is doomed to disappointment if they expect me to provide fodder for the gossip mill. I am not that interesting."

Judd laughed. "You keep telling yourself that, buddy boy." His radio crackled to life. He answered the dispatcher and turned for the door. "Duty calls. See you in the ring Wednesday morning?"

"I'll be there." Liam bumped his fist, watched him go.

Free of interruptions, he finished up measurements for the floor plan, made notes about which were the load bearing walls, and locked up. He circled around front, but the pharmacy was dark other than the security lights. Looked like Riley actually had gone home.

Liam didn't like the thought of her alone in the pharmacy this late at night. Defenseless. Or mostly. This was Wishful and the crime rate was low compared to the rest of the country. But she was still guardian of all kinds of controlled substances. What if somebody decided they wouldn't take no for an answer? She'd had enough experience with that kind of victimization. The memory of that had him clenching his fists.

It had been twelve years since he'd walked away from his self-appointed duty as her protector. She'd shown absolutely no indication she wanted him to resume that role, but Liam couldn't shrug off that sense of responsibility so easily. Knowing Riley wouldn't thank him for his concern, Liam made a mental note to check with his mom to make sure she'd upgraded the alarm system before she sold the business. If she had, well, it wouldn't hurt to make sure the system was still up to spec. And if she hadn't, he'd take care of it.

CHAPTER 2

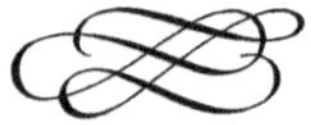

THE NUMBERS BLURRED AS Riley stared at the spreadsheet on her screen.

Should've done this last night, she thought with a jaw-cracking yawn.

That had been the plan, but everything about last night had been derailed by six feet two inches' worth of unwelcome testosterone. She'd been more rattled by contact with Liam than she had been by the near heart attack. There'd been no way she could settle down to work on quarterly taxes after that. Unfortunately, running on four hours' or less of sleep wasn't helping her get those taxes done either. Not even a trip on the Good Ship Caffeine was doing much to clear her bleary eyes.

The jangle of the shop bell drew her from the office. At the sight of Liam standing behind his mother in the open doorway, she almost ducked back inside.

You aren't a coward.

So Riley stood her ground, her hand gripping the travel mug of coffee like a lifeline. When Liam went on upstairs without coming inside, her knees went weak with relief. She sagged onto the stool behind the counter, pathetically grateful not to have to face him yet. Her nerves felt raw, and she needed more time to rebuild the walls he'd shaken so badly last night.

"Sorry I'm late." Molly shut the door and crossed to the counter.

Riley eyed the tell-tale green-and-ivory striped box in her hands. "If those are pastries from Sweet Magnolias, then all is forgiven."

"Blueberry streusel muffins."

Riley actually whimpered. She was supposed to be off sugar, but desperate times called for desperate measures. Retrieving a plastic knife from the back, she carefully cut one of the enormous muffins in half. It was all about moderation, right? Besides, her love of Carolanne Wheeler's muffins should overshadow her current discomfiture.

Molly accepted the other half. "Wynne called this morning, so I was late getting out the door."

For the first time since they'd graduated college, Riley was glad her best friend wasn't living in Wishful. Until Molly's youngest had moved off to New Orleans, she and Riley had been in each other's pockets since kindergarten. Most of the time, Riley used work to distract herself from the missing limb sensation of not having Wynne constantly around—there was always plenty of it to keep her busy. But just now, she was relieved. Wynne would absolutely cop to the fact that something was going on between her and Liam.

There couldn't be anything going on when it came to Liam. That had been decided long ago. Riley would just have to find a way to get over this—Thing. And it wasn't even a Thing. Her focusing on it was just prolonging the natural conclusion of…whatever it was. The insane attraction that had fairly knocked her on her ass at his welcome home party last December would fade in time. Exposure therapy.

A noise from upstairs had her gaze snapping to the ceiling.

"Liam. I should've called you last night to tell you I was having him do some renovations to the apartment upstairs."

He'd told her then.

"It might've saved me the heart attack I almost had when I thought he was a burglar."

Molly wrapped an arm around her shoulders and gave her a squeeze. "I'm sorry. He said he gave you quite a scare. What were you doing up here so late?"

"Some stocking. Since Ruby's out for the wedding, we're a little behind. It wasn't a big deal." She wouldn't let it be a big deal. Because it wasn't a Thing. "What motivated you to want to renovate?"

"It's been just sitting there doing nothing and Liam needed a project. The only time he doesn't seem to be restless these days is when he's building something. Plus, income from rent up there would help offset the cost of the building mortgage, and I can give you a break on the lease."

Riley had to fight the instinctive rejection of her kindness.

Molly laid a hand on her arm. "Don't fight me on this, Riley. You've been killing yourself to make this business work, and you could use a break from at least some of the responsibility. You have a habit of taking on more than the average person."

Having known her since she was five, Molly was in very good position to know exactly how much Riley had taken on over the years. That

Molly could and did look out for her as she did one of her own children humbled Riley, so instead of rejecting the offer out of hand, she said, "Thank you."

"You're welcome." Molly hesitated. "Have you heard from her?"

Riley didn't have to ask who "her" was. "Last night. She's in California."

The jingling of the bell again cut off that tangent of conversation Riley put on her best customer face and turned to greet Vivian Buckley, who was trailed by Ruby Fellowes. "And how are you this fine day, Viv?"

"Trying not to turn into Bridezilla, but I swear, my family is about to run me crazy."

"You's already there, baby," Ruby said.

Vivian shot her aunt a dark look. "Don't even."

Riley repressed a smile. "The wedding's next weekend, right?"

"It is. Mama's about beside herself with the details. Because, *of course,* Mama Pearl Buckley can't be satisfied with being the Goddess of Pie in this town. She can't *dare* let somebody *else* bake the wedding cake. Never mind that Carolanne's are amazing and we have a hundred and seventy five thousand other things to do between now and the wedding. Violet's on a tear because she's convinced Mama's trying to matchmake her for the reception—and who are we kidding? It's Mama, so of course she is. Omar and George are being Switzerland. And Ray and Carmen and their families don't get in until middle of next week." Vivian reached over the counter to take Riley by the wrists, a faintly crazed look in her eyes. "I'm desperate. Ruby tells me you've got a Chill The Heck Out kit for brides. Tucker says I'm not allowed to come back to the office or set foot in a courtroom until I get it, and I'm due in front of Judge Carpenter at three."

Riley said a silent prayer of thanks that she was an only child. "Deep breaths. I've got exactly what you need." She gathered up the essential oils for the Stress Away kit. "So where's

Darius during all this? Can't he take some of the heat?"

"Gettin' ready to leave for New Orleans for his bachelor party. I mean, at least he's doing it this weekend instead of right before the wedding, so he'll be recovered, but, Lord have mercy, I need all this to be over and *soon*."

"Breathe, baby girl," Ruby ordered.

"T minus a week and change to your honeymoon in Jamaica," Molly reminded her.

Riley took Vivian's hands and rubbed a few drops of the stress away oil on the undersides of her wrists, making slow circles over her pulse points. "Just focus on the finish line of those sandy beaches and lazy ocean waves. A whole week away from work, away from family, just you and your new hubby and an all-inclusive resort package."

Vivian closed her eyes and exhaled long and slow, some of the tension draining out of her shoulders. "I can do that. Vacation. Glorious vacation."

Riley continued to rub Vivian's wrists and

let the fantasy of a vacation seep into her own mind, imagined wiggling her toes in the sand and feeling salty breezes against her skin. Wouldn't that be lovely? Not that she had anyone to share it with, but at this point a vacation of any kind would be amazing.

"I feel better."

"Toldya." Ruby crossed her arms in satisfaction.

"What is this stuff?" Vivian picked up the bottle.

"It's a blend of lavender, vanilla, cedarwood, lime, and a couple of other essential oils designed to reduce your stress. Here, dab a bit more behind your ears and on the back of your neck. Like perfume."

"Smells wonderful."

"It does," Riley agreed. Deciding she could use some too, she added a few drops to the diffuser on the counter. "No side effects, no crash, no overdosing. Just use as you need."

"I'll take it! What do I owe you?"

Riley folded Vivian's hand around the bottle. "Not a thing. Consider it an early wedding present."

"Are you sure? Because this stuff is surely worth its weight in gold."

Delighted to share her passion for essential oils, Riley smiled. "Positive. Consider it a gateway oil. Come see me when you get back and I can introduce you to all the other zillions of things you can do with them."

"Deal."

"Come on, baby girl. We got an appointment with that florist in Lawley." Ruby began herding her niece out the door.

"Good luck, Viv," Riley called.

"See you after the wedding, Ruby," Molly added.

Ruby waved and shut the door behind them.

Riley picked her coffee back up, watching the two women disappear from view. "That. That right there is why some people should just elope."

"Is that what you'd do?" Molly asked.

Shrugging, Riley took her stool again.

"Would depend on the guy, I guess. It's what my parents did. But as I've already married the business, it's a moot point. Anyway, I think the oils will help her if she'll use them."

"I'd say that's been a great sideline you've added."

"If somebody likes one, they usually come back for more."

The bell rang again as their pharmacy tech, Jessie Applewhite, strolled in. "I come bearing mail."

"Early for that," Riley noted.

"I ran into Otis as I was crossing the green. He passed it off."

"I'll trade you for a muffin." She nudged the box toward Jessie.

Jessie handed over the bills—because what else would they ever get here at the business?—and pounced on the baked goods. As more customers came in, Riley passed that duty off to Molly and retreated into the office to see what the damage was.

She did the math, feeling anxiety creep up as

she compared the total of the bills and the balance of the business account. Payroll was due next week. She checked the due dates on the bills and started figuring how well she could manage her personal accounts to take a pay cut so everyone else could get paid in-full and on-time.

Molly stuck her head into the office. "Everything good?"

Riley offered a sunny smile as she shoved the bills into a drawer and closed the balance sheet on the computer. "Everything's just fine."

LIAM'S FIST connected with Judd's chin. The impact sang all the way up his arm. He checked his instinct to immediately press the advantage, hesitating long enough for his friend to stumble back toward the ropes and shake off the blow. A friendly sparring match wasn't the battlefield he'd lived on for more than a decade. This was all about exercise. And a little bit of payback for his torture about Riley.

From outside the ring, Reuben Blanchard shouted, "Keep your hands *up*, Hamilton! Montgomery's a sneaky son of a bitch. You've gotta protect your head."

Judd had barely reset his stance and lifted his gloved hands when Liam lunged forward, driving him back. Judd bounced off the ropes and ducked under Liam's jab, but not before catching a second body shot to the ribs.

"Break!" Reuben shouted.

Liam tugged off a glove and spit out his mouth guard. "What is up with you, man? Your head is not in the ring."

Judd slid down to a stool in the corner. "Lot on my mind. They finally opened the search for the new Chief of Police."

"Yeah?" Liam tugged off his other glove. "Bet Chief Curry's happy about that. Didn't he announce he was ready to retire back in January?"

"Yep. I'm gonna throw my hat in."

Reuben climbed through the ropes and

handed both of them bottles of water. "You got much competition?"

"Locally, no. But they're opening it up to a nationwide search. I don't know how much of a shot I've got. They'll probably go with somebody older, more experienced. But pulling somebody in from outside…no guarantee they'll stay for the long haul. So that's in my favor. We'll see."

Liam envied him. It might be a long shot, but at least Judd had a vision for his future, for what he wanted to do with his life. That was more than Liam himself had managed since he left the Marines.

"Good for you, man. I'll be rooting for you."

Judd offered his fist. "Hey, if I get it, that'll leave a hole open in the department. You could always trade your desert camo for blue. You'd make a helluva cop."

Reuben snorted. "SWAT maybe. Not local PD."

Liam bumped the offered fist. "He's right. I'd be bored out of my mind. Rematch soon?"

"You know it. And next time you won't get in so many lucky shots."

"Lucky my ass."

Judd grinned. "See y'all at poker night."

"We look forward to taking your money," Reuben assured him.

As Judd disappeared into the locker room, Liam climbed out of the ring. He considered putting in some time on the speed bag to get his heart rate up.

"I'll go a few rounds if you want," Reuben offered. "Or listen. Either way, somethin's gnawing at you."

"Not sure either would actually help."

"You sleepin'?"

"Mostly." He hadn't been afflicted by the night terrors and flashbacks that plagued many of his comrades. "Can't shake the habit of rising at zero dark thirty."

"That's not what has you in here every morning. Or not all of it."

Liam stuffed his gloves into his gym bag.

"How long did it take you to settle in to civilian life when you got out?"

"Didn't settle until I started up this place." A former Navy SEAL, Reuben had returned to Wishful five years earlier and opened the boxing gym. "But I knew exactly what I wanted when I got out. Your situation's a little different."

"Yeah."

Liam had enlisted in the Marines the summer after graduating high school and never looked back. If not for his father's unexpected death, he would've been a lifer. But as the eldest, with both his brothers deployed and his baby sister moved off to New Orleans, Liam couldn't see leaving his mother alone. So he'd come home.

Never mind the fact that Molly Montgomery could've given any Brigadier General a run for his money.

He'd been going slowly crazy ever since.

"You ran out of projects at your mama's,

didn't you?" A knowing smile creased Reuben's dark face.

"Cleaned out the garage, the attic, repainted the house, replaced the gutters, and wiped out her *entire* honey-do list going back to everything Dad had been meanin' to get around to for the last five years."

"Damn, son. We gotta find you a proper job."

"Been lookin' since I got back, but I haven't found anything that would be more than just killin' time. I just can't figure out what I want to *do.* Meanwhile, Mom's decided she wants to rent out that apartment above the pharmacy, so I'm digging in to start demolition on that this week." He checked his watch. "I probably ought to get on myself. If I can get some of the noisy work done before start of business, Mom and Riley would probably appreciate it."

The sun had just cleared the horizon when Liam caught sight of a familiar POS Honda parked on the shoulder, with an even more familiar set of full-figured curves peeking out from beneath the lifted hood. He pulled his

Dad's pristine '69 Mustang onto the opposite side and stepped out, appreciating the view.

Her voice floated back to him from where she leaned over the engine. "Now Jo, I know you're tired, girl, but this is not okay. I need you to pull yourself together."

"Who you talkin' to, Riley?"

She jolted, banging her head on the hood. "Son of a monkey!"

Liam wisely swallowed down his amusement as she swung around, eyes shooting daggers.

"Where do you get off sneaking up on people?" She didn't wait for an answer. "What are you even doing here?"

"On my way home from the gym. As nice a scenic stretch as this is, I didn't figure you'd be on the side of the road having a heart-to-heart with your car at this hour just for the hell of it."

"How would you know? I might. Jo and I have had a long and meaningful friendship."

Given his dad had been working on her car since she got it at sixteen, Liam knew this to be true. The bigger shock was that the thing still ran at all.

He ducked under the hood himself to take a look, aware of Riley edging back. "Did you check your gas gauge?"

"I didn't run out of gas. It's not my battery or my spark plug wires. Your daddy taught me that much."

He ignored the affronted tone. "Doesn't ever hurt to start with the basics. What was she doing?"

Riley said nothing.

Glancing over his shoulder, Liam found her glaring at him, arms crossed, every inch shouting *irritated female.* The fact that he found it attractive rather than off-putting either made him a perverse bastard or was evidence of the incredibly long dry spell he hadn't broken since he came home.

"I didn't ask for you to come rescue me."

No, Riley Gower didn't ask for help. Ever. Even when she needed it.

"Would you be this ornery at an offer of

help from anybody, or is it me in particular you object to?"

She dropped her arms, face momentarily stricken. "I don't object to you."

He didn't know what made him push rather than leaving it alone. "Really? Because your default attitude toward me since I got home has been dialed pretty much consistently to pissed off."

Riley closed her eyes, and he had the distinct impression she was praying for patience. "I'm sorry. It's not you. I've hardly even seen you since you got back. And when I have, it hasn't been under the best of circumstances. It's been…a stressful year."

Liam wondered what that meant but decided not to press the issue.

Riley continued to babble. "And I was on my way into work to prepare the monthly reports because they're late, and my accountant needs them so she can prepare the quarterly taxes on the pharmacy. Taxes. At 6:30 in the morning. And there's no coffee." She finished in a tone that suggested this was acceptable grounds for homicide, let alone a little bitchiness.

"You gave up coffee?"

"God no. I'd sooner give up sex."

So if I brought you coffee, there's a chance... Liam mentally slapped himself. *Bad idea, buddy boy. She isn't for you.*

Why was he even thinking of her like this at all? For twenty years, she'd just been his little sister's best friend. Sweet, tender-hearted Riley. A kid he had the urge to protect.

Except that was the thing, wasn't it? Once that urge to protect had become necessity, it had changed things between them, added a dynamic they'd never discussed. Liam didn't know how or even if he should bring it up now.

Either way, she definitely wasn't a kid anymore. And his feelings toward her were decidedly *not* brotherly since he'd come home and found that she'd matured into a 1940s pin-up model. That combination of inherent sweetness and guileless, oblivious sex appeal had fueled more than one fantasy and had him turning down offers for companionship any other man would've taken without hesitation. Damned if he understood why, since he knew he couldn't act on this insanity. She had no business showing up in his dreams like some silver screen sex goddess.

Liam realized he was staring and that Riley's cheeks were flushed, her expression pinched with embarrassment.

"Christ. I don't have a functional brain without coffee. No filter. Please, just go on about your day. I can take care of this."

He turned back to the engine. "In the military, not asking for help when you need it is a good way to get yourself killed."

"I'm not in the military. And this is hardly a life or death situation."

"Given the age and shape of your car, I don't know that your assessment is accurate. Go crank it."

"Really, I've got this."

Liam straightened, deliberately using his full

six feet, two inches to loom over her. "Get in the car and crank it, Riley."

For three long seconds, she stood toe-to-toe with him, chin lifted toward his in challenge. The stubborn cast of her lips had him wanting to back her against the car for a good long taste. Before he could give in to that lunacy, she broke eye contact and scurried around to the driver's side.

Get a grip, Montgomery.

The Honda's engine coughed and sputtered, something in the internal workings giving an ominous grind before it wheezed back to silence.

"Okay, stop," he called.

Riley hopped back out as he closed the hood. "What is it?"

"Nothing I can fix on the side of the road. Get your stuff. I'm taking you in to work."

"But—"

"And then I'm coming back with the truck and trailer to haul this home for a closer look."

Though Liam was positive she wasn't going to like whatever he found.

"But I don't—"

"Riley, don't argue. You can't fix this. You said yourself, you have things to do. I'm giving you a ride."

Liam's brain took a sharp left turn into fantasy territory that had him handling a whole different set of curves than the ones he preferred to hug in the Mustang. His body stirred. Since his basketball shorts would do nothing to hide his reaction, he didn't wait for Riley's acquiescence, just strode toward his car.

Safely blocked by the driver's side door, Liam called back to her, "You comin'?"

With an exasperated look to the heavens, she grabbed her purse and a second bag out of the passenger seat, then stalked around to the front seat of the Mustang. "You're bossy."

He made a U-turn back toward town. "You're welcome."

CHAPTER 3

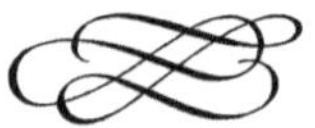

AT THE TAP ON the front door of the pharmacy, Riley happily abandoned the spreadsheets currently fueling a tension headache. On the other side of the glass, Autumn Buchanan lifted an extra-large General Burke from The Daily Grind and made *hurry up* motions. Riley unlocked the door and tugged it open, grabbing the coffee in one hand and her friend in the other, yanking both inside.

"Whoa. Take my arm off, why don't you," Autumn said with a laugh

Riley took a long swallow, feeling instantly

steadier with her favorite stimulant in hand. "I love you. Thank you for bringing me coffee."

"It was no trouble. Since they cut my hours at the library to the bone, I'm not due in until noon."

"They cut your hours *again?* What are you going to do for income? And Jesus, let me pay you back for the coffee."

Autumn waved that off. "I've got savings. Things aren't dire yet. I'm doing some freelance editing of dissertations for grad students at Ole Miss and MSU. That's making up the difference for now. And keep your money. This is complete bribery for gossip. How is it that the very sexy Liam Montgomery brought you to work this morning?"

Because the Universe hates me.

"Jo broke down on my drive in. He just showed up and started ordering me around, telling me what was going to happen. 'Get in the car, Riley.' 'I'll pick up your car later, Riley.' 'Stop being so damned stubborn, Riley.'"

"Did he actually say that?"

Riley scowled. "He might as well have."

Autumn sipped at her own coffee and pursed her lips. "Might I point out that most women would have absolutely *no* problem with the likes of him ordering them around? Preferably in bed?"

Well hell. She'd only just managed to turn that thought off. At Autumn's remark, the whole fantasy started up again in high definition, on repeat.

"Liam Montgomery is not interested in me. Never has been, never will be." Not sure she could control her face, she headed back to the spreadsheets and ledgers.

"Is that why you're so irritated with him?"

"I'm irritated because my stupid car ended my quite successful streak of avoiding him."

"It's a small town, Riley, and you still work part-time with his mom. It was bound to happen sometime."

"Later would've been better than sooner." Though never would've been preferable.

"You ever going to tell me *why* it is you're so

hell bent on avoiding him?"

"Not today." And maybe not ever. Her reasons for staying far, far away from Liam Montgomery were no one's business but hers. That embarrassment did not need to be spread any further than Liam himself.

And who needed old embarrassments? She'd already started adding new ones after less than two minutes in his presence this morning, with all that babble about coffee and sex.

Stupid.

"So he's going to fix your car?" Autumn prompted.

"Apparently. I tried to tell him I could call a tow, but he just rolled right on over me. Forget what I want. Liam knows best."

Never mind that Liam probably did know more about cars and engines than the mechanic who'd taken over care of Jo after Uncle John died.

"Well, I think it's awfully nice of him."

It *was* nice. The overgrown Boy Scout. More than nice, it was exactly what his father would've done, and probably either of his brothers. But none of *them* made her nervous. Grown adult Liam wouldn't be as oblivious to that fact as teenage Liam had been. Being around him made her feel fifteen again—gawky and awkward with a terrifying desire to depend on him. She'd been able to do that once, but going back there would be a mistake of epic proportions. That she even thought about it just pissed her off. Riley knew she'd been ungrateful and rude in her haste to get away from him. But she'd deal with the necessary apology later.

"I don't want him to be nice," she groused. "I don't want him to be anything but out of my hair."

Which was a complete and total lie. She wanted Liam any way she could get him. God, this had been so much easier when all she felt was the impassioned hero worship of her early teens. Adding sexual awareness to the mix was killing her.

"Methinks the lady doth protest too much."

Unwilling to rise to the bait, Riley closed the ledgers and carted them back to the safe. Clearly, she wasn't going to finish these reports before start of business.

Naturally, Autumn followed. "You like him," she drawled.

"You are an incurable romantic and want to see love everywhere." Ledgers stowed, Riley went into the storeroom to grab the next box of stock.

"That doesn't make me wrong. Remember, I'm the librarian. I know your reading preferences. He pretty much fits your hero type to a T." She gave Riley a knowing smirk.

Riley pointed a finger at her. "You know perfectly well that's confidential. You're supposed to be like a priest." She marched past Autumn to the appropriate aisle. Nobody else need know about her penchant for steamy romances with Marine heroes.

"Why don't you just ask him out? You're both available."

Riley attacked the seal on the box with more

force than necessary and managed to slice open several packages of Band-aids. She set the box cutter aside before she created reason to use them. "Look, it's complicated. We have a history."

"Oooooooh. Dish, girlfriend."

"Not that kind of history. The *known each other forever, and he's never going to see me as any-thing but another little sister* kind." Or maybe it wasn't that he saw her as a little sister but as a victim. "You, of all people, should know how that can get in the way."

Autumn's long and complicated history with Judd Hamilton had certainly seemed to do more to ensure that they stay permanently in the friend zone rather than catapulting into connubial bliss, despite everyone's expectations to the contrary.

"Then maybe it's time you *made* him see you as something else," Autumn declared. "You are a confident, sexy woman." She waved her hands in an hourglass motion. "A real woman's woman. Men love that."

Riley fisted both hands on her hips. "And how, pray tell, do you suggest I show him that? Dance on a table in my corset?"

"Well, that would do it. But no, I had something a bit less revealing in mind. Drool Night."

"What, pray tell, is Drool Night?"

"It's a relic from my college days. An excuse to dress up in all your finery and go out on the town. It's a ritual all about female empowerment and favorite dresses. And if it also serves to show the guys exactly what they're missing, so much the better."

Riley could see the appeal. There was no confidence booster like a favorite dress. "Unless you're planning to kidnap him to make sure he's wherever we decide to *go* on Drool Night, I fail to see how this is a viable plan."

Autumn waved that away. "Details. There's also the time-honored tradition of just planting a big one on him. With tongue. Because if you lick it, that makes it yours. Be hard to look at a woman as a sister after that."

In that case, Liam had a lot of inches she

wanted to lick. *So. Not. Happening.* She shook her head to clear the image. "No, then he'd just think I was a crazy person."

The bell on the door jangled.

Riley turned to say good morning to Jessie, but the words died as she saw Liam striding her way.

Why didn't I lock the door?

He'd changed out of the workout gear that had so wonderfully displayed his muscles in the early morning light. Not that the cargo shorts and plain black T-shirt did anything to hide his impressive physique.

"Morning, Autumn."

"Liam." Autumn nodded a hello in his direction. "I'm just gonna leave you two." She waggled her eyebrows at Riley and skedaddled out the door before Riley could come up with a reason why she shouldn't be left alone with him.

Damn it.

And then it was just the two of them.

Before she could do anything stupid, like

reach out to run her hands over his pecs, Riley blurted, "Please tell me you have good news." He opened his mouth, but she kept right on talking. "That is not your good news face."

Shut up, Riley.

"I'm afraid you should probably be planning funeral arrangements."

Riley closed her eyes against that blow. She'd known it was coming. Jo's cantankerous heart had broken when Uncle John died. But God, she'd thought she had a little time to recoup her savings after the latest string of disasters had completely wiped it out. And that was *before* she'd brought her bank balance too low to buy a cup of coffee in order to rescue her mother. Again.

"I can't afford a new car, Liam. Isn't there anything you can do? Something you can cobble together? Duct tape? Prayers?" It killed her to ask, but desperate times.

When he said nothing, she opened her eyes. He had his *wrestling with a problem* face on. It hadn't changed since he'd taken AP chemistry in high school. She would know. They'd had the same study hall that year, and she'd spent countless hours watching him instead of doing her homework.

"I could probably manage something. But whatever I do is going to be borrowed time and it's really throwing good money after bad. You're gonna have to start making some kind of arrangements for a new one in the not distant future."

"Any time you can buy me is appreciated." And maybe she'd have pulled off some kind of miracle to bring in extra income to pay for it by then.

Knowing she needed to keep her hands busy, Riley picked up the carton of Band-aids and went to put it away again. Never mind that she hadn't actually put any on the shelf. She added it back to the pile and turned. Liam had followed her into the storeroom, and the already over-crowded space suddenly shrank.

Riley took an instinctive step back and stumbled. Her feet snagged, sending her flailing. Before she could crash into the piled up junk, Liam's hands closed around her hips, yanking her flush against him. All her soft parts were pressed up close and personal against all his hard parts and, oh dear God, she couldn't breathe.

"Careful."

The rumble of his low voice vibrated that magnificent chest, which she felt because hers was plastered up against him. Her nipples went instantly, painfully hard. She couldn't speak or move, so she just stood there, staring like a complete moron, waiting for him to let her go. Except he didn't. His hands tightened on her hips, as if getting a better grip. Instinctively, hers tightened on his arms and, yep, they were every bit as hard and cut as they looked.

Through sheer force of will, Riley managed not to drool.

If you lick it, that makes it yours.

Before she could stop herself, she licked the seam of her lips. Liam's eyes tracked the motion, and his mouth curved in a little half-smile that spawned a whole host of other wicked thoughts. Her cheeks burned and the synapses responsible for coherent thought exploded from sexual overload.

"You're on my foot."

"What?" Riley managed.

Apparently tired of waiting for her to move, Liam picked her up bodily and shifted her over into the free space. He held on just long enough for her to lock her knees before turning away to survey the storeroom. Another minute of that and the fire in her face would've spread to her hair. This was why she'd avoided him!

"I see you haven't had any better luck with clearing this space out than Mom did."

Riley blessed him for not commenting on the awkward moment and desperately seized the change in topic. "I haven't been able to get to it. Our hands are plenty full with the day-to-day running of things."

At some point in the old building's past, this room had been part of the one that now housed the pharmacy. Some previous owner had blocked the whole thing off for storage. When the five and dime went belly up, the remaining stock that hadn't been sold off had been piled in here, and Riley wasn't certain the space had been cleared since. Like Molly before her, she kept meaning to get to it, but as a priority, it fell way down at the bottom of the list.

"I'll do it."

"You'll do what?"

"Clear it out. All this crap is a fire hazard. I've been telling Mom that for years."

"You don't have to do that." *Please God, don't let him do that.* "You're already dealing with my car. And the renovation upstairs."

"And I'll deal with this after."

Her brain scrambled to find some way to say no, to shove him out the door. "But I can't afford to—"

Liam turned back, one brow lifted. "I know you're not about to insult me by suggesting I expect to get paid for doing a favor for a friend."

They were hardly friends. One friend did

not come near to spontaneously combusting in the presence of another friend.

"Let me help you Riley."

He could've ordered her. That would've been more his style, Mr. Alpha Marine I Know What's Best, So Fall In Line as he'd done that morning. But he was giving her a choice—or at least the illusion of one—proving that as long as it had been, he still knew her, too.

That was a real pisser.

Riley took a bracing breath and made herself meet his gaze. "Thank you. I appreciate it. All of it. I know I probably don't seem like it. I'm really bad at accepting help from people."

The lightning quick smile lit his gray eyes like sunbeams, and Riley had to lock her knees again, grateful he didn't unleash it often. The damned thing was deadly.

"I know. Why do you think I'm being so bossy?"

"You're the oldest. You were always bossy."

"Just sharing the benefits of my maturity."

Riley snorted at that, and pushed out of the

storeroom. "Take all that maturity and go sweet talk my engine. I've got work to do."

"See you around, Riley Marie."

She watched him go, waiting until he'd walked out of sight before sinking down onto a stool. Like it or not, he was going to be in her space, so she'd better find a way to live with it.

I am in serious trouble.

Quite apart from the fact that Riley's engine was toast and he'd just promised her he'd figure something out, he'd violated his strict look-don't-touch policy—again—to keep her from landing on her fairly spectacular ass. As if that wasn't bad enough, she'd stared up at him with those big, blue, drown-in-me eyes and licked her lips, like maybe she wondered how he tasted. It had taken every ounce of his self control to set her away from him rather than dipping his head to kiss her and exploring the rest of those sweet curves with his hands.

"Maybe I should dunk my head in the fountain," he muttered.

"Well, you could, but a coin is the more traditional offering for a wish."

Liam jerked his attention away from the issue of Riley to find Autumn perched on the edge of the post-Civil War fountain that was the focal point of the town green.

"I wasn't making one."

"Oh come on," Autumn teased. "It's all the rage

"Right now, the only thing I need is a miracle to tell me how I'm going to fix Riley's car."

"What's wrong with it?"

"The damned thing needs to be buried. But she can't afford a new one, so I'm trying to perform a Dr. Frankenstein miracle and resuscitate it." And he knew exactly what it had cost Riley to ask him.

Autumn rose from her perch and looped her arm casually through his as they continued across the green. "Can you?"

"My dad could and did on a regular basis

before he died. It's the least I can do to try." He owed Riley, more than she could possibly know.

"And if you can't?"

The last thing he wanted to do was face that look of heartbroken disappointment on Riley's face.

"Can't isn't really an option. I'd rather just buy her a newer used car that I know is road-worthy, but she'd never accept that."

Autumn lifted a brow at that. "You'd buy her a car?"

"I'd do the same thing for my sister."

"Do you take this active a role in ensuring Wynne's well being?"

Liam brushed that off. "Lack of opportunity. Wynne would be the first one to applaud my trying to help. The two of them have been joined at the hip since they were five."

"Not so much the last couple of years."

That gave him pause. He hadn't seen his baby sister since his welcome home party in December, but he'd assumed she was better at keeping up with Riley than she was with the rest of the family. "Are they on the outs?"

"Not deliberately, but with Wynne being all caught up in her life down in the Big Easy, she doesn't come home often and Riley's tied to the business."

Liam wondered if she felt as abandoned by his sister as she had by him. "So who has Riley's back?"

"I do. And your mom does. But she misses Wynne."

"For a long time it was like they were two bodies who shared one brain. They were always so tight."

Autumn nodded. "And was Wynne the reason you looked out for Riley back in school?"

Liam paused mid-step. "I didn't think I was obvious about it."

"You weren't. But I notice that kind of thing."

She would.

"Riley hasn't had the easiest life. There

haven't been too many people she could really count on, and she's always been considered a part of my family." Which was the absolute truth, even if he hadn't thought of her as a sister in years.

"So now you're home, you're just falling back into that old pattern, huh?"

Autumn was an incurable romantic. Always had been. She was clearly fishing to find out more about his interest in Riley. Liam knew better than to bite.

"I'm just helping out a friend. That's it." His protest did nothing to wipe the look of speculation off Autumn's face. Time to redirect. "I didn't know you and Riley were all buddy buddy."

"We weren't growing up. Since she's younger, we didn't run in the same circles any more than you did. But when she came back to Wishful after college, she moved into the other half of the duplex I live in, so we've gotten to know each other pretty well over the last few years. I like her."

So did he, despite the fact that she was more apt to bite than smile at him these days.

As they reached the Mustang, Liam patted Autumn's arm and disentangled himself. "I gotta be gettin' on. Have to figure out how I'm going to perform an automotive miracle."

"Liam?"

"Yeah?"

"It's a kind thing you're doing for Riley. The latest in a long line of kind things you've done for all sorts of people since you came home. But remember it's also important to take something for yourself."

"Do as you say, not as you do?" He gave her a pointed look.

She looked suddenly weary. "What I want isn't an option. What you do is."

"You can't know that. *I* don't know what I want." He tried to forcibly shut out the image of Riley that popped into his mind.

Her lips curved. "You're a smart man. You'll figure it out."

Shaking his head, he waved goodbye and

slipped into his car, his mind full of the impossible.

He had no right to act on this attraction, no right to complicate Riley's life when his own was such a damned mess. Even if the attraction was returned—and it appeared that it was—he had nothing to offer her. He had nothing to offer anyone, for that matter. Until he figured out what the hell to do with his life, he didn't have any right to look at a woman like Riley.

No. Fantasies aside, Riley Gower was off-limits. And the sooner his brain got the memo, the better.

A GREASY NAUSEA gripped Liam's gut as he stared up at the faded lettering of the sign. *Montgomery and Sons Auto Repair.*

He'd avoided this, like a goddamned coward. His brothers, his mother, and sister had been the ones to deal with the accounts, tidy up business affairs in the wake of John Montgomery's death. Liam hadn't managed to set foot inside since it happened. He couldn't shake the sense of guilt that if he'd lived up to the legacy of the sign, if he'd been that kind of son, he'd have been there the day his father keeled over under the hood of his beloved '69 Mustang. The same Mustang Liam now drove.

But Liam had taken his own path, joined the Corps. His brothers had followed suit. And no one had been there that fateful Thursday afternoon. The others were able to cling to the fact that it had been quick. Painless, according to the doctors. He'd gone while doing something he loved. But Liam could only see a life ended far too soon. That was a reality he lived with in war. Not something he was ready for on the home front.

The garage was locked up tight, as it had been since the weeks following his father's death. Quiet. His mother hadn't sold the place. It was there, waiting, in case any of the Montgomery sons wanted to pick up their father's mantle and carry on the family business. He could do it. He had all the skills, the love of engines and puzzles. And he certainly had need of a legitimate vocation now that Uncle Sam wasn't calling the shots.

But to come here, every day? To be faced with all those reminders that his father wouldn't be swinging through the door or hollering for a tool ever again? Coward or no, it was more than he could bear.

Under other circumstances, he wouldn't be here now. But he'd promised Riley. Though her car was at the house, he needed the service records his dad kept here, along with the supplier contacts. Maybe he'd luck out and some of the parts would be in the remaining inventory.

Stale, musty air assailed his senses as he stepped into the office. The pin-up calendar hanging above the counter was still turned to October. Out of long-ingrained habit, Liam kissed his pointer and middle fingers and pressed them to the image of Jane Russell, his dad's particular favorite, before moving to switch on the window unit air conditioner.

Liam had always been more a Lana Turner, Loretta Young kind of guy, but he'd take the whole platoon of curvy, old school divas over today's starved, waifish offerings. To his mind, a woman was ultimately the grounded center of a man, and as such, ought to be substantial.

His hands flexed at the memory of Riley's hips. Glorious, solid curves.

"Focus."

Tugging open the ancient file cabinet drawers, he began to flip through. Why the hell hadn't his father believed in alphabetizing? Or computers? He'd worked halfway through the second drawer by the time the door opened. Braced to say, "We're closed," he trailed off at the sight of his mother.

"What are you doing here?"

"Saw the car. Wanted to check on you."

"I'm trying to find Riley's service records." She hadn't asked, but Liam felt compelled to explain what had finally gotten him through the door.

"They're in the family files." Molly reached past him and opened another drawer.

Given the direction his thoughts had been running, he sure as hell needed a good reminder of where Riley had always fit in his life. She was family. It wouldn't do for him to forget that.

"Is she having trouble?"

"Broke down on the way in to work this morning. I towed it to the house, but she needs a resurrectionist, not a mechanic."

"You're thinking you'll find the name of one in the file?"

"Wanted to check the dates when Dad last replaced some stuff."

"Over the years, I think he probably replaced at least half of that car."

"Yeah, well, the other half needs to go now. Pretty sure the engine is shot."

"But you're still going to try to fix it?"

"Riley gave me the face." Riley Gower, the woman who never asked for anything, had looked up at him with those deep blue eyes and he'd caved.

Molly laughed. "What face?"

"The face that, I'm sure, had her daddy wrapped around her pinky finger as long as he was alive. Damned thing's lethal. Like the people version of that cat in *Shrek.* And here I am promising to bring her car back from the beyond. I don't know what the hell I was thinking."

"I expect you were thinking she never asks for help, so when she does you'll do just about anything to deliver. We all would."

"Yeah, there's that. So anyway, here I am. I guess I was hoping for some sort of miracle. Be nice if Dad were here to tell me what to do."

In a gesture that was purely Molly, she squeezed his nape and stroked the length of his spine, automatically soothing the same way she'd done since he was a punk troublemaker come to live under her roof. "He's here. Just not quite as vocal as you'd like him to be."

"If he were here, he'd have some kind of sneaky ass plan to deal with this."

"Why do you need a sneaky ass plan?"

"Because in truth she needs a new car, period. And since she bought the business from you, she's taken on all she can handle."

His mother frowned. "I worried she bit off more than she could chew buying me out completely. But she wanted so much to prove that she could do it on her own. For the most part, she's done that. Made some expansions in product lines, modernized a few processes."

"Do you ever regret selling?"

"I don't regret relinquishing control. I steered that ship for a long time. But sometimes I'm bored with retirement. It's part of why I've been so active with the coalition. It gives me something to do, keeps me active in the community. You understand that need to keep busy or you wouldn't be taking on projects everywhere."

Liam grimaced. "Busy isn't necessarily productive."

Molly stroked a hand over his hair. "You know if you want the garage, it's yours, no questions asked. Your brothers wouldn't take issue with it."

He looked around the office, where he'd spent countless hours growing up, doing home-work, answering phones, helping out. So many memories soaked these walls, but he couldn't get past the bitter to the sweet. "It wasn't for me at eighteen. It's not for me now. I know dad was disappointed—"

"You know no such thing," she snapped. "Your father was proud of you. He never once took issue with the fact that you chose a dif-ferent path. Neither did I. I'm not upset you don't want the business, baby. I just wanted to put it out there as an option. I'll support what-ever you choose now, just like I supported you joining the Corps."

"Thanks Mom." Liam slid his arms around her, thinking that for all she was half his size, she still gave the best bear hugs.

"I'll let you get back to it. I've got a meeting

with Norah to go over some final details about the playground renovation at Waldrop Park."

Alone again, he took a breath and opened the file. As his dad had been working on Riley's car since she got it in high school, the stack of paperwork was thick. Every oil change, every tire rotation, every new part or repair was recorded in John's neat block print. He'd rebuilt the transmission six months before he died, so that, at least, was probably okay. The list of repairs and replacements made to the engine were extensive, increasing in frequency over the last couple of years. At the last service, he'd made note of problems he expected to be facing before the year was out, and Liam thought Riley had been lucky that they hadn't popped up until today. In the margin he'd written, *Rebuild or replace?*

That was the question, wasn't it?

As he flipped to the next page, a loose Post-it note fluttered to the floor. Retrieving it, Liam read the brief notation he knew referred to a location in the parts racks on the far side of the garage. There was no indication what was stored there. It might've been from a repair already completed. But he had to check it out.

The fluorescent lights flickered and caught, illuminating the wide, cavernous space. Industrial shelving lined the walls, most of them still filled with an assortment of parts his father always kept on hand for regular jobs. Years of oil and engine cleaner scented the close, hot air. He checked the shelves, looking for the relevant section. The crate had been shoved aside at some point, so somebody could retrieve something else. It was tucked in a corner, half beneath a tarp. Liam muscled it around and found the manifest from one of the parts auctions his dad sometimes attended. Sliding it out, he read the contents and began to laugh.

"Sneaky, sneaky, Dad." Still laughing, he went to get a crowbar to uncrate Riley's new engine.

CHAPTER 4

"**W**ELL, IT'S HAPPENED!" RUBY made this pronouncement in tones of *The end is nigh,* as she marched up to the counter.

Riley looked up from the computer. "What's happened? And what are you even doing here? It's your day off."

"Walgreens is opening a store out on the highway."

"What are you talking about?"

"I just had it from Pearl." Ruby's sister, Pearl Buckley—Mama Pearl to everyone else in town

—ran the local diner, Dinner Belles, and was the undisputed queen of gossip in Wishful.

Jessie paused in the midst of inputting the prescriptions that'd been called in. "How on earth did we not know this?"

Riley wondered the same.

"I don't got a clue, but what are we gonna do about it?" Ruby demanded, shifting her attention back to Riley.

"What do you mean do about it?" It wasn't like they could engage in some kind of corporate espionage or something. "We're going to carry on with business as usual. It'll take them time to build and stock a store. We're fine."

"They're not building. They bought up the old WingStop building. Won't take much to convert that. Pearl says they're supposed to be open in a month."

Jessie's eyes widened. "A month? That's not much time to prepare."

"Y'all, nothing's going to change," Riley assured them. "This has been the only pharmacy in town for half a century. Almost everybody comes here. That's not going to change just because Walgreens opens up on the other side of town. People aren't going to be so easily seduced."

She hoped like hell that was true.

"I think we oughta call in Norah," Ruby said.

Earlier that year, Norah Burke had waged and won a war against a warehouse store that had threatened their small town way of life. She'd mobilized the citizenry to form a citizen's coalition and made huge strides in the revitalization of downtown Wishful—and that had all been *before* she'd been hired as the new City Planner. She was a woman who made things happen. But even she couldn't put a genie back in its bottle.

"Norah has bigger things to do than be bothered about something that can't be changed," Riley said. "If Walgreens is already in the process of retrofitting the building, they're coming. Even she's not going to be able to stop that. Our customers are loyal. We're going to be fine."

A steady stream of patrons put an end to the discussion and seemed to prove Riley's point. They were exceptionally busy for a Saturday, with everybody trying to get in before the pharmacy closed at noon. As the lunch hour drew near, Riley cut Jessie loose to go work on the latest city beautification project, so she was alone as the last customer of the day wandered in.

"Tara! How good to see you."

Tara Honeycutt crossed to the counter with an unconscious grace that Riley envied. "I come bearing a special delivery of legal stimulants from Cassie. Just got off my shift at The Grind."

Pleased, surprised, Riley accepted the coffee and took a deep inhale. "God, I have such a weakness for these. Thanks. Those are really fabulous earrings, by the way."

Tara lifted a hand to the funky chandelier earrings made up of long, fanciful twists of wire. "Thanks. They're just something I've been playing around with in my spare time."

"You *made* those?" Riley leaned in for a

closer look. "Those are amazing. You could absolutely sell something like that."

"I did for a while on Etsy before they screwed the marketplace by removing the handmade requirement. These days it's too hard to get found there, and I don't have all that much time in the first place, juggling both jobs and the kids."

"Where are they today?"

"Vacation Bible School this week. Not that Austin is any happier about that than he has been about anything he's done this summer." She rolled her hazel eyes. "I am not, as he likes to point out, his parent."

"Raising your siblings has to be hard on you."

Tara shrugged. "It's better than the alternative. They need someone in their life who's stable and responsible. Anyway, I needed to pick up some more syringes for Ginny before I teach my one o'clock class at the gym."

"Which is it today?"

"Pilates. Then yoga at two-thirty. You should come."

Riley snorted with laughter. "I am not bendy, nor am I graceful."

"You can't *get* bendy without trying," Tara pointed out. "There's a beginner class Tuesdays and Thursdays at seven. Great way to unwind from the day."

"I'll think about it. Now. Syringes." Riley retrieved them. "How's Ginny doing on that new dosage? Are you having any trouble?"

"Her blood sugar's pretty stable, but we're fighting the athlete's foot again."

"Bless her. There's an oil for that. Several, actually. But probably your best option is Melaleuca."

"Mela what now?"

"Melaleuca. Tea tree oil. It's likely to work when the over-the-counter stuff doesn't. Want to give it a try?" Seeing her brief hesitation, Riley added, "It's really affordable. A little bit goes a very long way, so a bottle is likely to last you up to a year."

"Okay. How do we use it?"

Warming to her subject, Riley all but bounced. Essential oils were a personal passion. She retrieved the oil and scribbled down instructions on application to send home with Tara. As she launched into an explanation of carrier oils, the bell over the door jangled. Even though she didn't look, even though she was very focused on her customer and her pet subject, Riley knew Liam had just walked in. The store suddenly felt ten degrees warmer, the air thicker and harder to breathe.

Done with the instructions, Riley held them out, keeping her gaze fixed on Tara. "You should also use it to make a shower spray to use between showers. It'll help kill the bacteria that keeps reinfecting her feet."

As Tara took the offered paper, Riley caught sight of Liam standing patiently off to the side. God, he looked good. She hadn't seen him in days, and it was a struggle to keep her attention on the sale. Pathetic. Up until January, she'd hardly seen him in twelve *years*.

She finished ringing Tara up. "Let me know how it works out for you."

"I will. Thanks." She waved on her way out the door.

Riley wished she had some lavender oil in the diffuser at the register. She needed something to take her heart rate down a notch as Liam ambled over, hands tucked in the front pockets of his jeans. His sandy hair, grown out some from the military buzz, was rumpled, making him look younger, if no less a badass. The rumpled, boyish thing worked on him. Hell, everything worked on him. She couldn't read his face to gauge whether the news about Jo was good or bad.

Riley shoved her own hands into the pockets of her lab coat. "Well? Out with it. What's the final prognosis on my baby? I assume that's why you're here."

"It is."

He crossed his arms, which made his impressive biceps flex, straining the sleeves of his polo shirt in a way that had Riley's mouth watering. "Frankly, your baby is a stubborn bitch."

Riley winced, her attention dragged back to the matter at hand. "Your dad used to say she was a special snowflake."

"She's a special something. I just spent the last week tearing her almost completely apart and putting her back together. Rebuilt the engine, put in all new seals and fluids from front to back, a new battery, new spark plugs."

She reached out and grabbed hold of the edge of the counter, praying he hadn't done all that only to have the car stay dead. "And?"

He pulled her keys from his front pocket. "She's had the tires rotated, the front end aligned, and a bath. You'll need new tires by winter, but I doubt she's run this good for you since you got out of college."

"Oh, thank God." But her relief dimmed almost immediately as her mind tried to tally up the cost of everything he'd done. "What's the damage?"

He pulled out his wallet and fished a folded

paper from inside. "Just the cost of parts and fluids."

She couldn't read most of the items scrawled on the receipt he handed her from Wishful Auto Parts, but the total at the bottom had her looking back at him in suspicion. "You did not just do all that to my car for $293.74."

"New fluids and seals cover a multitude of sins," Liam said easily, his gray eyes level on hers.

Jesus, the man had a helluva poker face.

"Cost of parts aside, your *time* is worth something."

He shrugged that off. "Consider it the cost of my therapy. Wrenching is good thinking time, and I had a problem to work out."

"Did you figure it out?"

"Think so."

"Well, that's great, but I still can't let you just do all that work for free." Not that she could really afford to pay him more than the bill he'd handed her. But it was the principle of the thing.

His brows angled down. "I don't expect my friends to pay me for a favor."

He kept saying that. Friends. But they'd never been friends. Not like that. Not even after he'd slipped into the role of her own personal hero. She'd only ever been in his orbit at all because of Wynne. Now they were both grown, Wynne was gone, and what he'd done for her had become the stuff of Things Best Left In The Past. Which made them…well, nothing at all.

"Besides," he continued, "being in the garage all week was the closest I've felt to Dad since I got back. I needed that."

He hadn't even been able to go into the garage in the months after Uncle John's death. And he'd gone there for her? Riley's heart softened. Anything else she could've argued about but not that. Of all of them, Liam had taken his father's death the hardest. During the final eleven months of his last tour, Riley and Molly had both been worried sick that the unresolved grief would dull his edge and land him in harm's way.

"How did it go?" she asked softly.

He gave a nostalgic half smile that was still a little pained around the edges. "I kept expecting him to come in to help, start bossing me about what he'd do different."

Riley ached to step out from behind the counter and slip her arms around him. But after what close contact with him had done to her last time, she didn't dare give in to the impulse. "I miss him, too." Uncle John had been on her incredibly short list of men who could be counted on.

Liam flipped her keys around his pointer finger and didn't quite look at her. "This is the first time I've been able to really talk about him without wanting to hit somebody or blow something up."

Riley did move around the counter then to lay a light hand on his arm. All that smooth, hard muscle was bunched with tension. "Healing takes time, Liam. Your daddy was a good man, and there are a whole lot of great memories of him. You're really lucky to have them."

He did look at her then, covering her hand with his. "I hadn't thought of it like that. Do you remember your dad?"

Those big, strong fingers were warm and gave her a comfort she hadn't even realized she wanted. "Some. I was only five when he died. Some of what I think I remember is probably more my mom telling me stories over and over. Showing me pictures. And some I know are really my memories." She smiled. "I have a lot more of your dad. All good. Eventually, you'll get to where that's what comes to mind when you think of him, instead of the hurt."

He studied her, as if she were a puzzle he couldn't quite figure out. "You're an intuitive woman, Riley."

She had no idea how much of it was intuition and how much was the fact that she'd been a student of this particular man for years. For all that they'd never *really* been friends, she knew him. Better than he probably realized.

She stepped away before things got weird.

"He was so proud of your service. And he'd have been proud of you for taking the hard road and getting out of it in the name of family."

Liam huffed. "Oh sure. His eldest son, the combat engineer, still unemployed six months after telling Uncle Sam to take a hike."

"I gather that's not the problem you were working out on Jo's guts."

"Thinking about that one would've more likely resulted in Jo's guts being obliterated. My specialty is demolition and urban breaching. Not a lot of use for that around here."

The trilling of her phone put an end to whatever opportunity she had to reply to that—not that she knew what to say.

"I know it's not your strong suit, but try to have some patience. You'll figure it out. Meanwhile, thanks for fixing my car." She held her hand out for the keys as "Crazy Train" continued to jangle from her pocket.

As he laid them in her palm, his fingers brushed her wrist and a bolt of heat shot up her arm. Riley managed not to tense, but a shiver worked its way from her tail bone up her spine.

Liam frowned faintly before dropping his hand "I'm gonna go look around the storeroom and sort out the best plan of attack."

She pocketed the keys and left her hand there to hide her trembling fingers. "A few pounds of C4 might be quicker than actually cleaning out. And, hey, you'd know how to repair the resulting damage."

"Ha ha," he said flatly, but the corner of his mouth quirked.

She tugged out the phone. "I've gotta take this." He wandered over to the storeroom as she answered. "Mom?"

"Hi, honey."

She headed into the office for a little more privacy. "Where are you? I thought you'd be back by now."

"I'm still in Fresno.'"

"What?" It'd been almost a week.

"Well, I got back in touch with Hal."

"So you're back together?" Riley guessed.

"No, no. But I got my things. Put them all in the mail to ship home."

"Okay, so when can I expect you?"

Her pause had Riley's gut tightening. "Well, that's the thing. Between the shipping costs and the motel and food…I don't have anything left of what you sent me."

"Are you kidding me?" But Riley knew she wasn't.

Sharilyn got immediately defensive. "I couldn't just abandon my things. That's everything I have."

Except for the stuff still in storage in Wishful. Riley was footing the bill for that, too. But there was no sense in bringing that up now.

"I just need a few hundred more for that bus ticket."

After she paid Liam back, Riley's personal account would have all of $32 in it. Her savings had flat-lined months before, and the business account was doing a constant tango between profitable and nail-biting. She wasn't about to jeopardize her ability to make payroll. Her employees didn't deserve to be shorted. She could buy the ticket herself on her almost maxed out credit card—and, in fact, that was what she should've done in the first place—but she wouldn't put it past her mother to cash in the ticket and do something else to squander the money.

She was tired. So incredibly tired of this whole scenario.

"I'm done, Mom."

"What?" Riley could practically hear her reaching to clutch the pearls perpetually at her throat.

"I'm done. I'm tapping out. I have paid and paid and paid for your mistakes and bad judgment, and I just can't do it anymore. I don't have it to give. Every penny I have has been sunk into the pharmacy."

"You're…you're just going to leave me out here?" Sharilyn's voice shot high with incredulity and not a little bit of fear.

"I'm telling you I don't have any money I can loan you. You'll have to pick up some kind of temporary work. Earn enough for a bus ticket home."

"But I don't have any skills!"

Right. Because professional damsel in distress was not exactly the most stellar career move.

"You can wash dishes. Wait tables. It's time you learned how to take care of yourself." Because God knows no one else had ever made her.

"But Riley—"

"I have to go, Mom. Good luck."

She hung up before the tears could start.

LIAM FOUND Riley in the office, her head pressed to the desk, her shoulders slumped.

"Everything okay?"

She jolted upright as if he'd shocked her. "Fine." But he could see the strain around her eyes and hear the slight catch in her voice that said otherwise.

He might've thought that had something to do with him, except he'd heard enough to know it was her mother on the phone. They hadn't had an easy relationship back when she was younger. Liam doubted that had changed. He considered asking about it, bullying her until she spilled whatever was on her mind. But she hadn't pressed his tender spot about his dad, and he didn't think she'd welcome the intrusion.

Riley got to her feet. "Did you sort out whatever you needed to on the storeroom?" She held herself stiff, clearly waiting for him to get the hell out of her way.

He didn't need to know the why to help. "Yep. Come here." Without waiting for her acquiescence, Liam tugged her into his arms.

She shoved at his chest, trying to step back. "What are you doing?" Was that a faint trace of panic in her tone?

"You're upset about something. Figured you could use a hug."

"I'm fine," she insisted.

It didn't seem worth pointing out that he'd always been able to read her better than that. "Riley, you don't have to talk about it. You don't even have to acknowledge it. But for once in your life, lean for two damn minutes. I promise I won't tell."

With an annoyed sort of growl, she gave a half-hearted shove before finally giving up, dropping her head against his chest and sliding her arms around his waist. He stroked a hand up and down her back. Degree by slow degree, she relaxed. Liam tried his damnedest not to think about how good she felt against him or to notice the pretty floral scent to her hair.

"I forgot what good hugs you give," she murmured.

She'd been very much still a girl the last time he'd hugged her. She wasn't a girl now.

"What're friends for?"

She gave him an odd look as she stepped away. "I don't know what the hell we were, but it was never anything so simple as friends."

That was undoubtedly true.

He probably should've let it go, but this was as honest as they'd been with each other in twelve years. "I'd like to be."

It was the truth, if not the whole truth, and it was all he dared hope for after how they'd left things when he'd enlisted.

Riley inclined her head. "Well, you're certainly holding up your end of the deal."

Not exactly a yes, but he'd take it.

She shrugged out of her lab coat and hung it on a hook behind the door. "Can I give you a ride somewhere? I assume you drove Jo here to deliver her."

"I'm on the demolition crew for the city playground." Which had been slated to start at noon, so he was officially late.

The playground at Waldrop Park was Norah's latest cause. On seeing the patchwork of rust and warped wood that constituted the play space, she'd orchestrated a picket fence fundraiser. Seemed like more than half the town had bought a picket to raise the money for replacement of the equipment that hadn't been touched since Liam himself had been in elementary school. Once the new playground was built, the pickets would each be inscribed with the name of the donor, and a new fence built around the park. It was pretty ingenious, really.

"Jessie left for that about an hour ago."

Liam eyed the shorts and t-shirt that had been hiding beneath her coat. "Why don't you come with me?"

"Beg your pardon?"

"Come to the work day with me. Bunch of folks are gonna be there. I think it'd be good for you." It would give her a chance to work off some of that frustration still simmering below the surface.

Riley frowned.

"You have something else to do this afternoon?"

"Well, no, but—"

"Then come break stuff with me, Riley Marie." He tweaked her pony-tail, much as he'd done when they were kids.

"You're *such* a guy." But the corners of her luscious mouth twitched.

"What? Breaking stuff is fun."

"You think I don't remember you had exactly the same expression when you, Jack, and Cruz thought it would be a good idea to blow up pumpkins with M80s?"

A lot of the best times with his brothers had involved blowing things up. "Blowing stuff up can be fun, too." Liam took her arm and started steering her toward the door. "I volunteered to rig the explosives, but Norah vetoed that plan."

"Well, it's not exactly safe to be exploding things in the middle of town."

"Not if you know what you're doing. Which I do. Mitch thinks she's running a secret op to get sweaty, shirtless pics of the available bachelors in Wishful for a fund-raising calendar."

Riley snorted. "You know she wouldn't make a secret of it. She'd give some kind of compelling presentation about the marketing benefits and everybody would jump to do her bidding."

"This is probably true," he conceded. "So how about it? You coming with or are you gonna wuss out?"

She shot him a narrowed-eyed glare. "Watch it, Boy Scout, or I'll *suggest* that calendar to Norah."

He held up his hands in surrender. He'd had enough trouble after his mother's announcement at his welcome home party about taking applications for the mother of her future grandchildren. She'd been joking. He was pretty sure.

As he shoehorned himself into Riley's car, his phone buzzed with a text.

Speak of the devil.

Mom: **Just heard from Jessie. Walgreens is opening out on the highway.**

Well, that explained part of Riley's mood.

He texted back, **I'll mention it to Norah at the demolition.**

They both knew Riley would never say anything herself.

When they got to Waldrop Park and

climbed out of the car, Norah called, "You're late!"

"Doesn't count." He and Riley crossed to join everyone. "I brought more helping hands."

"We haven't gotten started yet anyway," Norah said. "Figured we'd wait on you, given demolition is your area of expertise."

"That'd be a lot more relevant if you'd let me make things go boom," Liam told her. "Mitch is more than capable of telling people how to tear a structure down."

Mitch Campbell, a local architect and one of Liam's oldest friends, lifted his hand. "Dude, I build stuff. I don't destroy."

"I suggested we kill some time by using it for target practice with those old potato canons we built senior year," Judd said.

"Best physics project *ever*," Liam pronounced. "Pretty sure that's when Cruz knew he wanted to be a sniper. I found mine in the shed when I cleaned it out a couple months ago."

"You boys gonna keep running your mouths

or are you planning on doing some work?" Riley asked. "I was promised I could break stuff."

"You heard the lady." Liam made quick work assigning people to various posts, making a rapid plan of attack before grabbing a hardhat. He plunked it down on Riley's head and handed her a pair of safety goggles and some leather gloves.

Riley eyed them for a moment before slipping both on.

"I can't believe this thing is *finally* coming down." Mitch looked fondly at the wreck of a playground, a sledge hammer balanced on his shoulder.

"Remember when we used to play Star Wars out here?" Liam crossed to a broken swing and slapped at it. "Looks like our Millennium Falcon is busted."

"Ooo, maybe I should tweak the design," Mitch said.

"Oh no you don't," Norah interrupted. "The castle and turret design was finalized and all the materials were bought based on those specs."

"Spoil-sport," Mitch grumbled. "Your fiancée is no fun," he told his cousin.

Cam Crawford laughed and looped an arm around Norah's waist, drawing her in for a smacking kiss. "You know my girl is gonna keep us on budget. That's a good thing."

Liam watched them, amused and a little envious at their obvious joy in each other. His parents had loved like that, and he only hoped to someday be half as lucky.

"Fine, fine. No Millennium Falcon."

"Let's get this show on the road," Mitch's sister, Miranda, said. "I've got an ER shift later, and I want time to shower and take a nap."

"Your wish, Randa Panda."

Miranda gave him a withering look that had him grinning in return. She'd crushed on him as a teenager. Unlike Riley, Miranda had always felt like a sister to him, so nothing ever came of it. But, God, it was still fun to poke at her.

"Okay, she who just found out Walgreens is

opening out on the highway gets the first swing."

Riley's gaze flashed to his, but she didn't ask how he knew.

"Man, seriously?" Norah asked.

"Look out," Cam said. "She's got that war-mongering look in her eye again. GrandGoods left her with a taste for blood."

Riley jerked her chin toward Autumn. "Save your war-mongering for a campaign to save the library and the job of the head librarians. The pharmacy is fine."

Liam was reasonably sure she'd say that up to and possibly including the place burning down. "War council can wait." He led her toward a section of semi-rotten tunnel. Built in the days before the widespread use of plastic components, the thing was entirely wood, missing a few slats along the roof and sides.

"Stand back." When she did as he asked, Liam demonstrated the correct hold and swing. "Think you can manage that?"

Riley held out a gloved hand for the sledgehammer. After making certain she had the proper grip, Liam moved well out of the way himself and watched her heft the thing. Her first swing had her turning a complete circle, missing the target completely.

Mitch laughed and started toward her. "You need a *real* man to show you how it's done."

Liam held up a hand. "No, give her a minute."

Eyes narrowed, Riley readjusted her grip and swung. This time the blow landed true, slamming into the side and caving in two slats at the first blow, a testament to exactly how bad a shape the playground was in. Eyes narrowed, she swung again, and then again, finding her rhythm and steadily destroying the entire length of the tunnel within her reach.

"Hooo-eee," Mitch remarked. "Remind me never to get on her bad side."

"Let's get our piece of this." With a war whoop, Judd threw himself into the cause.

"Oo rah," Liam said, and dove into the fray.

Soon, there was a cacophony of thuds and

crashes as they all set to demolition. The steady flex and stretch of muscle felt good, even in the heat of the sun. Before his tour in Iraq, Liam had thought Mississippi was hot. A hundred and twenty degrees in the shade had changed his perspective.

"We're gonna need a chainsaw for the bridge ties," Judd observed. "These bolts are long since rusted in place."

"There's one in my truck," Mitch called.

"I'll get it." Liam set his own sledgehammer aside, glancing over to check on Riley as she went after the walls of the crow's nest.

Judd followed his gaze. "She's gonna be super sore tomorrow."

"Yeah, but her head will be clearer."

Judd trailed him over to Mitch's truck. "Maybe you should offer to massage out the kinks. Since this was your idea and all."

Liam gave him a flat stare and checked the fuel level in the chainsaw.

"Fixing her car had to have gotten you back into her good graces."

"That's not why I did it." Though it probably hadn't hurt that particular cause.

Judd grinned. "Sure it wasn't."

Liam flipped him off. "Grab those bolt cutters. We'll need them for the chains holding the suspension bridge."

Hard, noisy work kept him occupied for another hour. By the time the pieces of the bridge had been relegated to the dumpster hauled on site, he was ready to pour the entire cooler of water over his head. He guzzled a couple of glasses before switching over to the sweet tea Mama Pearl had sent over from Dinner Belles. They'd made good progress. In another hour, all the detritus would be cleared and they'd be done for the day.

Grabbing another glass of tea, Liam took it over to Riley, who was breathing hard and glaring in triumph at a splintered support post.

"Okay, I admit it. You were absolutely right. Totally cathartic."

"Sometimes you just need to beat the shit out of something. Feel better?"

She took the tea and drank deep, watching him over the rim of the cup. "Some."

"It's not just Walgreens, is it?" he asked quietly.

Not even surprise in her big blue eyes this time. Just resignation. "Sometimes your perceptiveness is a real pain in the ass."

"Want to talk about it?"

"I really don't."

Liam tried to ignore the sting of that. He'd been out of her life a long time. He couldn't expect easy entry back into it. "Fair enough."

Riley drained the tea. "I'd like to take you to dinner."

That stopped him. "What?"

"As a thank you," she explained. "My car. Demolition therapy. It's the least I can do."

His traitorous brain supplied a quick montage of other things she could do that had absolutely nothing to do with dinner.

Not on the menu, he reminded himself and immediately began to mentally tear apart a Beretta M9 as a distraction. "Sounds good."

"Tonight work for you?"

"Sure."

"We'll go to Magnolia Heights."

"All the way in Lawley?"

"I know how much you love their prime rib." She dropped her voice low. "You said you want to be friends. If you're serious about that, there are things we should probably talk about, and I'd just as soon not do it where anybody in town can hear."

Clearly she was done dancing around the issue. Good.

"Pick you up at 6:30."

CHAPTER 5

SAFELY ENSCONCED BACK IN Jo, it was all Riley could do not to hyperventilate. What the hell had she done? In *what world* was it actually a good idea to face this head on? To invite him to dinner to talk about the past *on purpose?*

The heat had fried her brain. That was it. She was under the influence of dehydration and the sight of all his muscles in action. Between that and feeling gooey toward him over all the nice things he'd done, she'd suffered a massive lapse in judgment.

There was no way out of it. You didn't cancel a thank you dinner. Postponement wouldn't help anything. If she never went through with it, she'd look bitchy and ungrateful. Which meant her only possible option to potentially avoid this conversation was distraction.

She thought of what Autumn had said about Drool Night and picked up the phone. "I need your help."

Autumn was waiting when Riley got back to the duplex.

"I've lost my mind."

"You've found your gumption," Autumn corrected. "Way to go for asking him out."

"It's just a thank you dinner for fixing my car. It's not a date."

"You did not call me over here to help you prepare for a non-date. You wanted help in making Liam see you as something other than a little sister or a friend, and I'm going to deliver. Get your ass in the shower, while I peruse your closet."

Grumbling, Riley did as she was told.

As the heated spray beat on her tired muscles—she was going to feel the effects of wielding that sledgehammer for at least a week—Riley reflected on all the many ways this dinner could blow up in her face. He could think she was throwing herself at him and not catch her—coming up with all new reasons for them to feel awkward around each other. He could relegate her permanently to the friend zone. He could admit he'd really only ever seen her as another sister. He could not be distracted by whatever Autumn came up with to make him drool and want to actually *talk* about the letter. Or she could cave and bring it up only to find out that he'd never even gotten the thing and didn't have any idea what she was talking about. Worst of all, he could believe she was like her mother, trying to woo him in order to find some kind of protector or caretaker.

As if.

She'd rather give up chocolate for life than ever follow in those footsteps.

Wrapped in her robe, Riley stepped back into her bedroom and nearly tripped over her cat as Valium twined around her legs. She picked him up for a cuddle. "This is a terrible idea I don't have any idea what to say to him. I'm going to trip all over my tongue."

"It's an opportunity," Autumn corrected. "And you're not going to trip over your tongue because he's going to be too busy tripping over his."

She emerged from the closet with a little black dress. Knee-length, with fluttering cap sleeves, the princess seams and sweetheart V-neck played up every asset Riley had, clinging to her curves like a second skin. She'd never had excuse to wear it.

"This dress is sex on a stick. We'll do up some Veronica Lake hair, smoky eyes, siren red lips, and Sergeant Montgomery won't know what hit him."

Riley rocked the dress. She knew she did. She'd bought it because it made her feel feminine and sexy. Confident. God knew she could use some confidence when it came to Liam. And yet…

"I don't know." Maybe she should just go casual—or at least as casual as one ever went to Magnolia Heights.

"You are not required to know, you're just required to wear the outfit."

Riley took a long look at the dress. It really would be a shame to let it go to waste. "Tell me how to do the hair."

"Go ahead and dry it. I require tools and product. Back in a jiff."

The pile of supplies she returned with was mildly alarming.

"Did you go to beauty school when I wasn't looking?"

"No, but my mom was a beautician. I know a thing or three." Autumn gestured to the edge of the bed. "Sit here."

"Not in the bathroom?"

"Oh no, no mirrors. You don't get to see until I'm done with you."

Riley looked askance in her direction.

"Come on. Would I steer you wrong?" Autumn demanded.

"You are a serial matchmaker. I know this about you. You might not deliberately steer me wrong, but you want to see love everywhere, whether it exists or not."

"It exists, and my role in life is to help nudge it along. Besides, tonight is not about love. It's about inspiring lust. Now sit."

Riley sat, back to the dresser mirror, and felt like she was going to crawl out of her skin.

"Stop fidgeting."

"Sorry. I'm just…"

"Nervous. I get it. Do all these doubts have to do with that complicated history you won't talk about?"

"Yeah."

"Well sugar, you're going to have to either get some resolution there or let it go entirely. Otherwise, you're gonna be stuck in this weird-ass limbo. Given he's back for good, I'd say that's a pretty uncomfortable place to be." She did something with the curling iron. "You might feel better if you talked about it."

God, maybe she would. Autumn would tell her if she was being an idiot, maybe save her some embarrassment tonight.

Riley took a bracing breath. "You didn't know me when we were younger, but you know I've always been up in the middle of the Montgomerys. Wynne and I were thick as thieves from first grade on. Her brothers were my brothers and her folks were another set of parents—a much appreciated, much needed second set, since Mom and I were on our own."

"Your dad was military, right?"

"Air Force. He was killed in action when I was five. My mom didn't take it well. They had a really traditional marriage, with traditional gender roles. Despite the fact that he was deployed a fair bit, he still managed to take care of everything. So, when he died, she not only had to cope with the devastation of losing the love of her life, but she was suddenly responsible for all this stuff that she'd never had to worry about before. She tried. She really did, for a long time." Riley had to acknowledge that. "But she just…couldn't deal. She started looking for a replacement for Daddy. Somebody who could fill his role and take care of her. Of us."

"That doesn't seem so surprising."

"No. And it might've been fine under other circumstances. But she…wasn't as discriminating as she should've been. She had this complete fairy tale with my dad. He swept her off her feet and made it so she never had to deal with any harsh realities. And she was naive enough to believe that most men were as good as he was. So from the time I was about seven, there was this parade of men through our lives as she tried to find the stability she was missing. Some stuck longer than others. But it wasn't until I was thirteen that one of them got serious and asked her to marry him."

To buy a moment and gather her thoughts, she dipped her hand into a jar of moisturizer and began to smooth it over her skin. "I didn't like Cliff from the beginning. He didn't say or do anything wrong. I just had a…vibe. Mom thought I was just being difficult and that I wasn't going to like anybody who wasn't Daddy. I'll admit there was some truth to that. But this was something else. Not that it mattered. She said yes, and he moved in."

Autumn stayed silent, curling a hand around Riley's shoulder.

"He didn't do anything overt. Nothing I could point to and say. 'This. This is not okay.' He just made me uneasy. He…watched me." Even thinking about it now made her skin crawl. Riley waved to her body. "This developed early. I was already catching harassment from the boys at school, and because there wasn't anything specific, when I mentioned it to my mother, she convinced me that I was overly sensitive and imagining things."

Autumn winced.

"Anyway, Molly and John ended up throwing an engagement barbeque for Mom and Cliff. Mom was so damned happy." It hurt to remember that.

"I don't know what Liam saw. It's odd, I guess, that I never asked him. But before we left that night, he cornered me and told me to leave my bedroom window unlocked, that he was coming by later. It was such a strange thing and he was so deadly serious, even at that age, that it didn't occur to me to ask why or to do any different. So when he came later, I let him in. He told me he was sleeping under my bed, and even though he didn't ask any questions or offer any explanations, I *knew* that he knew. That he'd somehow sensed the creeper vibe."

"*Under* your bed?"

"It was on risers and he wasn't as burly then. In case he was wrong, he didn't want me getting in trouble."

"So he stayed. What happened?"

"Nothing. I thought that would be the end of it. But Liam wasn't willing to let it go that easily. Bless him, he slept under my bed for a *week*, sneaking out every morning before breakfast. The first night was...weird. I mean, my best friend's big brother was sleeping *under* my bed.

After that, though, we talked. Late into the night. Stupid, inconsequential stuff at first. I think he was trying to put me at ease. I don't know that we'd ever had any real conversations before that." And those talks had given her a whole different view of Liam.

"The weekend after the party was some anniversary or celebration or other. Cliff brought home a bottle of wine to drink with dinner. My mom's never had a head for alcohol, but he just kept refilling her glass, until she'd had about three-quarters of the bottle. She passed out. And he came after me."

Autumn had gone pale. "Oh Riley."

Riley shook her head. "He never got to put a hand on me. Liam was on him the moment he unbuckled his belt." She closed her eyes, remembering the thud of fists on flesh as Liam beat Cliff with a terrifying precision and efficiency. "Liam made sure that he left. Packed his stuff and got him out of the house before my mother ever woke up. And he made it clear that if Cliff came back, came anywhere within a hundred feet of me, he wouldn't stop with a beating."

"Jesus. What did your mother say?"

"Nothing. She never knew. As far as she's aware, he decided he couldn't handle an insta-family and bailed on her."

"Riley! How could y'all not tell her? What if she brought someone else into the house?"

"Because she didn't believe me when I tried to talk to her about it before."

"You had Liam as witness."

"I had Liam as a vigilante who beat her fiancé to within an inch of his life. I was terrified he'd get into trouble over it. So we didn't tell anybody. Ever."

"Didn't you worry it could happen again?"

"Of course. I was scared to death of every guy my mom went out with for a long time after that. But Liam looked out for me, taught me self defense, until he was sure I could take down a guy twice my size. He made me feel... safe. He was the first guy I could depend on since my dad. Which, actually, isn't accurate. I could absolutely depend on his dad, too."

"But it wasn't the same." Yeah Autumn would get that, given her relationship with Judd and his family.

"No. It wasn't the same. And then he enlisted. Without telling me. I found out from Wynne. And I couldn't even say a word about how I felt about it because she didn't know he and I were…whatever the hell we were."

"You must've been devastated."

Riley shook her head, though she had been. "I was furious. Looking back, I didn't have a right to be. Not really." She'd thought a *lot* about that over the years. "We weren't friends like you and Judd. We weren't…anything, really. And just because he saved me from a would-be rapist once, didn't make me his lifetime responsibility."

"I'm sure none of that made you feel any less abandoned."

"True enough," she admitted. "But I wasn't mad because of that, so much as terrified that he'd be killed like my daddy. I was so *angry* that he deliberately put himself in harm's way, I wrote him this letter and shoved it into his bag before he left for boot camp."

"What did it say?"

Riley shook her head. Some details were better kept to herself. "A lot of things I had no right to say. A lot of things I'm ashamed of and embarrassed about."

"So you've been avoiding him all this time because of a letter you wrote him when you were fifteen and upset?"

"In a nutshell? Yes."

Autumn paused, an eyeliner pencil in her hand. "And here I thought it was because you have the hots for him."

Riley barked out a laugh. "That complication didn't get added to the equation until he came home for good."

"Well, we're going to dial up the complication on his side tonight." She leaned in, stroking the pencil along Riley's eyelid.

"Are you sure about this? I feel like a painted lady."

Autumn continued shading Riley's eyes. "Something you may not know about Liam—he has a deep love of old movies. So this vintage look you're rocking is totally going to work for him. You are exactly his type."

"I don't want to manipulate him."

"Playing up your God-given assets isn't manipulation. Never forget, with a positive attitude and a great pair of ta-tas, you can do anything. And you, darling, have a fabulous rack."

Riley snorted.

"There." Autumn laid down the eyeliner and surveyed her handiwork. "One of my better efforts, if I do say so myself."

Riley started to get up

"No. No, you have to see the entire package. C'mon, get dressed. I raided your underwear drawer and pulled out some sexy lingerie to go with the dress."

"Why? I'm not sleeping with him."

"Well, of course not. Although there'd be nothing wrong with it if you did. But sexy lingerie is a confidence booster. You'll know you're wearing it, and it'll impact how you carry yourself. Plus, he's going to wonder what's under that dress, and it makes it all the better if it really is something awesome. And in the event you change your mind and go for the hot monkey sex, you're set."

The idea of Liam peeling her out of the dress to find thigh highs and a garter belt almost had her hitting the shower again for a cold one, but the clock was ticking and she didn't have time. Not to mention Autumn would murder her for ruining all her hard work.

Only when she was dressed and zipped and had stepped into the sky high heels did Autumn let her near the mirror on the back of the closet door.

"Holy crap." Riley stared at the reflection and barely recognized herself. "You're like my own personal fairy godmother. I owe you."

Autumn grinned. "You can pay me in details, when you get back."

The doorbell rang. Riley rode out the quick clutch in her belly. She let out a long, slow breath. "Pray for me."

"Oh, I will."

Riley gave her a quick hug before picking up her purse.

"Promise me something," Autumn said, suddenly serious.

"What?"

"Don't waste this opportunity. If you do, you'll always wonder." Without giving Riley a chance to actually answer, Autumn shoved her toward the stairs. "I'll lock up after you're gone. No reason for him to know I was involved."

"Thank you! Oh, could you feed Valium?"

"Of course. And Riley?"

She paused at the bottom of the stairs. "What?"

"Condoms in your purse, just in case!"

Oh God.

Bracing herself, she went to answer the

door. One way or another, tonight was bound to change things. For better or worse.

THE M16/M4 Carbine rifle is a 5.56mm, magazine-fed, gas-operated, air-cooled, shoulder-fired weapon that can be fired either in automatic three-round bursts or semiautomatic single shots...

Liam continued his mental recitation of the characteristics and components of Marine weaponry. It was the only thing keeping him from embarrassing them both with his reaction to Riley's appearance. But he couldn't stop himself from giving her another appreciative once over as she passed by him into the air-conditioned restaurant.

Her toenails were scarlet, peeking out through the toes of strappy black shoes with sky high heels. His gaze skimmed up shapely legs to the hem of her little black dress. But it wasn't just any little black dress. It was the empress of little black dresses, elegant and form-fitting. And, oh God, what a form. A perfect hourglass, crowned with the most magnificent breasts, framed by a plunging neckline. But it was her face that had glued his tongue to the roof of his mouth since she walked out. Her full lips matched her toes, and her eyes looked almost electric with the smoky shadow and impossibly long lashes. If she'd stepped directly out of one of his erotic dreams, she couldn't have looked more perfect

But in the ensuing forty-five minutes, while he'd been busy reminding himself of every single reason why he shouldn't just blow dinner and find the nearest hotel to show her exactly what kind of fantasies that dress inspired, the confidence and vivacity she'd greeted him with had evaporated, leaving her obviously ill-at-ease. He was pretty sure it had something to do with a text she'd gotten on the drive. At least, he hoped it was the text and not him and his less-than-brotherly reaction. Surely she didn't think of him as a brother if she'd worn *that.*

Her hands were clamped around her purse

as if she expected it to get snatched. If she'd been any other woman, he'd have put an arm around her, flirted until she relaxed. But Riley wasn't any other woman, and Liam wasn't sure exactly what tonight was about. The last thing he wanted to do was misread the situation and screw things up.

Inconsequential small talk got them through being seated and placing their drink orders.

As the waiter scurried away, Liam sat back and sent her a smile that he hoped came off as friendly rather than *I am the Big Bad Wolf, and I want to eat you up.* "You look really amazing, by the way."

Her cheeks pinked. "Thanks. I spend most of my time in a lab coat or yoga pants, so it seemed a shame not to take advantage of the ambiance to wear something more fun." She went back to hiding behind the menu.

Liam didn't think she meant the kind of fun he'd been imagining.

Once they'd placed their orders, he picked up his beer and opted for a full-frontal assault of the elephant in the room. "I owe you an apology."

Distress flickered across that beautiful face. She shook her head. "You don't owe me anything, Liam."

When she began to pluck at a tiny, loose thread in the tablecloth, he covered her hand with his. He said nothing, waiting until she lifted her gaze to his. "I abandoned you, and I'm sorry."

At the faint jerk of her fingers, Liam tightened his hold. In twelve years, neither of them had ever spoken of the letter she'd left in his bag the day he left for boot camp. But he was tired of having the past lingering like some noxious smoke between them

Riley ducked her head and winced. "I'm ashamed of the things I said."

"You weren't wrong. I didn't think about you when I made the decision to enlist."

"And you shouldn't have. One noble act didn't make me your responsibility for life, and it wasn't fair of me to say anything to you that implied that I was. It wasn't fair of me to try and make you feel guilty just because I was afraid. I'm the one who should apologize."

Liam frowned. "You said you hadn't had cause to pull out that self defense since then."

"I haven't. I wasn't afraid for me. I was afraid for you. I was furious that you'd chosen a path that was going to put you in constant danger and terrified that you'd be killed in action like my father. I barely remember him, but I remember life was good and stable when he was alive. I didn't have a lot of stability after that. Not until you, anyway. I knew I could count on you, and that was an exceptionally rare thing in my world."

Had he realized that at eighteen? His motivations for protecting her had nothing to do with providing stability. She'd been so self-contained, so together. It never occurred to him that she'd looked to him for more than physical protection. Or maybe he hadn't wanted to believe she needed more than that because it made his decision to walk away easier.

"All the more reason I should've at least talked to you about it before I enlisted."

"Why did you enlist? I've never asked. Why the Marines?" She sat back and he regretted the loss of her touch.

"I wanted to be selfish."

Riley blinked. "I don't think anyone would ever think that joining the military is a selfish act, so you'll have to explain that one."

He'd never talked about this. "Did Wynne ever tell you how Jack and I came to the family?"

"Other than the fact that all four of you are adopted and that you and Jack are actual blood brothers, no."

"I was eight when we came to Molly and John. Jack was six. They were our tenth foster home. We'd been in the system for three years by then, and it was a damned miracle we hadn't been split up. I was what they euphemistically referred to as a 'difficult child,' which really meant that I was a smart ass little punk with no respect for authority." Liam jerked a shoulder.

"None of the so-called authority figures we were exposed to deserved any respect, as far as I could see. I learned quick that nobody was going to watch out for us but us. So I had one mission: Protect my brother—no matter what."

"From what?"

"Anything. Everything. Bullies. Negligence. Abusers. Child predators."

"That's how you knew about Cliff," she said softly.

"Yeah. That's how I knew. We didn't have a pretty life before we got to John and Molly. But I was the big brother, so it was my job to take care of him."

Riley sipped at her wine. "That didn't change once you became a Montgomery."

"No. We were some of the lucky ones. Our parents are amazing. But I could never just turn that part of me off. So the mission expanded to cover Wynne and Cruz. Then you."

"I imagine that was a heavy responsibility."

"That's just it. It wasn't. Life here was good. It wasn't like I had the same level of danger to look out for here as I did when Jack and I were in the system on our own. But I'd been in this constant state of threat assessment since I was five. Having that…awareness of the world and not doing anything with it was driving me slowly nuts. I didn't talk about it. Mom would've worried that she'd done something wrong, and it wasn't anything to do with her or Dad. It's just how I was built."

He took a long swallow of his beer, surprised to find his throat dry. "Everybody thought I'd work for Dad at the garage. I liked the work, and I was good at it. But the idea of staying here, locked into that life, felt like watching a cage door close. My whole life, up to that point, felt like it had been lived for somebody else. And I just—"

"Needed out?" There was no censure in her eyes, and he realized she got it.

"Yeah. Everybody I cared about was safe, so for the first time in my life, I was free to make a decision just for me. Everything that made me not quite fit in this world made me a born fighter. So, I enlisted and traded responsibility for one family for the responsibility of another, one where that mission-oriented focus is an asset and there's always somebody else to look out for."

"You miss it."

"Yes and no." He grimaced. "I'm not at all sure I'm cut out to be a civilian."

"Is it the structure you miss? The people?"

Most folks would've asked if he missed the action. But, as usual, Riley had a way of jumping past the obvious.

"Some of both. In some ways, life in the military is a lot more black and white than the everyday. There are always orders, hierarchy. And very clear lines that you don't cross."

His gaze was drawn to the thumb she stroked along the stem of her wineglass, and he wondered how it would feel along his skin.

Focus, Montgomery.

"Are the lines so blurry in civilian life?"

He thought of how much he wanted to touch her, how much he wanted her to be something other than his sister's best friend, and took a pull on his beer. "On some things, yes. Part of it's just that they gave me a place. I knew where I fit there." He sure as hell didn't know who he was if not a Marine.

"And you haven't quite figured out where you fit now that you're back. There's not a specific place outlined and waiting."

Liam lifted his beer. "Got it in one."

"So build your own place."

"You say that like it's easy."

"Easy isn't the right word for it. I've worked my ass off to build mine. But it's so worth it. To figure out that thing that you want and build your world around it."

He was having a hard time thinking about what he wanted beyond getting her out of that dress. What kind of underpinnings went with an outfit like that? Lace? Silk?

"Do you think you'd be happier if you went back?"

Liam jerked his attention back to the conversation and hoped like hell he hadn't been staring at her breasts. "If you'd asked me that a few months ago, I'd have said yes. Now, I don't know. When I enlisted, I was proud of what I was doing, felt sure that I was meant to serve my country. But this last year…I don't know what the hell I was fighting for that was so important, it was worth abandoning my family."

The arrival of their food interrupted the baring of his soul, and Liam was grateful, hoping to turn the conversation. But once their server had departed again, Riley reached out for his hand, expression fierce.

"You didn't abandon your family, Liam. If you'd never left, if you'd stayed and followed in Uncle John's footsteps at the garage, if you'd been there that day, you couldn't have done anything to change what happened. You know that, don't you?"

Of course, she'd know that'd been kicking around in his head. Objectively, he knew she was right. According to the doctors, the aneurysm had killed his father all but instantly. But it didn't mitigate the guilt. He'd walked away from the place he'd been given and his father was dead.

Liam turned his hand up, curled his fingers around hers. "Knowing that in my head and knowing it in my heart are two very different things. Either way, I've had enough of war. That being the case…"

He reached into his shirt and pulled out the engraved Celtic shield knot medallion.

Riley inhaled an unsteady breath. "I wasn't sure if you ever found it."

"You said your dad always wore it. Except the one time he didn't."

"It was the only thing I had left of him," she said softly. "Mom got rid of almost everything else over the years."

And she'd given it to him to keep him safe. "I've never taken it off." He did so now, slipping the cord over his head and folding the medallion into her hand. "I figure, it's time you have this back."

She rubbed her thumb over the surface of the knot before lifting her eyes back to his. "It's probably nothing but superstition, but thank you for wearing it."

He credited that superstition for saving his life on more than one occasion when he should've died, so he figured he owed her. "I got home safe, so I'd say it did its job. Thank you for caring enough to send it."

"You mattered. Still do, even if I haven't exactly shown it since you came back."

Simple words that he wanted to mean more than she probably did.

"You were angry with me. I get it."

"I shouldn't have been. It's hard for me to think about back then. The fact is, I should thank you for leaving."

It was the last thing he expected her to say. "Why?"

She pulled her hands free and slipped the medallion over her head, wrapping her fist around it against her breastbone. She closed her eyes and something in her face relaxed, some subtle tension he hadn't even realized she carried until it was gone.

"Because I'm stronger now than if you'd stayed."

He frowned, lifting his gaze back to her face. "How so?"

"I learned to rely on myself. No parachute, no fall back, no net. My mother has spent twenty years looking for that. It was all she knew from her parents, from my dad. She never moved beyond that. I did. And I'm so much better off because I learned how to stand completely on my own."

She sat back, obviously relieved. "So consider tonight both a thank you and an apology. And if it's all the same to you, I'd like to forget about the rest. Clean slate."

Clean slate. No reminders of their complicated past.

Translation: I don't need you anymore.

And why should she? She'd built a life for herself with no help from anyone. Liam admired the hell out of that indomitable spirit, understood the need to prove oneself. The last thing she needed was any kind of hindrance to her goal of establishing independence, and the last thing he wanted was to somehow drag her back to something she was trying to get away from. He owed her that, if nothing else.

So though it pained him to do so, Liam tapped his glass to hers and forced a smile. "Clean slate."

RILEY DIDN'T KNOW what she'd expected from asking for a clean slate. To feel better, somehow. More at ease with the situation and with him. Maybe even for both of them to pretend they'd never met and were on an actual first date.

But she didn't feel better. After finally finding out what drove Liam into the Marines in the first place, she felt like even more of a bitch than she already had. Add to that the nerves that kept jumping every time he laid his hand over hers, and it was a wonder she managed to get out coherent sentences.

He wasn't looking at her like a victim, and she was grateful. But he wasn't looking at her like a date either. That hadn't *really* been the point of tonight. The whole distract him with sex appeal plan had flown out the window when he brought up the past straight out of the gate. But sitting there across from him, sharing a lovely meal and good conversation—once they'd left their complicated history in the past —she'd wanted more than the friendship he'd asked for.

He'd returned the medallion. As the dark miles rolled by, Riley wrapped her fist around it again. She didn't care that it looked ridiculous with her dress. He'd brought back a piece of her father that she'd lost and grieved for years ago. And now, it was a piece of Liam, too. Despite everything, he'd worn it all these years. That had to mean something. Didn't it?

She glanced at him, skimming her gaze over the strong line of his jaw, down his arms to those very capable hands on the wheel.

Did she have a right to push for more? To

complicate things when both of them were aiming for something simple? And did she really, truly *want* to push for more than friendship after what he'd told her? He'd said he was done with war, but could he really be happy in Wishful, in a life without a mission? If she pursued this and he walked away again…

"Are you busy tomorrow?"

Startled out of her thoughts, Riley sat up a little straighter and realized they were pulling into her driveway. "Nothing that can't be moved around. What did you have in mind?"

"Can you meet me at Blanchard's Gym?"

She blinked at him. "At the gym?"

"I'd like to do some refresher training with you on your self defense."

"What?"

Liam looked over, but there was no flirtatious smile to suggest he was thinking about anything other than actual training. "You did pretty well, considering you haven't practiced in years, but I'd feel better if you brushed up on things." At her hesitation, he added, "It's closed on Sundays, so you don't have to worry about the other guys. I've got a key."

"I suppose so." What else was she going to say? She didn't want to insult his kindness again just because it wasn't the sort of sweaty, up-close and personal time she'd had in mind.

"Great. Two o'clock work for you? Plenty of time for coffee that way." He flashed a teasing grin.

"You sure? I'm meaner without coffee. I'd probably fight better."

Liam laughed. "I'll test your mean after I'm sure you've got your techniques down."

Riley followed when he got out of the car. As this clearly hadn't turned into a date, there was no reason to wait for him to circle around to open her door. Still, he walked her up the front steps of the duplex, waiting as she slid the key into the lock.

"Thanks for dinner."

"Thanks for fixing my car."

Dressed for a date. Felt like a date. Still not a date. What the hell do we do now?

Riley hesitated, her hand on the knob. "I'm glad we talked." No matter how things turned out, at least they'd cleared the air and she wouldn't have to spend the rest of her life avoiding him.

"Me too. I missed you, Riley Marie." He leaned in, and Riley's heart began to thud. Then he wrapped an arm around her shoulders in an awkward, brotherly sort of hug.

She slid an arm around his waist and squeezed. "I'm glad you made it home safe."

Liam stepped back. "See you tomorrow?"

"Yeah. Tomorrow." When she realized he was going to stand there until she got inside, she opened the door, offering a little wave before shutting it again. On a long sigh, she leaned against the other side, listening to the sound of his car pulling away.

She didn't believe in playing Cinderella, so why the hell should she be so disappointed that the prince didn't respond to a makeover?

At the knock, Riley jolted. Had he changed his mind? With her head full of visions of Liam coming back and ravishing her mouth without a word, she yanked open the door.

The sight of Autumn's expectant gaze deflated her fantasy as quick as a pin prick.

"Hey."

"I come bearing chocolate in lieu of the sex you're not having." Autumn pushed past her into the entryway and squealed. "You're wearing Liam's necklace!"

Of course, she'd zero in on that. "It's not what you think. It was my dad's good luck charm. I put it in Liam's bag when he left for boot camp. He was returning it to me."

"And he's worn it faithfully, all these years," Autumn said softly. She had that look in her eye that meant she was extrapolating a lot more out of the action than it merited.

"Don't you dare go off on some romanticized tangent about a knight wearing his lady's token in battle or some crap. It wasn't like that."

She handed over the chocolate. "Clearly you need this."

Riley scrubbed a hand over her face. "I'm

sorry. Operation Sex On A Stick was a miserable failure. He was a complete, uninterested gentleman." She'd thought, maybe, the outfit had gotten his attention when he picked her up. But other than telling her she looked nice, he'd steered completely clear of flirtation.

Autumn pouted. "That's not how this story is supposed to go."

Irritated, Riley bent to unbuckle the shoes that were killing her feet. "There's no supposed to about it. Life isn't one of your fairy tales or romance novels. I stopped looking for a prince a long time ago." And why the hell should that have changed? "For all that I love them, those stories are dangerous things. They set up completely unrealistic expectations."

"Well that's all kinds of cynical and just plain sad."

Riley stalked into the living room, tossing her shoes by the coffee table and flopping onto the sofa. Valium emerged from beneath it to crawl into her lap. At least someone loved her. "It's realistic. Fairy tales aren't real. They don't last." She'd do well to remember that instead of letting her brain run amok with romantic fantasies fueled by sexual starvation and a high school crush that should've died long ago.

"Them's fightin' words, baby girl. But you've had a disappointing evening, so I'm going to pretend you didn't just say that." Autumn folded herself into the opposite corner of the couch. "Did y'all talk about…stuff?"

"Yeah, we cleared the air."

"That's it, then. You killed the mood with all the serious stuff. Which needed to be said so that y'all can move past it."

"There wasn't a mood to be killed. He's not harboring some secret desire to strip me down and drizzle me in honey." *More's the pity.*

"Not a bad thing. Honey's delicious, but hella sticky. You don't want to mess with getting that out of your sheets."

"Doesn't matter, as he's not going to be anywhere near my sheets." Riley dropped her head back. "We're friends. That's all we'll ever be."

"So that's it? You're just going to leave it at that?"

"I'm not going to throw myself at him. He said he wants to be friends, so I'll honor that." It was the smart thing. The sensible thing.

"Even though you're totally undressing him with your eyes every time he walks into a room?"

Riley draped an arm over her eyes. "I'll get over it." *Somehow.* In the long silence, she could feel Autumn's eyes on her. "Feel free to offer up suggestions as to how I can speed that along."

"You and Liam sizzle when you get within ten feet of each other."

"Not useful, Autumn. I'm pretty sure you're delusional." The only one of them spontaneously combusting was her.

"Okay, okay, I know. Not helping. But maybe this will. Be right back." Autumn came back a few minutes later with a stack of books. "If you're serious about not going after him, then all you've got left is sublimation into more socially acceptable means."

"Which are?"

Autumn set the books on the table. "Smexy romance novels with Marine heroes."

Riley picked up the top one, Tawna Fenske's *Marine For Hire*. "It's sticky tabbed."

"I marked the really good parts."

Riley eyed the bristling pages.

"There are a lot of good parts," Autumn said. "Anyway, since you're determined to walk the safe path, it's all I've got for you."

Riley shot her a sympathetic look. "I guess you're pretty familiar with that."

Autumn bit into the bar of Godiva. "Girl, I'm so deep in that rut, I can hardly see out."

"Well, at least you'll have company. Where should I start?"

CHAPTER 6

GOT A JOB. :) :) :)

RILEY stared at her mother's text from last night. She still hadn't answered. What was the right response? Was it true? Or was Sharilyn just telling Riley what she wanted to hear? And if it was true, what kind of job was it? What on earth sort of work could she have found in less than twenty-four hours? Was it horrible? Did she want Riley to ask just so she could play martyr and show what new lows she'd sunk to in order to garner sympathies and force Riley to roll right on past the new boundary she'd set and rescue her again? Okay, maybe that was over-thinking. If it was horrible, she probably wouldn't have added the smiley faces. But Riley couldn't make herself call to get the details. She was too afraid of what she might hear. Her faith in her own resolve was running thin. But she had to say something.

Proud of you. Take care.

As Liam came out of the locker room and dumped a bag by the mats, Riley hit send and reached for the medallion around her neck. She brought it to her lips and said a little prayer. *Daddy, look out for her. I'm trying to do the right thing.*

"Problem?"

"No. Yes. Maybe. I don't know." Thinking about it was giving her a headache.

Liam straddled the bench beside her, looking all big and tough as he leaned toward her. "Talk to me."

Riley shook her head. "I don't want to dump on you."

"It's not dumping if I asked."

She needed to talk to someone about it. Wynne would've been her first choice. But Wynne wasn't here, and much as she tried to stay in touch, calling sporadically when she surfaced between clients, her life was in New Orleans now. Autumn would listen, but it wasn't the same as telling someone who'd been around almost from the beginning, who'd seen what she went through. Liam had been there. She'd agreed they could be friends. Friends talked. Maybe it would get easier with practice.

Riley pivoted, swinging one leg over the bench to mirror his position. "That phone call I got yesterday, when you dropped off Jo, was my mom. She's in California, where her latest ex dumped her off with nothing."

"Do we need to go get her?"

This was his immediate response. No questions. No details needed. Just an unequivocal offer of help. Was it any wonder she'd wanted so much to depend on him growing up? Looking at him now, Riley realized exactly how easy it would be to slide back into that expectation. That solid dependability was beyond seductive. She wanted to frame his face in her hands and brush her lips over his, just for making the offer.

To keep from giving into the urge, Riley curled her fingers around the edge of the bench between them. "No. I already sent her money for a bus ticket last week. Which she blew instead of coming home like she was supposed to. Yesterday she called asking for more money." She took a breath. "I cut her off. Told her to find some kind of short-term work to earn enough for a bus ticket home. I just *left* her out there, Liam. Entirely on her own."

"Good for you." His easy conviction surprised her.

"Really?"

"Your relationship with your mama has always been wonky. She never *really* had to take responsibility for anything because you did it for her. This will push her to do that.'"

"But what if—" A dozen disaster scenarios

rolled through her mind, each worse than the last.

"Has she texted or called to say she's in trouble?"

"No. She says she's found a job."

"Well, then she's doing exactly what you told her to do. What's the problem?"

Riley knit her fingers together and twisted. "As you said, I've always taken care of her. What if she can't make it on her own? If anything happens to her, I'll never forgive myself. Weird as our relationship is, she's all I've got left."

Liam folded her hands between his to stop their wringing. "You're doing the right thing, Riley. And unlike some people we know, your mama has no problem asking for help if she gets in over her head."

She narrowed her eyes. "Ha. Ha."

He grinned and chucked her lightly under the chin before sliding off the bench. "C'mon. You'll feel better once you work some of that tension out of your system."

"Yeah, about that. I'm pretty sure even my

hair hurts from that sledgehammer. It took me nearly an hour of yoga this morning just to un-kink my back."

"All the more reason to get moving before you knot back up again."

She followed him over to the mats, pulling her arm in a cross body stretch that left her hovering at that threshold between pleasure and pain, until the muscle finally released. She shifted to the other arm, then bent at the waist to touch the floor, stretching out her back and hamstrings.

Liam made some sound behind her.

Spreading her legs slightly, she peered at him between her knees. "Did you say something?"

"No. Just muttering to myself."

Was he redder than he had been a minute ago? Had he been checking out her ass?

Straightening, Riley moved to the center of the mat. "Instruct me, oh Obi-wan."

He was all business as he came to join her.

"Okay, to start, let's review the release you tried on me."

His hand clapped down on her shoulder from behind. Riley grabbed his wrist, pulling him forward and ducking.

"Stop."

She paused, his arm slung around her neck. The hand attached to the wrist she still held dangled dangerously close to her breast.

"Do you know what you're doing wrong?"

"Um."

"Start again. Slower, this time."

Once again, she stepped back as she grabbed his wrist, pulling him forward, until that broad chest bumped into her back. And once again, she forgot what she was doing.

"Trade places," he ordered.

So Riley grabbed him by the shoulder.

He hunched down a bit, so as not to leave her dangling. "You've got this first bit right." His grip around her wrist was firm, but not bruising as he tugged her forward. "What you're forgetting is to step back with this foot—" He shifted his lead leg behind her. "—grab this hand between both of yours and *then* duck and twist, bringing your opponent's arm up." He followed through, and Riley found herself bent forward, her arm at an awkward angle behind her back. "And at that point, you grab the collar and drag backward, to the ground. Or you can take out a knee, whatever works. From here, you have complete control over your opponent's body." With careful motions, he proved his point "Got it?"

Riley flushed. *Stop thinking about his control over your body.* "Yep."

He made her go through it several times slowly, correcting small motions, until he was satisfied she had the technique down from both sides. Then he let her do it at speed. He ended up on his knees, a fact which left Riley feeling more than a little satisfied.

"Good job. Now let's try a double shoulder grab."

It came back quickly as Liam put her through the paces. He was a patient, thorough teacher. They progressed through basic releases, into some simple throws. He'd picked up some new tricks in the years since they'd last done this, and Riley enjoyed proving she was a quick study. Was there anything more satisfying than successfully tossing a Marine on his ass?

"Okay, so let's say all that fails. Somebody gets you on the ground in a compromising position."

At his direction, Riley laid back flat on the mat. He pinioned her arms above her head, pinning the rest of her with his weight against her hips. And oh, yeah, there was definitely something that would be more satisfying than tossing him on his ass.

Focus.

But his pupils had blown wide and his breath quickened against her chest as he stared down at her. It became rapidly apparent that she wasn't the only one having a hard time concentrating. Her core muscles tightened, everything in her wanting to grind her hips against the erection now pressing between her thighs.

"Compromising position?" she prompted.

"Right. What are you going to do?" His voice was rough and low.

Struggling to think past the haze of lust, Riley considered her options. There was no getting her hands back from here. She had only one real alternative that she could see. Wrapping her legs around his waist, she squeezed him tighter against her center. Liam dropped his head and let out a strangled moan, and she took advantage of his distraction, shifting her hips and rolling until their position was reversed.

Now what? Was there an actual protocol for when your sparring partner was sporting a hard on? It probably wasn't licking his throat and begging him to strip you down to get to know every sweaty inch better.

Liam yanked, and what leverage she had was lost. She collapsed on his chest with a whoosh. He rolled and then he was on top again, his breath hot against her throat.

Oh please, yes.

"Mistake number one. Never let somebody get this far."

Riley blinked up at his shoulder. Okay, so he was sticking to instructor mode. They were not going to acknowledge what was going on in his pants.

"But if they do," he continued, "you're going to shrimp out of it."

"I'm going to what now?"

He rolled off her, onto his own back, and Riley kept her eyes firmly on his chest as he demonstrated the technique. By the time they'd gone through the escape again, from every point at which she could stop an attacker, all the way to where they'd started, he'd managed to get himself under control. But he didn't quite meet her eyes as he suggested they call it a day. It was a strange and fascinating thing to see Liam Montgomery embarrassed about something, and it left Riley wondering if Autumn wasn't on to something after all. Was this about her? Or would he be just as turned on doing this kind of training with any woman?

"Thanks for the refresher." She gulped down water.

"No problem. You remembered the original stuff pretty well, and picked up the new quickly."

"I could probably use some more practice. Some of those techniques I'm not going to remember in an hour. I'd feel better with some more drills." *Neutral face. Neutral face. Neutral face.*

"Sure. We can do that."

"Great." They'd keep getting hot and sweaty together, and she'd put the theory to the test.

LIAM WAS FINISHED with demolition on the apartment. Which was really too damned bad because he wasn't anywhere near done working off his sexual frustration.

He slapped the next two-by-four across the saw horses and measured, marking the cut, and lining up the blade of the miter saw.

This whole *just friends* thing with Riley was going to kill him. Liam couldn't decide whether to be insulted or envious that she found it so easy. He sure as hell didn't. Thanks to their weekly training sessions, he knew exactly what all those curves felt like—heaven. Keeping his hands off her these last two weeks—off the mats anyway—as he plowed ahead on the apartment renovations had proved a helluva lot more difficult than he'd expected. That probably would've been made easier if he actually stayed *out* of the pharmacy, but despite his best intentions, he kept finding reasons to pop in and see her. Attraction aside, he genuinely *liked* Riley. Always had. And it was a pleasure to be at a point where their age gap no longer mattered.

Or it would be if he could get other kinds of pleasure out of his mind.

Liam carried the wood over to the new wall he was building and tested the fit. No dice. He was going to have to rip it for the tie-in to be neat. After a few more measurements, he took the stud over to the table saw, lined things up for the cut and turned on the saw.

Why the hell had she worn that dress?

All he'd been able to think about since their dinner was peeling her out of it and finding out what other surprises lay underneath. Which was so obviously not in the cards. He needed the image wiped from his brain. Instead, he found himself wondering if she was hiding something sexy under that lab coat she worked in every day.

The saw whined and snarled, and the two-by-four jerked beneath Liam's hand. The next thing he knew, he was seeing stars. The saw cut off.

"Son of a bitch!"

What the hell had happened? He picked up the two-by-four—now on the ground—and saw the knot on the bottom side. The knot he should've noticed before he ever tried to rip the damned thing. Goddamn it. He needed his head on the job, not on the woman he couldn't have.

Blood was dripping onto the floor from his thumb. Despite the mess, it didn't look to be too bad. Because it was the only thing handy, he grabbed a sweat rag and wrapped it around his hand. There was no mirror to check the damage to his head—he hadn't put a new one up in the bathroom yet. He could still see out of both eyes, so that was probably fine, too, but he wasn't going to get any more work done until he dealt with this. Irritated, he headed downstairs and into the pharmacy.

Riley was on the phone when he walked in. At the sight of him, her jaw dropped open. *What the hell did you do?* she mouthed. Into the phone she said, "Sure thing. Yeah, thanks. I have to go."

She hung up and pointed at him. "You, sit. I'll deal with you in a minute.

Ignoring her order, Liam strode toward the first aid aisle, while she dealt with the irritated woman at the counter. Riley spoke to her in a quiet voice, then the shredder whined.

The customer shrieked. "That was *mine!*"

Abandoning his search for Band-aids, Liam headed toward the front, ready to intervene if necessary. He didn't catch Riley's reply.

"What am I supposed to *do* without my prescription?"

"Sorry, Ms. Tomlinson. That's a matter for you to take up with Dr. Campbell. You're welcome to try the new Walgreens, when it opens."

"You can be sure that I will." On a huff, the woman turned and stalked out.

Before the door had fully shut, Riley hurried around the counter. "What did you *do?*"

Embarrassed, Liam scowled at her. "Stop looking at me like I've whacked off a finger. I just need some gauze and tape."

"What you need is to sit down and let me look at it. Damn it, you're bleeding all over my floor." Riley herded him back behind the counter and into the office. "Sit."

Heaving a long suffering sigh, Liam sat on the desk. "The saw blade caught a knot on the bottom side of the wood. Yanked it right out of my hands." *Because I was thinking about getting you naked instead of focusing on what I was doing.*

With a moue of disapproval, she unwrapped his impromptu field dressing and examined the wounds "And apparently took a chunk of your thumb and several layers of skin with it. Not to mention gave yourself a nasty goose egg on your head."

Said goose egg was throbbing in time with his thumb.

Riley shut the office door and retrieved the first aid kit from the cabinet behind it. They were, he realized, alone.

"Where is everybody?"

"Ruby had a dentist appointment, and Jessie went to pick up lunch."

Quick and efficient, she wadded up the bloody rag beneath his hand to catch drips and doused the thumb with peroxide. He took a moment to be thankful she hadn't chosen the rubbing alcohol.

"Does that kind of thing happen often?" he asked.

"What kind of thing?"

"People doctor shopping, trying to get more pain meds or whatever?"

"Mmm, a fair bit. Since they clamped down on Sudafed, people shifted from meth to prescription pain meds. Mississippi has one of the worst abuse rates in the nation."

"How did you know?"

"We've got an electronic database. Any time somebody comes in with a prescription for controlled substances, we run a check to find out when and where they last got them. If it's too close together, we call the prescribing doc and verify. In this particular case, the doctor requested the prescription be shredded." After the thumb stopped bubbling, she dabbed it clean with some sterile cotton and examined the wound, which still bled sluggishly.

"You shouldn't be alone here."

"I rarely am. But I'm completely fine, Liam. I know how to handle that kind of thing."

He could too easily imagine how such a situation could go south in a hurry, and he didn't like the idea of her facing it by herself one bit. "I don't like it."

Her mouth quirked, but she didn't look away from what she was doing. "You don't have to like it. It's part of the job. Your mom's dealt with it for years and never had any trouble. Neither have I. And there's a panic button if anything goes sideways. *And* you've already made sure I've been getting a refresher on self defense."

Liam frowned. "I guess I never thought much about Mom having to deal with stuff like that. She never talked about it."

"Because it's never been a problem. We're fine. I don't think you have any wood splinters in here. You could probably do with a stitch or two."

He'd already been over the security and it was solid, so he let the subject drop. "I'm not going to lose the entire afternoon of work just to get a couple of measly stitches." This renovation was the first time he felt like he'd accomplished something since he came home. "Just slap a Band-aid or three on and be done with it."

She rolled her eyes. "You are such a man."

"I'll take that as a compliment."

"It was more commentary on your pig-headedness." But she bandaged the thumb as requested.

After taping off the gauze bandage on his thumb, Riley turned over his hand to examine the abraded knuckles. The sense of déjà vu swamped him as she paused, fingers curling gently to hold his. She'd done this before, that long ago night. Cleaned and bandaged his bruised and bloody knuckles. Her hands had trembled then. They'd both trembled then, in the wake of what he'd done to protect her.

Riley traced a finger along the unabraded skin, and he knew she was remembering, too. Liam brought his free hand up to trap her hand between his and gently squeezed. Lifting her gaze to his, she offered a fleeting smile before resuming her ministrations with cool efficiency.

"There." She released him.

"Thanks."

"Now, let's take a look at your head." Moving in close, she probed around the knot with light fingers.

Liam hissed, though it was more from the feel of her body brushing his than from the pressure of her touch.

"Sorry. It's definitely going to bruise." She stepped back. "But you didn't break the skin, so that's something."

"That's it?"

"That's it. Unless there's some other injury you're hiding. I know you're not about to sit here with an ice pack, even though you should."

He pointed to his temple. "Mom would've kissed it."

Riley's lips quirked. "The big bad Marine needs that kind of special attention?"

Liam gave her his best puppy dog face.

"Fine." She laughed and cupped his face in both hands, tipping it down so she could reach.

Her lips pressed his wounded temple, soft

and smooth, and Liam closed his eyes with a sigh. Something inside him settled, even as his heart stumbled and sped up. He wanted to wrap his arms around her. Wanted to bury his face against her throat and lose himself in the scent and taste of her skin. He just plain wanted. But he curled his hands around the edge of the desk instead, accepting the small thing she offered without pushing for more than she wanted to give.

When her lips brushed his, Liam froze. Had he been hit harder than he realized? Was he hallucinating now? But the pressure came again, her hand sliding around to cup his nape as she settled her mouth more firmly over his.

"Well butter my butt and call me a biscuit."

Riley shot away from him as if she'd been electrocuted.

"Mom. You're back."

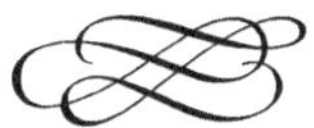

CHAPTER 7

HE DIDN'T KISS ME back.

Mortification burned through Riley so hot and fast, she wondered the floor didn't collapse beneath her feet. Except, of course, it didn't. Because that would mean the Universe was giving her some kind of an escape from this God-awful situation. She hadn't earned enough good karma in this lifetime for that.

Her mother stood in the open doorway, expression bright with curiosity as her gaze flickered between Riley and Liam. Riley didn't meet her eyes, and she sure as hell didn't look at Liam.

He slid off the desk. "Mrs. Gower. Welcome home."

"I think I should be saying that to you." Sharilyn stepped forward to give him a quick hug. "I'm sorry I missed your party back in December. I know your mama's so glad to have you home."

"Yes, ma'am. I've been steady working my way through her backlogged honey-do list. Speaking of, I should get back to it."

In her periphery, Riley saw him lift his bandaged hand in her direction.

"Thanks for fixing me up."

She kept her eyes on the door frame and wrapped both arms around her middle. "Sure."

He hesitated for a moment, and Riley could feel him looking at her, but she simply couldn't bear to look back and see the awkward or the embarrassment or the *what the hell were you thinking, you crazy woman?* After a couple of eternal beats, he nodded a polite goodbye to her mother, who stepped out of his way, and beat a hasty retreat. Riley watched him go, the big bad Marine she'd taken a chance on, who'd let her fall flat on her face. Because she'd listened to Autumn's optimism and misread him.

Her lip wanted to tremble. Aware of her mother's attention, Riley bit the inside to keep it still.

"I never thought I'd see the day you'd go for a military man."

Riley closed her eyes and counted to ten, waiting for the muscles in her back to loosen. They didn't. "I'm not going for a military man, Mom."

"Then what was that?"

"That was—" *A mistake. An aberration.* "—nothing."

"Uh huh." Sharilyn crossed her arms, her lips twitching in amusement.

"How did you get here, Mom?" Riley asked, determined to change the subject. "I expected you to call me to come pick you up from the bus station in Lawley."

"I didn't take the bus."

Riley frowned. "Then how did you get home?"

"I hitched a ride with a trucker."

"You did *what?*" Riley's voice shot high with disbelief as she imagined all the worst iterations of that scenario, most of which ended with Sharilyn dead in a ditch and Riley left alone.

"I was working third shift at an all-night diner to earn my bus fare. Which was taking a while, since I had to pay for living expenses meanwhile."

Riley ignored that subtle jab. "And, what? You decided you were tired of waiting, so you *hitchhiked?*"

"I got to talking to one of my customers and noticed *her* southern accent. Turned out she's from Alabama and was headed home to Dothan. She offered me a ride, and I took it."

The clutch in Riley's chest loosened somewhat. "Oh my God, Mom, she could've been an axe murderer."

Sharilyn waved a dismissive hand. "Don't be silly. Billy Jean is a twice-divorced grandmother of two. We had plenty to talk about across country."

I'm sure you did.

As the shop bell jangled, Riley pushed out of the office, struggling to put on her friendly customer face. She thanked God it was only Jessie with their take out from Dinner Belles. She wasn't ready to face anyone else until she'd had some privacy to process her shame.

"Mrs. G! Didn't know you were back."

"Only just. Hello, sugar." Sharilyn walked back around the counter to give Riley's tech a hug.

Jessie set their food on the counter. "How was the Great American Road Trip?"

Her mother's smile faltered only briefly before coming back full wattage. "Got to see all kinds of amazing sights and go to places I'd only ever heard of. It was an experience. But I'm glad to be home. The long-term open road is not for me."

"What about Hal?" Jessie asked.

"We parted ways, and he drove off into the sunset." She said it like he was a lone-wolf cowboy riding off at the end of a movie, instead of an asshole who'd abandoned her thousands of miles from home

Riley studied the dreamy expression. Was it a facade or had she really convinced herself it'd been tragically romantic? How could she be okay with what had happened?

Sharilyn hopped on the counter to perch. "So tell me, any funny pharmacy stories lately?"

"Oh, well yesterday Riley compounded muscle relaxer for a squirrel."

"Get out. Really?"

"Jessie, we really aren't supposed to talk about this."

"What? It's not like HIPPA covers rodents. Poor thing has puncture wounds in her leg. The squirrel—whose name is Roxy—also needed some Valium because her bladder was so distended that she couldn't teetee. When her owner showed up to pick up the meds, he said he'd spent over $240 on her at the vet. The bill here was over $50. He said they'd bottle fed her from a baby and that his son would be really upset if they lost her."

"Well, if she was a pet, I guess I understand that. How old was the son?"

"Thirty-one."

Riley's mom, who had no poker face to speak of, stared in disbelief. "Now, I've heard everything."

"Oh no." Jessie pointed with the straw she was unwrapping. "There's more. She starts physical therapy next week. And they're still planning on releasing her into the wild when she gets better."

"My Lord. What did y'all say?"

"Good luck with that," Riley replied. "Listen, the stuff you shipped is at my place. It'll be a little while before I can shake loose to drive you to the house. Molly's at a citizen's coalition meeting until three and won't be able to relieve me until then."

Sharilyn crossed her legs. "Oh, don't you

worry about that, honey. I've got orientation for my new job."

Riley managed not to do a complete double take. "Your new what now?"

"Matthew McSweeney hired me as a checker at the market. He told me to come on in when I got back to town to learn the system."

Riley stared at her. When had she even talked to Matthew McSweeney? "You only just got back. How did you already land a job?"

"You probably don't remember, but Matthew was an old friend of your daddy's. They were in the service together. He always said if I ever needed anything, I just had to call. So I did, and he happened to have a position open."

Dear God, don't let her have set her sights on Matthew. "Does he know you don't have any retail experience?"

"That's the entire point of the orientation. I officially start day after tomorrow."

"Well that's—" *Surprising. Astounding. Got disaster written all over it.* "—great, Mom. It'll be good for you to be working with the public. I know how much you love people."

"I'm looking forward to it," Sharilyn said breezily. "It'll take me a little while to save up enough for my own place, but as soon as I do, I'll be out of your hair. I'm not going to be a burden to you."

Riley didn't believe that for a minute. As soon as she found another sugar daddy, she'd fall right back into old patterns. Riley forced her lips to curve and prayed it didn't look like a grimace. "I wish you the best of luck." Sharilyn was sure as hell going to need it. Riley just hoped she didn't lose her own mind in the meantime.

Riley was avoiding him.

Nearly a week had passed since that unexpected kiss, and Liam still hadn't had a chance to talk to her about it. Her mom was staying at her place, and in light of that, Riley had thrown herself into work like it was the only thing tethering her to sanity. Given her relationship with her mother, maybe it was.

The pharmacy had been covered up, which pleased Liam, since Walgreens was due to open in a week. But it meant they hadn't had a moment alone. Riley had made absolutely sure of that. Every time he came into the pharmacy, she was on the phone, holed up in the office, or tied up with a customer. Which was part and parcel of running a business. But she wouldn't even look at him.

She had the wrong idea.

Looking back, perhaps pretending nothing had happened just because her mom had shown up was not the best course of action. But she'd seemed so embarrassed. What else was he supposed to say under those circumstances? Excuse me, Mrs. Gower, I need to shut the door in your face so I can finish kissing your daughter brainless. Yeah, no.

Liam could've called or sent flowers or some kind of note, but this was a conversation that needed to be had in person—without starting the kind of courting behavior that would get the entire town buzzing before they'd even sorted out what was what.

But setting Riley straight required some privacy. Since she wasn't cooperating, he was going to create the opportunity. He'd thought about inviting her up to see the progress on the apartment upstairs, but she wouldn't leave the pharmacy unless his mom was there to relieve her. With her current streak of luck, the Board of Pharmacy would drop by for an impromptu inspection and dock her for not having a licensed pharmacist on premises for fifteen minutes. She didn't need that. So it was on to plan B.

Liam reached the pharmacy as Babette Wofford was stepping out.

"Oh Liam! Just the man I was looking for."

He worked up a smile for the pint-sized spitfire, who owned the local bridal shop. "Afternoon, Mrs. Wofford."

She beamed at him. "Your mama showed me

the renovation you're doing on the apartment above the pharmacy. It's just gorgeous."

That was a stretch. "I've only just got the new walls in and the built-ins started. There's a ways to go yet." He waited, wondering where this was going.

"I've got apartment space above my shop as well, and I want to hire you to renovate it. Norah's gearing up for a push to really sell downtown living, and having the space all duded up would allow me to bump up the rent a bit."

Surprise struck him momentarily speechless. Why would she want to hire *him* as a contractor when there were others in town more qualified? "Well, I certainly appreciate you thinking of me, Mrs. Wofford. It's one thing for me to do that kind of work for my mother, but I'm not licensed or bonded. That kind of liability is dangerous for you."

Babette fisted both hands on her hips. "Nonsense. I saw that apartment. Your work is quality. I'm not at all worried that anything would go wrong."

Some people were way too trusting. If she had that kind of attitude toward renovations, she was in prime position to be taken advantage of.

As he geared up for a polite way to tell her exactly that, she interrupted, "Tell me you'll come by and at least look at the place to give me an estimate."

He could do that much, at least. And his quote would give her a yardstick to judge other offers for fairness. "All right I'll have a look."

Babette clapped her hands together with glee. "Excellent."

They made arrangements for a time and chatted briefly about Babette's grandchildren—her eldest granddaughter Delilah was doing something big with fashion in Paris—before Liam finally managed to break loose to slip inside without attracting Riley's attention.

She moved behind the counter, hands quick and competent as they sorted and filled and dropped the pill bottle into a white paper bag and folded the top neatly over. "Here you go, Mr.

Tolleson. You don't owe a thing. It's all on your insurance now that you've met your deductible." She passed him the bag and leaned forward conspiratorially. "And I snuck in a handful of those butterscotch disks Winnie likes."

Howard Tolleson's wrinkles swallowed up his faded blue eyes as he shot a mostly toothless grin at Riley. She grinned back, and Liam reflected how well-suited she was to this job. She had a way of radiating genuine compassion with even the most agitated or irritating customers, and he thought that had as much to do with people's healing as the medications she dispensed. It was so different from his mother's no-nonsense pragmatism, yet no less effective. People loved and trusted her.

Howard lifted a plastic shopping bag onto the counter. "Winnie sent you this as a thank you for keeping up with us."

"Oh now, she didn't have to do that," Riley said. "I'm happy to help. You two are some of my favorite customers."

"Still. She wanted you to have it."

Riley slipped some kind of fabric out of the bag and her cheerful expression shifted to stunned delight. "Oh. Oh, this is exquisite!" She slipped off her lab coat and slipped on the fabric, which turned out to be some kind of cardigan deal that hit below her hips. "This must've taken her ages to knit."

"She enjoys it. And enjoys you. So. You enjoy that sweater."

"Thank you! You tell Winnie I love it!"

Riley waved as Mr. Tolleson shuffled toward the door, cheerfully swinging his rubber-tipped cane like an umbrella. As soon as he hit the sidewalk, she turned to Jessie and Ruby. "Oh my God, can you believe this? Look at the craftsmanship."

Jessie fingered the sleeve. "I totally want one. Winnie Tolleson's knitting is a thing of legend."

"She spends a lot of time in doctor's offices," Ruby added. "Knitting is something she can still do without too much trouble. Takes a lot of joy in it."

"Do you know, Howard and Winnie have been married for fifty-eight years?" Riley asked.

"Really?" Jessie asked. "I can't even wrap my brain around that. That's amazing."

Liam absorbed the brief stab of pain at the thought that, if not for his father's aneurysm, his parents would've been just like them. "We should all be so lucky."

Riley didn't squeak, but she did jolt at the sound of his voice, one hand pressing to her heart. "I swear to God, you need a bell around your neck."

"Didn't mean to startle you. Got a minute?"

As he expected, she immediately opened her mouth. "I really need to—"

"I just wanted to talk to you about the storage room. Work out a plan for when would be the least disruptive time for me to move everything out and where you want me to put your stock in the meantime. It'll only take a few minutes."

"Go ahead, Riley, baby. We've got things covered." Ruby gave him a wink.

Liam worked to keep his own expression neutral. No reason to give the sister of the biggest gossip in town additional fodder for the mill.

"I guess I can spare a couple of minutes."

She preceded him into the stock room, wrapping the sweater tight around herself despite the fact that the AC wasn't pumping that hard. He wondered if he could shut the door without making anybody suspicious and figured the answer was no. In her current state, Riley was liable to bolt. So he followed her inside.

She jumped straight to business. "I hate to make you do any work on a weekend, but Saturday afternoon or Sundays are the best time since we're closed."

He had no trouble reading between the lines. *And if we're closed, I won't be here and have to see you because I'll see to it your mom is the one to supervise.*

"The playground assembly is coming up this Saturday and next. We're cementing in posts this weekend, doing the full assembly the weekend after."

"Oh right, I forgot about that."

"You coming? Seems like you ought to have a hand in the finished product since you helped tear down the old one."

"I'll have to talk to your mom to see if she can cover the pharmacy."

"I'm sure she'd be happy to, if you asked."

Cue awkward silence. Because she looked completely miserable, Liam walked on by her, weaving his way through boxes of new stock back to the piles of other crap that had been accumulating for years.

He moved a drop cloth to peer beneath. "I think there are display shelves under all this mess."

"Your mom said before this building was the pharmacy, it was a five and dime. They had need of more space than we do."

"You ever think of tearing down that wall

they put up and expanding back into this section?"

"I don't have enough stock to justify it. Not to mention the expense."

"If money were no object?"

"It's definitely an object."

"Humor me."

She shrugged and plucked at the lapel of the sweater. "I'd thought about turning it into a space for local craftspeople to sell their wares. There are a lot of people who make and sell things who don't have large enough business to justify a storefront but could easily lease booth space. There's not really a place for them to do that right now."

"Hmm," he murmured. "Be easy enough to build you a proper stockroom in the back, with industrial shelves and organization. Then this front part could be more retail space. Wouldn't take much to set up other shelving or counters as need be." Despite the mounds of stuff, he could see how it could be converted. "It's a good idea."

"It's a moot point." She'd followed him past the stacks, seeming to relax a fraction as he got her talking about other things.

"How are things going with your mama?"

Well, there went the relaxation. Her shoulders cranked up a good inch with tension and she winced. "I haven't killed her yet, which is a minor miracle."

"There's not really room at your place for somebody else, is there?"

"No. And she doesn't understand the importance of not talking until the coffee pot is empty." She looked up at him with those deep blue *I need you* eyes. Which was purely projection on his part because she didn't need him. "Silence before caffeination is *sacred*."

Liam chuckled. "Your self-restraint against committing bodily harm is commendable."

"Damn straight. No jury of my peers would convict me for that."

"You've been working too hard." He itched to reach out and rub her shoulders.

"That's what you do when you own a business."

"It's also what you do when you're trying to avoid people."

She flashed a humorless smile. "It's a better alternative to matricide."

"I wasn't talking about your mother."

Her back stiffened. "Listen, Liam—"

"I don't want—"

She held up a hand to stop him. "No really, listen."

Liam fell silent. His impatience faded as he heard what she'd heard.

"Is that water?" she asked.

Moving quickly, he searched the room, finding the start of a puddle at the base of one wall. Following the trail of wet upward, he saw the spreading water stain on the ceiling.

"Shit!"

He bolted into the pharmacy just in time to see the ceiling burst. Water poured out of the hole, soaking displays, slicking the floors. He dimly heard Jessie's "Oh my God!" and Riley's sound of alarm as he raced for the door. Taking the stairs three at a time, he tore into the apartment. The sound of water was louder here. He found the source readily enough in the hall closet. Water spewed from around the drainage valve of the ancient water heater, pooling in the base of the closet and draining through the floors.

"Oh, Jesus." Riley had followed him upstairs.

He shot past her, scrambling to turn off the main water valve.

"Why isn't it stopping?" she asked, an edge of hysteria to her voice.

"That only keeps the tank from refilling." There wasn't a damned thing he could do to stop the entire eighty gallons from pouring out into the pharmacy below. "Come on."

Running back downstairs, he sloshed through the water to start muscling displays out of the direct stream. Riley and Jessie threw themselves into the cause, as did a couple of other patrons who happened in during the chaos. As soon as the displays were moved, he began snapping out orders.

"Jessie, is any of the medication in the back in danger of getting wet?"

"No, it's high enough off the floor."

"Good. Make sure it stays that way. Then call ServPro. The insurance information should be in the office. Ruby, call my mother and let her know what's going on. She can bring towels, sheets, whatever she can find to soak things up."

Liam put in a call to Mitch.

"What's up, buddy?"

"Flood at the pharmacy. I need every shop vac and box fan you can get your hands on."

"On it."

Within half an hour, the pharmacy was full of people springing to action to try and minimize the damage. By the time the water slowed to a drip, the floor was inches deep and water was flowing out the front door. The entire over-the-counter painkiller and allergy/sinus section was a lost cause. So was a huge chunk of the first aid supplies. Product boxes swollen with water floated by.

Riley wasn't crying, but she was obviously close. Her face was dead white, and she was shaking. Somewhere along the way she'd gotten rid of the sweater. Liam hoped it hadn't been damaged.

He took her by the shoulders. "Look at me." When she didn't move, he tipped her face toward his himself. "I'm going to fix this."

"I don't—"

"Riley, don't argue with me. This is my fault. The damn thing was ancient and has been on the list of things to replace. I didn't get to it fast enough. I'll fix it. I swear." He could offer her that, at least.

It was a mark of her level of upset that she didn't argue, merely gave a reluctant nod. She took a hiccuping breath and pressed her forehead to his chest. But before he could wrap his arms around her, pull her in, she straightened and turned away, mechanically going through the motions of trying to salvage what she could of her business.

Cursing himself and the situation, Liam wondered if he had any more likelihood of salvaging his chances with her.

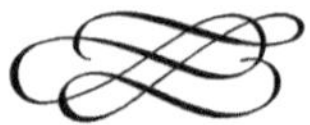

RILEY'S SHOES WERE SOPPING. They'd rubbed blisters on her heels and the instep of one foot. The hems of her pants had mostly dried, but in the heavy, humid air inside the pharmacy, everything felt damp and sticky. Exhausted, heartsick, she methodically counted the boxes of ruined over-the-counter allergy meds and marked the tally down on the inventory sheet before she added them to a bag for proper disposal.

It seemed like half the town had sprung into

action at Liam's call for help. But it wasn't enough. Everything was falling apart.

Above her, the ceiling gaped open, the occasional drip of water hitting her shoulders and head like spittle from some kind of hellmouth. The variable-width wood floors, original to the century-old building, were warped and buckled. Though water no longer stood in puddles, it had wicked up the drywall, which was more like wetwall now, the top layer bubbling and peeling in places. Chunks had been removed to allow the air to circulate, so that the fans and dehumidifiers could do their job, which would take days. The insulation that dangled reminded Riley of nothing so much as the guts of her business, spilling out of a mortal wound.

It was an apt comparison. How much revenue had been lost today? How much would be lost tomorrow, while they were closed so that more clean up could proceed and the remaining displays rearranged for some kind of functional layout? How much stock had she lost that insurance wouldn't cover because of the deductible?

Thinking about the numbers had a migraine pricking behind her eyes, which didn't at all help the tears she'd been fighting all day. At least she'd be alone soon if they spilled over.

"The claims adjuster on the building insurance will be here tomorrow," Molly announced, coming out of the office. "We should have a check to cover the damages pretty quickly."

Liam emerged from the storeroom, his clothes a patchwork of wet and drywall dust from where he'd been ripping open walls. "That's something, though I can't get started on repairs until things dry out."

"You can get started figuring out how much you'll need of materials and make arrangements to get them here. That way you'll have a plan and be ready to hit the ground running as soon as they clear out all these fans." Molly wrapped an arm around Riley's shoulders. "We're going to get this taken care of."

"I know." God she missed having Molly take

an active hand in the business. Sliding an arm around her waist, Riley leaned in for a hug. "My priority tomorrow is to get things arranged into whatever temporary state we're going to have to live in so that the business can still open. Revenues aside, people need their medications. I already started a box of products from the front to donate to the women's shelter. There's a fair bit of stuff that had damaged packaging, but the contents are still usable. It might as well go to somewhere it can still be used instead of in the trash. I'd like to take that over tomorrow, too."

"That's a good idea. Meanwhile, I'm pulling mom rank on both of you. Jessie and Ruby actually listened when I sent *them* home an hour ago. Let's all get out of here and go *home.* Get some sleep. We're all exhausted, and there's nothing more we can do here tonight."

Riley had absolutely no desire to go home. With her mom in residence, it was no longer her sanctuary. She just couldn't handle Sharilyn's well-meaning concern on top of her own worries. But Molly was right. She couldn't stay here.

"I'll walk you to your car," Liam said.

Was this another attempt to talk to her alone? If it was, Riley wasn't interested. She couldn't take anything else tonight.

"That's really not necessary."

"It's late, Riley."

"And last time I checked, the only person skulking around and scaring me to death lately was you."

Molly gave her another quick squeeze. "Humor your other mother. You're parked at the other end of the block, it's dark, and I raised him to be a gentleman."

How was she supposed to argue with that? "Yes, ma'am."

The three of them walked out together, locking the door against the engine roar of a dozen fans. Riley could feel the faint vibration against the glass. She was pretty sure she'd hear the drone in her sleep. If she managed to sleep.

Molly opened her car door. "See you in the

morning, honey. I'll bring pastries from Sweet Magnolias for breakfast."

"Then I'll bring coffee." Lifting her hand in a wave, Riley watched Molly drive off.

Resigned to having an escort, she started walking.

Liam stayed quiet. Grateful for the reprieve, she listened to the echo of their footsteps as it mixed with the symphony of night insects and the sound of a car on a nearby street. After the tumult of the day, the summer silence soaked into her bones, unknotting something in her gut.

At her car, Riley turned toward Liam to see him reaching out for her. "Don't."

He stopped, one hand outstretched, hurt flickering over his face before he shut down to stoic mode again.

"I'll fix it, Riley. I'm going to make this right."

He thought she blamed him for all of this.

She tried to soften the rejection with an apologetic smile. "I know you will. You're not at fault here. It's just that, if you hug me right now, I'm going to start crying, and I really don't have time for that." Never mind the fact that curling up in his arms and bawling sounded pretty amazing.

For a moment, she thought he'd ignore her wishes and pull her into his arms as he had weeks before. A part of her wished he would so she could let go of the burden she carried, just for a little while. But he didn't move.

"I'm sorry."

Riley had the sense that he was apologizing for more than the soggy disaster that was her business, but she absolutely couldn't deal with that right now. She didn't want his apology for not being on the same page as she was. She just wanted him to pretend it hadn't happened. Someday, she'd get past the lingering mortification over the kiss he hadn't returned. But that day was somewhere far off in the future.

Still, she hated seeing him miserable too, so she made an effort to be the friend he wanted. "You've already helped so much. I can't imagine how much worse things would've been if you hadn't taken charge in the chaos."

His level-headed dependability had taken some of the pressure off so that she could actually do what needed doing on the business side as quickly as possible. The prescription drugs were protected, insurance had been notified, and as much stock as possible had been salvaged. Things were bad, but because of him, they weren't a complete loss. She needed to remember that.

"The fact is, I'm really glad you were here." Riley realized she meant it. And she wasn't at all sure how she felt about that.

Liam shifted toward her. "You want to get a drink? I figure we can both use one after today."

What she wanted was a long soak and a week to sleep. But those weren't in the cards either. She shook her head. "As you said, it's late. And there's lots to do tomorrow. I should head home. Thank you for helping today."

"I wish I could've done more."

Riley couldn't stop herself from laying a

hand on his arm. "You kept a level head. And that helped me keep mine. The rest can be fixed, and I know I can rely on you to do it. So stop beating yourself up for not being omniscient and knowing what was going to happen."

His lips twitched in a humorless smile. "Didn't you know? As the oldest, I'm supposed to be all-seeing, all-knowing."

"You've got that confused. That's your mother's job. Now go home and go to bed, Boy Scout. We've got a busy week ahead of us."

"That we do. Get some sleep, Riley Marie."

As she drove away, Riley thought maybe now she actually would.

LIAM MEASURED the stretch of wall a third time, making a notation on a small notepad before moving over to the miter saw to cut the next piece of moulding. He just wanted to finish up the bedroom before he called it a day and headed out to Judd's place for poker night. The guys would provide a much needed distraction.

In the week since the flood, he'd replaced the water heater, ripped out damaged flooring and walls in the closet that housed it, and generally eradicated evidence that anything had even gone wrong. The apartment was coming along nicely. The pharmacy below…not so much. He'd ripped out drywall down there, pulled down large chunks of the ceiling and wet insulation to help speed the drying process, but the shop was still filled with fans and dehumidifiers. He could hear the drone of them from up here.

Business was open, and, though it wasn't as usual, it was keeping Riley and his mother plenty busy. They'd managed to set up a narrower floor plan with the displays they had, funneling foot traffic away from the worst of the buckled flooring so that customers could get to the counter without injuring themselves. There'd been plenty of people coming through rubber necking the mess, but Liam knew not all of them were actually buying stuff. And the new Walgreens had opened. If he hadn't seen the ancient, rusted water heater himself, he'd have had Wishful PD looking into the coincidental timing of the flood in relation to their grand opening. As it was, Riley was winding tighter by the day.

Liam didn't know how to help her. He'd done everything he could to help things dry faster, and he already had supplies on order down at Edison Hardware so he could dive in with the crew he'd assembled as soon as they were given the all clear. She trusted him to do all that, but she wouldn't lean on him for anything else. And she sure as hell wasn't giving him the opportunity for a conversation of a more personal nature. At this point, he didn't know whether she was avoiding him out of embarrassment or if she'd changed her mind and wished she hadn't kissed him at all.

The compressor roared to life as he positioned the trim along the edge of one of the newly hung double-paned windows and lifted the nail gun. *Kshunk. Kshunk. Kshunk.* He ran a hand down the fluted moulding, feeling a sense of satisfaction that he'd managed to find some double-paned windows that maintained the character of the building, without the inefficiencies of the originals.

As the compressor kicked off, he heard footsteps and a female voice calling out, "Liam?"

"Back here."

A moment later, Norah Burke stuck her head into the room. "You've been busy."

"Making progress anyway. What brings you by? If Mom's not downstairs, I don't know where she's gone off to."

"I'm here to talk to you, actually."

"About?"

"How 'bout you give me the fifty-cent tour, and I'll tell you about it?"

"It's more like the nickel tour. You've already been through most of it just to get back here."

"Yeah, but I didn't get commentary on what you've done."

Shrugging, Liam took her through, explaining what had been ripped out, what had been replaced. He answered her questions about the bits of restoration he'd managed in keeping with the history of the century old building, modernizations he'd made without sacrificing the original character of the space, and described the rest of his plans.

"About the only decision I have to make now is whether the cabinet boxes in the kitchen are worth salvaging or if I want to build from scratch."

Norah's deep brown eyes lit with interest. "You can do that?"

"Sure."

"Babette Wofford tells me you're going to be doing some work for her, too."

"She seems to have made up her mind about that, and I haven't even seen her space yet."

"She likes your work. She's the one who sent me over here."

"You ready to tell me what for?"

"I have a Plan."

Liam laughed. "You always have a plan with a capital P. What's this one?"

"We've made some good strides with the Shop Local campaign and the downtown facelift from back in the spring, as well as working on getting the new website off the ground to promote rural tourism here. Part of that deals with the history of Wishful. We're lucky that such a significant chunk of downtown remains from the turn of the last century. Most small towns in Mississippi don't have that. I want to do what we can to preserve what's left and to restore the things that can be restored. I'm working on a proposal to put before both the Chamber of Commerce and the City Council regarding covenants about the kind of architecture that can be used downtown for future projects, so that the whole thing can retain the charm it's got, while we work on refreshing everything else. I'd like to be able to recommend you for the job."

Surprise struck him momentarily silent. Him do long-term historic restoration? When his gut didn't immediately discount the idea, Liam crossed his arms and studied her. "Why me?"

"You appreciate history. That's obvious in how you've dealt with this place. I think you'll see and agree with my vision. Plus, I like your work ethic and results. You're more concerned with doing something right than with doing it the fastest, cheapest way."

"No sense in doing something if you aren't going to take the time to do it right."

"Exactly. The project would be long-term and could be a really good fit for your skillset."

"You know I'm not a licensed contractor, right?"

"A formality easily dealt with if you want. You don't have to make a decision right yet. I know you need to finish the work here and at the pharmacy. Just think about it." She headed for the door. "I'll get out of your hair so you can finish up. You'll be late for poker night. I have it on good authority that Mitch is ripe for the fleecing."

Liam grinned. "I'll keep that in mind."

He finished trimming out the last of the windows before washing up at the kitchen sink and changing into the clean t-shirt and shorts in his gym bag, packed for the workout he hadn't gotten around to that morning. He was already late by the time he slipped into his truck. Running a fresh bead of caulk around all four windows had taken a bit longer than he'd expected. He could've put it off until tomorrow, but that part of the job didn't feel finished without it.

Judd lived about ten miles out from town, in a fixer upper on the banks of Hope Springs. The cedarwood board and batten siding was silvered with age, and the exterior was a testament to a style of architecture that held no characteristics worth preserving, but Liam couldn't find fault with the location. The sun was sinking low, gilding the little pier with its Adirondack chairs as he pulled up behind Mitch's truck. He could absolutely understand the appeal of living out here.

The card table was set up on the screened in porch, ceiling fans stirring the humid air, scented with good tobacco—which explained why they were outside.

"Cigar night?" Liam let the screen door slap shut behind him.

Judd's enormous mutt, Boudreaux, some kind of bloodhound mix, lifted his head and thumped his massive tail.

"I got definitively put on the short list for the position as Chief. Seemed worth cele-bratin'," Judd told him around the stogie clamped between his teeth.

Liam bent to scratch Boudreaux between the ears. "Congrats."

Mitch kicked back in his chair, the green plastic visor denoting him dealer for the night. "Didn't expect to see you tonight."

"Got as far as I can with the demolition in the pharmacy until things dry out. Should go quicker now that I've opened up the walls. I got a bit delayed by your future cousin-in-law."

"What's Norah trying to wrangle you into?"

"Tell you about it in a bit. Is there food?"

"We got bucket o'cluck and beer in the kitchen," Judd told him. "Might even be some cole slaw and mashed potatoes left, if Reuben didn't wipe them out."

Reuben snorted. "I got access to *good* cole slaw from my mama. You think I'm gonna waste my time with take out?"

Liam grabbed a beer from the fridge, nabbed the last of the fried chicken and potatoes, and took his place at the table.

"Want me to deal you in?" Mitch asked.

"Next hand. What do you know about Norah's Grand Plan for the historic restoration of downtown?"

Mitch dealt the flop. "Like all Norah's schemes, it's big. She and her intern Cecily have been working on grants to help fund various and sundry projects. I've helped with that some, giving them estimates of labor and materials and the kind of scope they'll be looking at once they actually get into things."

The others tossed in their chips.

"She wants to pitch me as the man for the job."

Mitch arched his brows as he dealt the next card. "Yeah? I hadn't thought of that, but it's actually pretty brilliant."

"You think?"

Judd examined the turn, burned two cards, and took two more into his hand before seeing the bet. "Seems like a good fit. Even when we were kids you were always more into fixing the old instead of buying new."

He'd learned that from his father.

Mitch burned a card of his own. "You've got the skillset. You like the work. And you've got the added bonus of war hero giving back to his community, which will push some of the more resistant over to her side."

"I'm hardly a hero."

"Pretty sure the Marines in your unit would disagree." Reuben met the bet and waited as Mitch turned over the river.

Judd swore and folded. "You think it's the kind of work you want to do?"

Liam had been mulling that since Norah left him. "I spent a lot of years destroying things in the military. The idea of bringing something back is pretty damned appealing."

"Plus, running a crew would maybe give you some of that sense of working with a team again." Reuben laid down his cards. "Queen high flush. You're used to leading men and organizing things. You'd be good at it."

Mitch grinned. "Full house, buddy boy."

"Shit. Next hand, Campbell."

"Keep dreaming. I'm hot tonight." Mitch gathered up his chips. "Anyway, if I know Norah, she's also thinking that since you'd be just starting out, you might cut everybody a break on pricing, while you build your reputation as a contractor. Nothing undercut, mind you, but she'll capitalize on your sense of fairness."

"I'd expect nothing less from her." Liam had worked with Norah enough back in the spring that he'd learned she knew how to work people to get the best results.

"So you gonna do it?" Judd asked.

It was an option. A good one, with long-term viability and the kind of parameters that would allow him to build a business as he saw fit rather than fitting into somebody else's box. And that would put him in a position to start thinking about other areas of his life. Like what he was going to do about Riley.

"Thinking about it. She's not lookin' for an answer until I'm done with repairs on the pharmacy." He finished off his chicken and washed it down with some Shinerbock. "Meanwhile, my more immediate priority is lightening y'all's wallets. Deal me in."

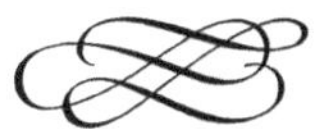

CHAPTER 9

"I'M AFRAID I'M GOING to have to call your line of credit due, Mrs. Lazore." Riley braced herself for the inevitable blow up from the third grade teacher, who'd made her elementary school life hell.

"Young lady, I have had this line of credit with the pharmacy for fifteen years. I've never been late with a payment, never had a single complaint from Molly Montgomery. What is the meaning of this?"

"Yes ma'am, I understand. But as you might have heard, the pharmacy flooded a couple of weeks ago. Repairs are going to be costly, so I'm sure you understand why I'm doing this."

"That's what insurance is for," the woman insisted.

And thank God for it. As Molly owned the building, her property insurance was dealing with the physical damage from the flood. But Riley still had the headache of trying to get her stock covered on her business policy, which wasn't going well. And even if they agreed to pay the claim, there was still the deductible, which was considerable. Plus the bi-monthly drug invoice was due next week, including the non-returnable chemo drugs she'd ordered for Karen Albert, who'd died Wednesday from the ovarian cancer she'd been fighting for a year. Her supplier didn't care about the grief of losing a long-time customer. They just wanted their $6,000 on time.

"Mrs. Lazore, I apologize if you're upset about this, but I'm running a business. Lines of credit are a courtesy, not a requirement, and at this time, that courtesy is not available. Consider this notice. I'll be expecting your payment by the first of next week."

Riley hung up the phone on the older woman's sputtering complaints. Probably not the most professional response, but she just couldn't take it anymore. In the wake of realizing she probably wouldn't be able to make payroll, she'd made more than two dozen similar calls in the last week. Nobody had taken the news well. And almost all of them had made the same inference—what had she done in the year she'd owned the pharmacy to screw up everything Molly had built?

When her cell phone rang, she didn't even lift her head from the desk as she picked up.

"It's time for your weekend sanity check."

Autumn's voice came over the line and left Riley with such a yearning for a hug, she almost cried. No shock. She'd been fighting tears for a week and a half, as everything she'd worked for threatened to implode. As Autumn was away at a rare conference, she hadn't been around to update.

"We're sorry, that cuckoo has flown the coop. Please try again in another lifetime."

"That bad, huh?"

"Walgreens opened last week. With half my stock ruined, people had no choice but to go there."

"They'll come back, Riley."

"What if they don't?" This was her fear. They were a national chain. By dint of sheer volume, they could offer greater discounts than she could. With the economy being so strained, she wouldn't even blame people for trying to save a buck. She of all people understood the need for that.

"Molly will help."

Riley knew she would, in a heartbeat. But Riley couldn't ask. She couldn't bear to admit how much she was struggling. Molly had sold her the business in good faith because she believed Riley could handle the responsibility of running it. Riley couldn't tell her she was in over her head. There was simply no other option than to find some kind of miracle to fix this.

"Molly has her hands full dealing with the insurance company."

Autumn was silent for so long, Riley knew she was biting her tongue.

"How are things going with your mom?"

Because that was a better topic? Riley sighed. "It's going…okay, I guess. She's stuck with the job at McSweeney's for a little over three weeks."

"You sound awfully skeptical about that."

"I just…I hope she's not taking advantage of Matthew McSweeney."

"Why should she be taking advantage of him?

"He's an old Air Force buddy of my dad's, and he made the egregious mistake of telling her at some point that if she ever needed anything, she should just let him know."

"Most people don't make that kind of offer if they don't mean it, Ri. Besides, asking for a job isn't the same as expecting some kind of handout."

"I know. It just worries me. She's barely been out of her last relationship a month. I don't think she should be moving on to somebody else."

"Do you think there's something else going on?"

"She likes him. And why shouldn't she? He's a super nice guy. But she has a history of continuing to ask for things—especially from nice guys. And since she's got that damsel in distress thing going on, they're usually all too happy to give them to her."

Autumn was quiet for a long moment "Which part of this bothers you more? That she doesn't have a problem asking or that she has no problem accepting?"

"What?"

"I love you, but you're terminally allergic to asking anybody for anything, and I know how much you despise anything you perceive as charity. Not everyone is like you, sweetie, and that doesn't make them bad people."

"I don't think she's a bad person. I just think she should take some more personal responsibility instead of always expecting someone else to bail her out and take care of everything."

"And it sounds like she's finally doing that. She came home, got a job right off. Has she asked you for anything since then? Other than to stay with you?"

Riley frowned. "Well, no, actually. Besides the fact that she just can't seem to *not* talk to me in the mornings, she's mostly been staying out of my way since the flood. I guess she realizes I'm about two inches from snapping."

"Then maybe give her the benefit of the doubt. Maybe she really is turning over a new leaf. All that aside, you'll feel better once the repairs are finished. Liam will make it right," Autumn assured her

"He's certainly trying. He's already replaced the water heater upstairs, and ripped open the walls and ceiling, but it's still not dry enough to fix yet without danger of mold." The chaos was getting to her. She could hear the drone of fans and dehumidifiers outside the office door.

"He feels really bad about what happened."

Riley sat up. "You've talked to him?" Had he told Autumn about the kiss? Of course not. If Autumn knew about that, she'd have been on Riley's doorstep as soon as he hung up the phone demanding to know why Riley hadn't spilled the beans herself.

"Yeah. He's kicking himself pretty hard."

"It wasn't his fault. He keeps saying it is, but it's not like he's psychic. He couldn't have known the water heater would blow up."

"Yeah, but since when does Liam ever admit he isn't all knowing, all seeing, and in control all the time?"

That would be the last time the Devil wore ice skates. So, never. They had that in common.

"Point taken. It's going to be a big job, when he gets to it, and I'll probably have to close for a little while." Riley couldn't think about that. "The wood floors are ruined and have to come up. The bottom of the sheetrock has to be replaced. And the ceiling. There's damage in the store room too, though, obviously, that's lower priority. It's…a mess."

And that didn't seem to phase him in the least. As her world had imploded, Liam had risen to the challenge and taken control. Which was exactly what he did, what he needed. A mission. Since things had gone all to hell for her, he seemed to have found a rhythm. Which was great for him. She just wished it hadn't happened at her expense. Remembering what he'd said about not being sure if he was cut out for civilian life, she wondered if having a crisis to deal with would make him miss the Marines all the more or if he felt more settled.

Regardless, once he got started, he was going to be all up in her space. As if she needed more opportunity to feel awkward. In the wake of the flood, he hadn't tried to talk to her about the kiss again, which was just as well. She didn't need the added mortification of him trying to gently explain why he wasn't interested. He hadn't kissed her back. That was all the explanation she needed. Message received, loud and clear.

"I know it's awful, and I know you're stressed. But you will get through this."

"I know. I know. This, too, shall pass. I just hope it passes before it bankrupts me."

Jessie stuck her head into the office, bringing with her the perpetual wind tunnel the pharmacy had turned into. "Molly's here."

"Hey, I need to go. Molly's here. I'm due to go work on the playground assembly at Waldrop Park."

"Oh good. You need to do something away from work and home. Get your mind off stuff."

"I don't have a lot of choice in the matter. Liam railroaded me." And since he was taking on all of the repair work, it wasn't in her to deny him much.

"Good for him. Back porch margaritas soon," Autumn promised.

"You're on."

The man himself was standing at the counter.

"Are you here to escort me to make sure I actually make it to the job site?"

"It's the only way I can be sure you won't go disappear somewhere to brood."

"I'm not brooding."

Liam's brows jacked up.

"I'm not. I'm dealing with obnoxious things, like insurance and bills and taxes and all the crap nobody tells us about when we're kids in an all-fired hurry to grow-up. That's not brooding."

"Then what is it?"

"Adulting."

Molly laughed and put an arm around her. "I believe that should officially be a word. Now why don't you let me take over the adulting for the day and go with Liam to work on the playground. And when it's finished, do something really radical and play on it."

Riley's instinct was to list all the things she should be doing instead, but the fact was, she'd made all the calls, filled out all the reports, done inventory. There was absolutely nothing else she could do now but wait. If she didn't do *something* to keep busy, she would fall into a brood. Her mood was bleak enough without going there.

But that didn't mean she wanted to be trapped in Liam's truck even for the short drive to the park.

"I can drive myself."

Jessie piped up, "Actually, no you can't. Your mom came to borrow the car. She said you'd said it was okay, so I gave her the key while you were on the phone earlier."

She'd said no such thing.

I will not lose my shit. I will not lose my shit. Riley mentally counted to ten and reminded herself she didn't look good in orange.

"Then I guess I am riding with you. Let me get my purse."

"Just a little bit higher."

In tandem with Judd, Liam shifted the slide on his shoulder.

"That's it," Mitch said. "Hold what you've got, while I bolt this bad boy in."

The work day was drawing to a close and the new Waldrop Park playground was almost assembled. Across the way, Liam could see Riley laughing with Miranda as they threaded the blocks of the tic tac toe game onto pipes. Her cheeks were flushed with heat and maybe a little sunburn. It was the first time he'd seen her smile since the flood, and the sight of it hit him straight in the gut.

"You want me to dump the water cooler over your head?" Judd asked.

"What?"

"You keep looking over there like that and the new playground's gonna catch on fire."

"I don't know what you're talking about."

"Sure you don't." Judd chuckled and stepped out from beneath the finished slide.

Jesus, he had to get himself under control.

What he really needed was a chance to corner Riley to *talk* to her. Although Liam was starting to wonder if that was the best approach. His last attempt to do that had been a disaster, and she was so stressed out and defensive these days, he wasn't entirely sure she'd listen.

"That's it. It's officially done," Norah announced.

Tools were set aside, and they all crowded around to look over the finished product.

Mitch had outdone himself with the design. In place of the old, boring playground, they'd built a veritable wooden Camelot, with turrets and bridges, climbing walls, slides, monkey bars, and two banks of swings. It almost made Liam wish he was a kid again.

"Well, the equipment is done, anyway," Cam said. "It'll take me another weekend to get all the landscaping done."

"And Tyler's still got to finish with the pickets for the fence," Mitch added.

"I'm on duty to help put that together when it's ready," Liam said.

"Oh shush," Norah scolded. "I'm enjoying the moment of having something *finished.*"

"Somebody's got to test it out," Liam remarked, eying the swings.

"What do you mean? It's safe. Mitch went over all the specs."

"As in make sure it will hold up to a proper swing long jump competition."

Norah cocked her head. "A what?"

"You know, that thing we did when we were kids, where you swing as high as you possibly can and then jump out. Surely kids still do this." Liam couldn't imagine sedately using the swings only as intended. Where was the fun in that?

"I get someone at the clinic at least once or twice a year with a broken limb from that," Miranda confirmed. "As adults, you're all supposed to know better."

"Psh. Knowing better is over-rated." Liam pegged Riley with a look. "Weren't you, like, reigning long jump champion in fourth grade?"

Brows up, she nodded. "I was. And how did

you, from your vaunted position in the far off seventh grade, know that?"

"Because Wynne was always mad you beat her. She couldn't figure out how you won since she was taller and should've had the longer reach."

"Reach isn't everything. It's all in the technique."

"You up for a little friendly competition?"

Riley narrowed her eyes in suspicion.

Liam upped the stakes. "Loser buys pizza."

"You're on, Boy Scout."

Of course, that led to bets being taken. Being a Marine, he was the clear favorite, but that didn't seem to put Riley off one whit.

Liam slid into a swing, feeling the sides dig into his hips. "Hope you like pineapple."

Riley sat down beside him, shoving back until she was straight-legged. "Pineapple doesn't belong on a pizza. Not that it matters because you're buying me chicken and bacon."

"Cocky."

"Confident," she corrected. "On three. One.

Two. Three!" She jumped back and swung forward.

Liam followed suit but was, as it turned out, at something of a disadvantage with his much longer legs. Riley laughed as his feet dragged, kicking hers until she rose higher and higher. Then he got the rhythm and figured out how to tuck his feet on the back swing and began to catch up. Liam swung higher, his stomach doing that altitude lurch as he neared the zenith of the arc. Beside him, he could see Riley preparing to jump, shifting her grip on the chains so her arms were free.

"Geronimo!" she shouted.

Riley went first, her sneakers leaving deep furrows in the rubber mulch as she skidded to a stop, arms pinwheeling. Liam readied for his own jump, eyes on Riley and the finish line. The moment he left the swing, he knew he'd miscalculated something. His body over-rotated, and he tried to twist in the air, to tuck and roll. His landing was an awkward, sideways crash of limbs. The impact radiated through his hip, his elbow, jarring loose a completely un-manly *Ooph.*

"Liam!" Riley dropped to her knees beside him. "Don't move. Are you hurt?" Her hands were racing over him faster than he could an-swer, and as he rather enjoyed the process, he wasn't in any hurry to stop her.

"Nothin's broken." Except possibly his pride. And maybe his ass

Miranda rolled her eyes at him. "Your head's too thick for any serious damage."

"Dude, I really hope you're more coordi-nated in the field," Mitch ribbed.

He didn't have the distraction of Riley in the middle of war.

Apparently satisfied he was in one piece, the distraction herself sat back on her heels. "You jumped too high."

"Huh?"

"You missed the optimal exit point of the arc. Instead of using your momentum to fling you forward, you wasted the energy by going up. That's how I always beat Wynne."

"The champion remains supreme," Mitch said. "Pay up, y'all."

Riley helped Liam into a sitting position. "You owe me pizza."

"It's not like pizza is a hardship under any circumstances."

"Okay, I can't take it anymore," Norah declared. "When are you two going to publicly announce that you're dating?"

Riley's mouth dropped open. "Don't be ridiculous. We're not dating."

"We're not," Liam confirmed, hating the embarrassed flush that crawled up her neck.

Riley threw her arm out in a "See?" sort of gesture, as if that reinforced her point.

"But we should be." Liam was acutely aware of the awkward silence that descended in the wake of that declaration.

Riley laughed, not quite meeting his eyes as she got to her feet. "Clearly you hit your head harder than we thought."

Norah pouted. "Well damn. I guess I lost that bet."

"Can't win 'em all, sugar," Cam told her.

Everybody suddenly got busy with the cleanup of the job site. Riley was already striding away from him. Liam followed her around the back side of the tower, where she was gathering up tools.

She started to duck around him, still not looking him in the eye, but he grabbed her arm. "Hold it."

"I need to—"

"You need to stop running away from me and listen." Liam kept his voice low.

"To what?" she hissed back. "To you trying to humor me? Make me feel less like an idiot? That's nice of you, Liam, but it's not necessary." Her tone indicated it wasn't even possible, and that just pissed him off.

He caged her in against the wall of the tower. "I have been trying to tell you for weeks, but every time I get close we have some kind of disaster or you bolt like a damned rabbit. So let's clarify something before there's another flood, fire, or parental invasion. You are not in this alone."

And then his hands were in her hair, his mouth on hers in a blistering, possessive kiss that poured out every ounce of the dark, desperate wanting that had haunted him for months.

Riley didn't move.

Heart pounding, Liam eased back. Her pupils were blown wide with shock. He was already cursing his rashness but he had to ask. "What do you think?"

Those eyes narrowed and her hands fisted in his shirt. "Oo rah."

She yanked his mouth back to hers, fingers clutching at his shoulders, sliding around to his nape to pull him closer as she proceeded to kiss him like she meant it. Like she'd stumbled out of the desert and he was the oasis designed for the sole purpose of quenching her thirst. His tongue traced the seam of her lips, and she opened for him. She tasted rich and sinfully sweet. Every cell of his body screamed, *Oh, hell yes*, and his brain supplied applause and cheers as accompaniment.

Wait, that wasn't his brain.

Their audience was hooting, hollering, and clapping with great enthusiasm.

"You go, Riley!"

She broke free, hiding her face against his chest. Liam turned his head to glare at the grinning onlookers, staying where he was as a wholly ineffectual shield.

"I *was* right!" Norah gave a fist pump.

"I called it first," Judd said. "Pay up."

More money changed hands—didn't they have anything better to do than bet?—and friendly ribbing ensued.

"Sorry. I didn't plan on an audience. You okay?"

She lifted her head and smiled at him—really smiled for the first time in he couldn't remember how long. Something buoyant and huge expanded in his chest, and all Liam could think was that he'd do just about anything to lighten her load and make her happy enough to do it again on a more regular basis.

"I feel like sending a message out to every teenage girl everywhere who ever had a crush on her best friend's big brother—don't give up."

"You had a crush on me in high school?"

Riley laughed "Buy me that pizza you owe me, and I'll think about telling you about it."

Liam swung an arm around her. "Now that's a bet I'm happy to pay up."

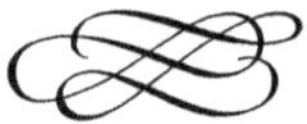

CHAPTER 10

"THIS WILL BE JUST lovely." Sharilyn shut the car door. "I haven't seen Molly in ages."

Riley hadn't seen her either since the news that she and Liam were a thing had swept through town like wildfire. Molly's response to that was to invite Riley and her mother over for a family dinner. Nothing Liam could say changed the fact that Riley felt like she'd been summoned, and she was more than a little nervous about it.

Hey, I know you're as much a mother to me as

my own, but I really want to do the horizontal boogie with your eldest son. That copacetic with you?

Riley had no idea how she'd react to this. Sharilyn had been ecstatic and hadn't been able to stop talking about what a fine, upstanding serviceman Liam was. Which was patently true, but had left Riley so on edge, she thought she might've ground down a layer of teeth.

Clutching the casserole dish in a death grip, Riley headed for the front door. The front door for company, not the side door she'd been using all her life. Happy-faced cosmos and zinnias lined the walk, and the beds were neatly mulched. Liam's doing, she was sure, along with the freshly-painted siding and trim of the house, and the newly-built planter boxes lining the windows. Since her hands were full, Shar-ilyn rang the bell.

Moments later, Molly pulled open the door, beaming. "Welcome! Oh, what have you brought here?"

"Corn casserole," Riley managed.

Molly leaned in to buss Riley's cheek and

tugged the dish out of her hands, leaving Riley wishing she had something else to hold on to. Her gaze flicked to Liam, standing barefoot in the hall behind his mother, looking completely at ease in a polo shirt and khaki shorts.

"Don't just stand there like a bump on a log, Staff Sergeant. Kiss your girl hello."

He bent to give Riley a chaste peck that bore no resemblance to their playground interlude but left her thinking all kinds of sweaty thoughts anyway. "Hi."

"Hi." *And the winner for best deer in the headlights impression goes to...*

Molly leveled a Look in Liam's direction.

He grinned. "Yes ma'am."

They hadn't been together long, but Riley recognized the expression in his eyes as he laced his hands behind her back and reeled her in.

"Liam!" Riley hissed. But he stopped her warning with another kiss that absolutely justified those sweaty thoughts.

She struggled to give him a stern glare when

he pulled back but was sure she missed by a mile.

Entirely unrepentant, he said, "I come from a PDA kinda family. You know this."

And she'd always loved the easy affection between John and Molly. "Yeah but…" What could she say to that?

Molly nodded, satisfied. "I swear, you two move slower than molasses in winter. It took me six months to even get you near each other."

Liam shifted his attention to his mother. "It…what?

"Well you weren't doing anything about getting together on your own, so I had to do something to push you together." She looked so pleased, Riley half expected to see feathers peeking out from her mouth.

"So you blew up the water heater?" he asked.

"No! Of course not. But that apartment's been sitting empty for ages. I figured having you renovate it would put the two of you in the same general vicinity and nature might finally take its course."

"You were *trying* to get us together?" Riley couldn't wrap her brain around the idea of that.

"Of course I was. I've been waiting years for you both to grow up enough to figure it out. It's about damned time, too. Honestly, I thought I was going to have to bring in reinforcements."

"Years?" Riley repeated. "But how did you…"

Molly tapped a finger to the medallion around Riley's neck. "Because you wouldn't have given this to him if he didn't matter, and he wouldn't have worn it all these years if you didn't." Smiling, she picked up the casserole dish and headed for the kitchen. "Sharilyn, tell me all about you."

Riley and Liam watched them go.

"You know, I used to think I was in control of my life," Riley said.

"She likes to leave people with that impression."

Somewhere in the middle of all her embarrassment, Riley felt a bit of a glow at the idea that not only had she earned Molly's approval to take over the business but also as a worthy match for her son. She respected Molly more than almost anyone else, so her approval meant a lot. But at the same time…what went along with that approval? Expectations of…what?

Riley shied away from that thought.

Liam combed both hands through her hair, massaging her scalp as he went. "Relax. It's just dinner. You've had dinner over here hundreds of times."

"I wasn't thinking about getting naked with you all those other times," she murmured. "Not most of them anyway."

Liam laughed. "Why, Miss Gower, have you been fantasizing about me?"

"It's the dimples."

Confusion flickered across his face. "I don't have dimples."

"Oh but you do. That summer you life-guarded at the city pool? You had these board shorts that rode really low on your hips so the dimples at the top of your very fine ass showed. You wouldn't guess half the things I've thought about doing with you because of those dimples."

"Your fantasies and my fantasies should talk."

"Given that we're more or less back in high school with our living situations, talking is about as far as they're going to get."

"There's always the back seat of the Mustang. Classic for a reason."

"I'm not that desperate yet."

Liam bent to press a kiss just above her collar bone. "Bet I could change your mind." His voice was a dark velvet promise that proved they'd both be winners of that bet.

"Liam, come set the table!" Molly called.

He winced. "I'm too old for this."

"Remind me again why you haven't gotten your own place yet?"

"Seemed prudent to settle on a job and known level of income first."

Riley couldn't fault the sensibility of that. She patted his cheek. "C'mon, Boy Scout. We have to go be good children."

They headed into the kitchen.

"—surprised you didn't do a big cookout," Sharilyn was saying. "I have such fond memories of cookouts over here."

"Oh we still throw them from time to time, but Wynne couldn't make it home and I thought the kids might appreciate not being paraded in front of half the town."

Liam walked over to squeeze his mother's shoulders. "The *kids* appreciate your self-restraint."

Molly tugged him down for a noisy kiss. "No matter how big you get, you'll always be my baby."

Riley relaxed as they finished setting out silverware, napkins, and serving dishes. It was hard to be anything but relaxed at this table, surrounded by the scents of fresh fried chicken, potato salad, and fried green tomatoes. Some of her best memories were here.

Beneath the table, Liam's knee nudged hers. How many times had that happened growing up, crammed around the table with him and the rest of his family? Always an accident then. It was very much on purpose now, a harmless, flirty gesture that kept distracting her from the conversation.

"How are things going at the market?" Molly asked.

"Really well. Matthew's happy, so I'm off the probationary period as a checker. That was a relief. I was worried about learning to run the register, but the computer actually makes it really easy."

"Technology is a beautiful thing," Molly agreed.

"When it works anyway. We had a young girl in the store today trying to buy her groceries and there was something wrong with her EBT card—wasn't anything to do with her, the system had been squirrelly all day—but the lines were pretty long and someone said something rude about 'some people' loud enough she could hear. Poor thing got so upset and embarrassed, she ran out of the store without any groceries."

Riley's heart ached for the girl. She well remembered the various sly comments and judgmental remarks heaped on her as a child when they'd been in dire straits.

"That's awful," Molly said. "Who was it?"

"I didn't know her. Really young. Nineteen or twenty maybe? Sandy hair. Dark eyes. Row of piercings going up one ear. I'll never understand why people need more than one set of holes."

Riley stilled. That was Tara Honeycutt. She had way more on her plate than anybody her age deserved. "Who was the jerk?"

"Gary Hopper."

"Clearly the apples don't fall far from the tree," she muttered.

"Amber Hopper was in your class, wasn't she?" Liam asked.

Riley's hand clenched around her fork. "Yes, yes she was. Her sister, Brandy, was two years ahead." And between the two of them, they'd made junior high a living hell.

Molly frowned. "Amber is the only fight

Wynne ever got into. She never would admit what it was over."

"I remember that." Liam forked up another tomato from the platter. "Cruz pulled her off. Said he was sure Wynne was going to pull half the hair out of that girl's head."

"Wynne was my little Zen child," Molly said. "It would've taken a lot to rile her to that point."

Riley realized everyone was looking at her.

"You must've been there," Liam said. "You and Wynne were always joined at the hip."

She dropped her gaze and poked at her chicken. "Yeah, I was there."

The silence dragged out, until she felt a twitch between her shoulders.

"She was a bully, okay? A stupid, hateful, privileged little snot, who liked to take pot shots at me."

"Over what?" Sharilyn asked.

"Wasn't important."

"Wynne wouldn't have been so mad if it wasn't important," Sharilyn said.

Riley sighed. "Fine. On that particular occasion, she'd called us poor white trash one too many times for Wynne's taste." She'd also implied that Riley's mother was sleeping with the pastor to receive preferential treatment among the church's charity cases. But Riley wasn't about to admit that. "It was a long running thing. Amber and her sister bullied me from about fourth grade on, always making sly, catty comments designed for maximum humiliation." This many years later, she could still feel the burn of shame.

Sharilyn clutched at her pearls. "But…Mary Ellen Hopper was the one who organized the fund-raiser so we didn't lose the house."

Yeah, Riley had heard plenty about that, too. That had been the year she'd taken over all the money management and turned her babysitting into a profitable enough enterprise to keep the wolf from the door.

"The whole family is a bunch of self-important, sanctimonious assholes. The kind of 'Christians' who do very public good works to be *seen* doing them, so that they get credit for it, not because they have a shred of actual decency or give a damn about helping others. Every single hand up they gave came with a price tag. And they never, ever missed an opportunity to remind me that they were better. The Hoppers and people like them are the primary reason you have to practically hold a gun to my head to get me to accept help. Because I *refuse* to ever be made to feel like less or that I didn't earn what's mine, ever again."

The moment the words were out, Riley wished she could take them back. The relief of having finally admitted it wasn't worth the anguish on Sharilyn's face pale.

"I had no idea. Why didn't you tell me?"

Because I was the one who did the protecting. Riley shrugged. "You had enough to cope with." And she hadn't managed that particularly well. "There was nothing you could do about it. There's no law against people being hateful."

"You didn't tell me, either." There was hurt and no little bit of temper in Liam's eyes, though Riley knew the latter wasn't directed at her.

"Stand down, Marine. It was a long time ago. And nothing you could've protected me from."

"I could've done something."

"You did. You taught me to stand on my own two feet." She smiled in an attempt to break the tension. "Besides, there's karmic justice. She married a guy with the last name Butts. So now she's forevermore Amber Hopper Butts. If that's not the Universe kicking her ass, I don't know what is. Maybe that's small and petty of me, but I'll take my entertainment where I can get it."

She stabbed the last bite of fried chicken, determined to put an end to the discussion. "Did I hear a rumor about cobbler?"

"LIAM! RILEY!"

Liam tightened his arm around Riley's

shoulders and kept his voice low. "Don't make eye contact. First rule of traversing enemy territory—keep moving and don't draw attention to yourself."

"Enemy territory?"

"Getting cornered by the Casserole Patrol this close to the start of the fireworks means we'd be guaranteed to miss the show."

Her arm snaked around his waist and she leaned into him. "My big bad Marine is afraid of three elderly ladies?"

"Three busy bodies, more like. If they manage to pin us down for a conversation, they'll have an engagement announcement in tomorrow's paper and names picked out for all three of our future kids. Rumor has it, they've already started knitting baby stuff for Cam and Norah, and they haven't even set a date for the wedding. No, thank you. They can interrogate us later. We're setting up at the perimeter."

"Lead on, Boy Scout." He was glad to see her eyes spark with amusement. She'd been sober and withdrawn since dinner.

He steered her through the crowds, studiously ignoring everyone he could, smiling and nodding at anyone he couldn't. But he didn't stop until they'd reached the outskirts of the throngs encamped on the banks of Hope Springs.

Across the water, the last vestiges of daylight bled to night, only a faint blush of orange left in the sky. There were still a good forty-five minutes until the fireworks started. People milled around them, chatting, snacking on the contents of coolers brought from earlier cookouts, wrangling kids. It wasn't how he'd planned to end the evening. His original intent had been to take her to one of his favorite haunts from high school, far on the other side of the springs, to encourage some private fireworks of their own. But in the wake of her admission about being bullied in school, she'd been too much in her own head. He could've distracted her with the physical, but that wouldn't get at the thing still gnawing at her. So he'd brought her here, where an audience would keep their libidos in check, and he could, hopefully, figure out what to do to banish this demon of hers.

He unfolded the blanket he'd brought from the car and spread it on the grass. Slipping out of his shoes, he sat, stretching a hand up to Riley. "Come here."

She toed off her sandals and stepped onto the blanket. Taking his hand, she sank gracefully down, smoothing her dress before crossing her feet primly at the ankles and settling back against his chest.

Liam wrapped his arms around her, everything inside him going quiet and content as he tucked his chin against her shoulder. "You smell...sort of lemony. What is that?"

"A blend of lemongrass and eucalyptus oils. Natural mosquito repellent."

Of course, there was an oil for that. It was Riley.

"Definitely more appealing than Deep Woods Off." Unable to resist, he pressed a kiss to her neck, pleased to feel her faint shiver. But she wasn't entirely focused on him. "What's going through that busy brain of yours?"

"I'm still trying to wrap my head around the fact that your mom has been shipping us since high school."

Not what he'd expected. "She's been what now?"

"Shipping. As in hoping two people will get together in a romantic relationship. Though usually the term is used in conjunction with fan fiction, books, and TV shows rather than real people. Like, I ship Oliver and Felicity on Arrow."

"That sounds like an Autumn-ism."

"Given her romantic leanings, it's a favorite word of hers."

"Huh." Liam turned that over in his head and decided he kind of liked the idea. "Does it bother you that Mom hoped we'd get together?"

"Not...bother, exactly. I'm kind of embarrassed, I guess."

"Why?"

"You have no idea how hard I worked not to

moon over you back then. *You* never noticed, and Wynne never said anything, so I thought I pulled it off."

"You mooned over me?" He smiled to himself, inordinately pleased by the idea.

"Having a crush on your best friend's big brother is a special rite of passage. And mine had a hefty dose of hero worship thrown in."

"I'm no hero."

"You were always my hero," she said softly. Abruptly she stiffened

He didn't have to ask why. "No, I never told her what happened. Whatever she saw between us, it was nothing to do with that." He rubbed light circles on the back of her hand until she eased again.

"Don't you find the whole thing a little…I don't know. Weird?"

"Not weird. I guess I'm surprised. And a part of me feels like I shouldn't be because she knows me—apparently better than I know myself, since she figured this out way before I did. She loves you like a daughter, and I guess I worried she wouldn't be okay with this. It wouldn't have stopped me if she did, but it's nice to have her approval." Of course, that came with a whole helluva lot of pressure not to screw it up.

"What about Wynne? I haven't heard from her, and, frankly, I'm just as nervous about her reaction as Molly's."

That was a whole other kettle of fish.

"Oh, she called and read me the riot act last weekend. Said she's glad I finally got my head out of my ass to notice you were awesome, and I'd better take care of you, or I'd be answering to her."

Riley opened her mouth, then closed it again, shaking her head. "Maybe I wasn't as good at hiding my crush back then as I thought. How did she even know about us?"

"Evidently quite a few pictures of us at the playground made their way to her on Facebook, and she saw the announcement that Ruby won the pool on who I'd pick."

She twisted around. "Ruby? Seriously?"

"Apparently *I* wasn't so good at not mooning over *you.*"

"Could've fooled me. I spent most of the last month wanting to die of embarrassment every time I saw you."

"If your mama hadn't shown up, we'd have been doing this a helluva lot sooner." Liam rubbed his lips over hers, a lazy, teasing kiss.

"We're gonna wind up on Facebook again," she murmured.

"Don't care." He just kept right on with that slow taste, thinking she was the perfect dessert.

Until something thunked him against the side of the head.

Liam jerked back, already noting the breathless, "Sorry!" being called, as he looked around for what had whacked him. He picked up the frisbee and winged it back to the little girl still chanting, "Sorry!" as she jogged over.

"No problem!"

Riley had gone very still. He followed her gaze to a young woman waving a second apology for the little girl. She stood near water's edge, gesturing for an older boy to move out of range of the crowd. The empathy in Riley's expression clued him in.

"That's her, isn't it? The girl from the market that your mom was talking about."

Riley offered a friendly smile along with her wave. "Tara Honeycutt. She's barely twenty and has sole custody of her two younger half siblings. Brother and sister. Austin is about ten, I think Ginny's seven."

"How did she end up with them?"

"Their mom dropped them off with their dad—which is Tara's dad—and disappeared. Then Wayne got busted for burglary and sent to prison. Tara quit school and came home to take care of them rather than see them go into the foster system."

"That's a lot of responsibility to take on at that age."

"She's busting her ass, working two jobs to make sure they've got everything they need. So somebody like Hopper coming along and implying she's lazy or some kind of reprobate would probably be enough to send her over the edge. I so completely understand that."

She'd tensed up again, so he began to stroke and soothe. This was the opening he'd wanted. "It explains a lot about you."

"Oh, you mean the fact that I'm mule stubborn?" She shot him a self-deprecating smile.

"Well there's that—" He gave her a squeeze to take the sting out "—and how you got to be so strong. A lot of people would've buckled under those circumstances."

"My mother did. And I probably would have, if not for your family." She tipped her head to his shoulder. "Y'all were my collective rock. Always. Not everybody's so lucky."

"Are," he corrected.

"Sorry?"

"We are your collective rock. What's between you and me may have changed, but that hasn't. I hope you know that."

"I do. But I'm not in this for you to take care of me. I hope *you* know that. That's my mother's M.O. Not mine. I don't expect that from a relationship."

He could've been offended. He could've argued that the entire point of relationships was taking care of each other. His parents had been a glowing example of that. But this wasn't about her not needing him. It was about her not being willing to need anyone. Chipping away at that wall would take time and finesse.

Liam brushed a kiss over her brow. "You're nothing like your mom. Doesn't change the fact that I'm here to support you. Whether you think you need it or not."

She relaxed into him. They lapsed into silence as the fireworks began. Throughout the show she spent more time watching Tara and her siblings than she did the festive explosives. Liam spent his time watching her. Something was percolating in that brain of hers. He waited, patiently, to see if she'd let him in on it.

When the last burst of color died away, Riley straightened. "What time is it?"

"Coming on close to ten."

"Will you do something for me?"

"Anything."

"Will you drive me to Lawley?"

"Sure. What for?"

"To pay it forward."

"STAY HERE, while I scout the perimeter."

"No way," Riley whispered. "This was my idea. I'm going with you." She wasn't about to admit she felt a little squeamish standing in the woods by herself in the pitch black dark of midnight. There could be…creatures and crawling things. Some things she was fine being a girly girl about.

She couldn't make out Liam's face in the shadows, but his long silence suggested he probably knew it.

"Fine. We'll come back for the cargo. Step where I step, and test each one before you put your full weight down."

Riley fell into careful step behind him.

Heeled sandals were absolutely *not* the correct footwear for a covert operation. The flirty sundress was hardly appropriate either, but going by her apartment to change would've meant running into her mother. There was no explanation for why she needed to be dressed in black from head-to-toe that Riley cared to give. The whole point of this mission was secrecy.

A single light burned in the back of the little one-story house. Tara, probably, taking some rare time to herself or maybe figuring out how she was going to make ends meet for another month. Riley was well-familiar with that kind of late night.

They crossed the yard at what felt like a slow crawl, until Liam finally motioned her to press up against the side of the house. He eased through the weedy flowerbed. Riley followed until they both crouched beneath the edge of the lit window. Using hand signals that she could only presume meant raise up slowly, Liam turned to face the house. Like a pair of cartoon robbers, they moved in sync, un-bending just enough that they could peer in.

Tara sat on a stool at some kind of work bench, an oversized t-shirt slipping off one shoulder. A bright desk lamp illuminated the small tools, wire, and other detritus scattered across the surface. Her jewelry making station, Riley realized. The long artist's fingers twisted and fastened, picking up a tool here, a component there, then checking the overall composition beneath a large magnifying glass mounted with a spring clamp to the lamp. A satisfied smile spread across her face, and, for once, she actually looked her age. As they watched, she set aside whatever she was working on and turned out the desk lamp, before crossing to the bed in the corner.

Liam tapped Riley's arm and motioned back toward where they'd left the supplies. As they made their way back toward the woods, the last light went out.

"We wait ten minutes. Let her get good and

settled, slide on into sleep. Then we make our move."

"You're good at all this stealth stuff," Riley whispered.

"Ought to be. Nice not to have to do it while worrying about IEDs or mortars."

Riley closed her eyes and swallowed hard. She'd been making a concerted effort *not* to think about what he'd faced in the Middle East. After twelve years of worrying about it, that part of his life was finished. Thank God.

Liam's hand tangled with hers. "You okay?"

"I used to keep a map."

"Of what?"

"The world. Every time we got an update on you or your brothers, I'd note down where you were supposed to be. But given Jack is military intelligence and Cruz is a sniper, we usually didn't know where they were, so it was mostly you. I've got a record of your entire service. What we knew of it, anyway."

He tugged her against him. The cheek he pressed to hers was a little bit rough with stubble, but the way he held her was anything but. "I'm sorry I worried you. I don't know if it would've changed anything if I'd known, but I'd have at least made more of an effort to let you know I was okay."

Riley pressed her face into his shoulder, holding him tight. "I know it's been hard on you, but I'm so glad you're out."

"I thought about writing you."

"Really?"

"A hundred times. I kept that letter you wrote with me all the time. Read it and reread it until it fell apart and had to be taped back together."

The idea that the words she'd written him in anger had been a constant companion to him in battle made her vaguely ill. "Why? Why on earth would you want to reread a guilt trip?"

"That wasn't the part I reread. Not most of the time, anyway."

That only left one part.

"Do you remember?" he asked softly.

As if she could forget. "Take care of yourself,

Liam Montgomery. You'd better come home safe to all the people who love you, or I'll never forgive you."

Liam stroked a hand through her hair, tipping her face up toward his. "I took comfort in the idea that you might be one of them. That's why I wore the medallion all these years. I didn't think you'd have given up a piece of your dad if you weren't."

She was. Of course she was. She always had been. And she'd never been able to handle it.

Riley closed her eyes. "God, I'm glad you didn't see me before you got out. I was hateful to you. I wouldn't have wanted you to take that back out into the field."

She could see his smile even in the dark. "Well, I admit I was disappointed you didn't fall into my arms at my welcome home party. But I consider myself damned lucky to have you here now."

"Me, too."

He pressed a kiss to her temple. "C'mon Let's get this done."

It took two trips to get it all. They'd gone, perhaps, a little bit overboard with the three styrofoam coolers and dozen bags of other non-perishables. Once Liam had realized what she had in mind, he'd gotten into the whole thing. There was enough here to feed the family for a month. They arranged the lot of it neatly in front of the main door to the house.

"That's everything. You ready?" he asked.

"Wait." Riley laid a hand on his arm. "Do you think we should really wake them up?"

"If you just leave the coolers, there's not enough ice to guarantee no spoilage by morning. And you run the risk of stray dogs or raccoons getting into them or the rest of it. You wanted anonymity, this gives it to you."

"Okay, fine. You're right."

"You go on ahead. Once you're back to the treeline, I'll pull a ding dong ditch and make a run for it."

"Oh wait, I almost forgot." Riley pulled the note she'd scribbled out of her pocket. Prying up the cover of one of the coolers, she wedged the edge of the paper in and closed the top.

Liam arched a brow in question.

"In case she's too afraid to open them. People pull mean pranks on those less fortunate with far more regularity than anybody likes to think about."

"Fair enough. Go on."

Using the same tactics he'd shown her to cross in the first place, Riley headed for the trees. As soon as she was safely hidden behind an oak, Liam rang the bell and bolted, his long legs eating up the distance, as a light snapped on in Tara's room. He made it to the woods just as the front porch light came on. The door didn't open.

"We probably scared the crap out of the poor girl."

"Just wait," he said.

The door cracked open and the barrel of a shotgun peeked out.

"Good way to lose your gun," Liam remarked.

"Told you we scared her."

Evidently assured no one was there to molest her, Tara opened the door further and caught sight of the bounty piled on her porch. Riley saw her jaw drop and felt the rest of the ice that had lodged in her belly at dinner melt. Yes, *this* was what she'd needed tonight. To do something kind for someone who needed it, no strings, no identity attached.

Tara stepped further out, looking around for her benefactor. Seeing no one, she took one quick swipe at her eyes and started hauling things in. They waited until she'd carried it all inside, before melting back through the woods the way they'd come.

Riley felt buoyant. By the time they emerged where they'd stashed the car, a laugh bubbled out. "That. Was. *Awesome!*" All the covert ops stuff had her blood pumping in exhilaration.

"Feeling better?"

"So much." She threw her arms around him. "Thank you for helping me."

"It was a worthy cause all around."

Feeling the hard press of Liam's body against hers, her heart came up with an entirely better reason to thud in her chest. "Seems like you've earned a reward."

"Oh yeah? What did you have in mind?"

"Well, there is that backseat you mentioned earlier." She skimmed her hands down his back to grip his very firm backside.

"Have I mentioned I like the way you think?" He opened the car door. "After you."

Riley tipped the seat forward and climbed in.

Liam followed, shutting the door behind him. "Now, I believe I had a bet to win." He shifted to crawl toward her and bumped his head, then a knee. "Damn it. I wasn't this tall in high school."

She swallowed back a laugh at his look of consternation. "Ah, I'm not the first girl you've had back here."

"You're the first woman I've had back here."

"Nice save, Boy Scout."

"And, to be clear, I've never gotten past second base in this car."

"I can see why. There's not any room to maneuver."

"I could send your mom on an all-expenses-paid trip to…I don't know. Somewhere."

She stiffened, shoving at him. "No."

He smiled, trying to put her at ease. "I was just—"

"I mean it, Liam. I know you have this need to fix things, and I appreciate it. God knows, I don't know where I'd be right now without that. But this is not yours to fix. Leave it alone."

"Yes ma'am." He shifted around again. "The quilt is still in the trunk. We're alone in the woods. We could absolutely have more room."

"Oh no. You hear those cicadas and crickets? We are very definitely not alone in the woods. Not the kind of alone I would require for the kind of activities we both have in mind. There is nothing sexy about bugs or snakes or any-thing else that's out there."

"So I'm hearing that you're never going to want to go camping."

"I'm fine with camping. So long as there is a tent. And sleeping bags. And a gallon of mosquito repellent."

Liam sighed and pressed a kiss to her throat before finally just sitting on the bench seat. "Just as well. When I make love to you, I want it to be in a bed, where I can take my time about it."

Riley felt her body coil with need and longing. She wanted that. Oh God, how she wanted that with him. She slid into his lap to straddle him, her knees bracketing his hips. "You should know I fully support that plan at the earliest possible opportunity. In the meantime—" She shimmied against the evidence of his arousal. "—I expect we can at least manage second base to take the edge off."

She gripped the hem of her dress and lifted it up and off.

"God bless America."

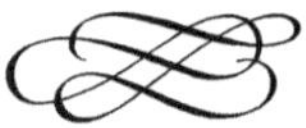

CHAPTER 11

RILEY WATCHED THE SERVPRO technicians roll the dehumidifiers and fans out the front door of the pharmacy. "Good riddance."

Ruby lifted her hands to God. "Amen. I ain't gonna know what to do with myself without all that noise rumblin' through here."

"Don't get rid of your earplugs yet," Liam told her. "I'll be making plenty of noise fixing the damage."

Ruby winced.

"I'll be doing as much as I can after hours to

keep from disrupting business any more than I have to." He turned to Riley. "You need to be deciding on a new wall color. Once the new sheetrock is in, the whole room will need re-painting."

"Oh, can we *please* have something other than some shade of antique white?" Jessie begged.

"There are flooring decisions to be made, too. These original wood floors aren't salvageable. You and Mom need to decide ASAP if you want to go with more wood, laminate, tile, or what, so we can get it ordered over at the hardware store. If there are any changes you want to make to the place, now's the time to do it while we're about to have it all torn up anyway."

"Decisions, decisions." Riley was getting damned tired of making them. "I just want everything dealt with as quickly as humanly possible."

"It'll look worse before it gets better. But it *will* get better. Promise." He chucked her softly under the chin.

"I trust you." And she did.

"Good." He pulled her in for a quick and entirely unsatisfying kiss. "I'm gonna run over to see Tyler and pick up flooring samples for y'all to think about. Maybe grab a paint fan too. Then I've got a few other things to see about, but after work, I'm taking you out to celebrate."

"What are we celebrating?" Liam was not the two week-i-versary type.

"The fact that repairs can finally proceed. And the rest is a surprise."

Riley lifted a brow. "A surprise, huh?"

"So suspicious." He grinned. "Just be ready to go by seven. And wear that little black dress. I have a particular fondness for that one."

She saluted him. "Yes, sir."

"You're so cute when you try to be official." Liam kissed her again, lingering this time in a way that had her way more curious about his surprise than she had been. "See you tonight."

He sauntered out the door, a spring in his step.

Jessie leaned against the counter and

propped her chin on her fist. "You know, I hate the reason he's in here all the time right now, but I do love having the eye candy."

Riley smiled and resisted the urge to touch her lips. "He is pretty exceptional eye candy, isn't he?"

"I wouldn't kick that one outta my bed for eating potato chips."

"Ruby!" Riley laughed.

"What? I may have thirty years on him, but I'm not dead."

"You two were looking mighty cozy the Fourth of July fireworks," Jessie noted with an eyebrow waggle.

That wasn't anywhere near as cozy as they'd been *after* the fireworks. Not content with second base, they'd ambitiously headed for third. And if they'd only had a bed…

"Earth to Riley."

She jerked her attention back to Jessie to find the other girl smirking in a way that let her know she'd mentally wandered off for a while.

"I'm just gonna assume by the dopey grin on your face that you two made your own finale."

An image of those broad hands on her bare skin had Riley's face burning hot.

Ruby's teeth flashed white. "Good for you, sugar. You need a little loosenin' up."

Riley glared at both of them. "Back to work, both of you. My love life is not up for discussion."

"You keep thinkin' that, honey." Ruby patted her arm.

The bell jangled and Tara Honeycutt walked in with her brother and sister. She went brows up as she took in the water damage and rearranged shelving.

"Wow. I'd heard you had a flood but this is…"

"Yeah. It's bad. But the good news is we're dry enough to finally start repairs, so hopefully all will be back to normal in fairly short order," Riley told her. Liam was a man of his word. If he said it would be so, it would be so.

Tara spoke a few soft words to her siblings.

Judging from Austin's hunched shoulders and baleful expression, it was something along the lines of "Don't touch anything," but he took his sister over to the candy display.

"What can I do for you today?"

They both looked around as the door opened again and Autumn walked in. She waved at Riley and headed toward the haircare products.

"How's the tea tree oil working out for you?"

"Really well." Tara paused. "I've still got your instructions tacked to the fridge."

"It can sometimes be hard to remember ratios for stuff. I have to check my references all the time for different oil recipes."

"Your handwriting is really—"

"Messy? Yeah, I know. Mom says I should've been a doctor."

Tara's gaze was intense. "I was going to say distinctive."

Riley blinked, then realization dawned. *Oops.* She'd forgotten about the note she'd stuck in one of the coolers.

No one should ever be made to feel less because of their circumstances or what they have to do to survive.

"Thank you." Tara's voice was soft but firm, and Riley didn't have to ask what she was referring to.

She laid a hand over the younger girl's. "You're welcome."

"I wanted to bring you something. Just a token."

"Oh, you don't have to…" Riley trailed off as she pulled the small white box out of her purse. Nestled inside were a pair of chandelier earrings, similar to the ones Riley had admired earlier in the summer.

"I did them in silver. It suits your skin tone better than the copper."

"They're wonderful." Riley slipped them on and immediately felt sassier. "Thank *you*."

Jessie wandered over. "Oh my God, those are *awesome*. Where can I get some?"

"Tara makes them."

"Well, I want to commission some," Jessie insisted.

"Really?"

When Tara left a little while later, the kids in tow, Riley waved them on their way, feeling like she'd added some positive karma to the world to balance out the negative.

Autumn stepped up. "You look like you're having a good day."

Riley tapped at her dangles. "I very much am."

"Well, it's about to get even better."

The door opened again.

"Hold that thought," Riley said.

Sharilyn breezed up to the counter. "Hey, baby."

"Hey, Mom. What can I do for you?" Riley couldn't stop the instinctive tensing.

"Not a thing. I'm on my lunch break. I just wanted to let you know I'd be away this weekend."

"Oh? With who?" *Please don't say Matthew McSweeney.*

"You remember Linda Buckner?"

"It was her wedding where you met Daddy."

Sharilyn beamed. "It was. She's in Lawley now and invited me for a visit."

Riley relaxed. "That'll be fun. How are you getting there? Do you need to borrow the car?" If she needed anything, Liam could probably take her.

"Nope," Autumn said. "Judd's Nanna's birthday is this weekend. He has to work, so he and Mary Alice are going for the party tomorrow and coming back late. I'm staying the weekend at the farm, so I told your mom she could hitch a ride with me."

"I just wanted you to know I'd be gone until Sunday. You know, so you don't worry." This last was said with a pointed look that had Riley frowning.

You're welcome, Autumn mouthed.

Translation: I'm making sure your mom will be gone all weekend, so she won't be around to barge in on you and your sexy new boyfriend.

Oh God.

"That's...very considerate," Riley choked out, knowing her face was flaming ten shades of crimson.

"Are you all packed, Sharilyn?" Autumn asked.

"Just need to swing by the house and grab my bag."

"Why don't we do that, and then I can drop you back by work for the rest of your shift."

"Sounds great. I'm off at six." Sharilyn popped her over-sized sunglasses back on and headed for the door "Have a good weekend, baby!"

With a final wave and a wink, Autumn followed her out.

Looked like Riley wasn't the only one getting a surprise tonight.

"IT REALLY SHOULDN'T BE TOO bad." Liam could already see how the place could look with some TLC. "There's no need to knock out walls or alter the floor plan. Updated fixtures, refinished cabinetry and trim. It can all be done very reasonably."

Babette Wofford crossed her arms and nodded. "What kind of timeline are we looking at?"

"Well, I need to knock out the pharmacy first thing, and that's going to take some time. And then finish up the apartment above it. Maybe a month or six weeks before I could start. But the job itself…a week. Maybe two."

"That's fine," Babette said. "You just let me know."

"I'll work up that estimate and get it to you in the next few days. You can get some other quotes in the meantime to make an educated decision."

Babette waved her hand. "I don't need other bids. You were a good, honest boy and you're a good, honest man. I'll wait until you're available to do the job."

Mildly exasperated and more than a little amused, Liam said, "I appreciate that Mrs. Wofford. But if you change your mind in the meantime, no hard feelings."

They headed down the stairs.

"I'm just happy to finally be doing something with it. Meanwhile, I'll be looking for a new tenant for the studio apartment down on Sutton. My last one up and skipped out on his lease last month. Moved his stuff out and didn't tell a soul. We didn't realize anything was wrong until he was late with his rent."

Liam's interest piqued. "What's the rent?"

Babette named a figure. "After this latest fiasco, first and last month's rent will be required up front. And a security deposit. Are you interested? Not to talk you out of it, but it's a real crackerbox of a place. I can't imagine a man your size fitting comfortably there."

He thought of Riley's insistence that he stay out of things with her mother. But giving Sharilyn information about a place that would suit her needs hardly qualified as actual interference. "I'm not, but I know somebody else who might be. Do you have time to show it to me?"

It really *was* a crackerbox, but it was clean and functional. More to the point, it was within walking distance of everything downtown, which made it affordable, even on an hourly wage, if she wasn't having to pay for a car. Sharilyn could probably swing it, and it would do her good to have a taste of the independence that her daughter prized above all else.

Because it was on his mind, he headed straight to McSweeney's Market. The after work, pre-weekend rush was starting. Since he didn't want to take up Sharilyn's time without even buying something, he swung through the floral department to grab one of the ready-made bouquets. By the time he'd picked between sunflowers, Gerbera daisies, and something hot pink and tropical looking, the crowds had thinned, and he caught Riley's mom alone at her register.

She gave him a broad smile when he approached. "Well, aren't those just the prettiest things? For Riley?"

"Yes, ma'am."

"Sunflowers are a good choice. They're a favorite. She'll just love those. It's the kind of little thing she'd never buy for herself but absolutely appreciates."

He was doubly glad he'd decided to stop. "I'd say she deserves a little spoiling."

"She absolutely does." Sharilyn rang him up. "Would you like to make a contribution to our Good Food for Good Neighbors program?"

"And what is that, exactly?"

"The program enables you to tack on a donation to your bill, either by automatically rounding up to the nearest dollar or by adding an amount of your choosing. The money then goes into a fund managed here at the store that can be distributed via gift cards for store credit so those in need can buy groceries. It's a way for people in our community to help those who need it without having to go out of their way or do anything complicated."

"And since the money is on gift cards, there's no stigma attached."

"Exactly," Sharilyn said.

"This was your idea." It wasn't a question.

A shadow of pain flit across her face. "If something like this had been around fifteen or twenty years ago, maybe Riley wouldn't have been harassed."

"This is a brilliant idea."

Sharilyn's cheeks pinked. "It's just experimental for now, but if it works out, Matthew's going to make it a permanent thing."

Matthew McSweeney strode over. "I can't imagine it not being a rousing success. So far the response has been really positive. People like the idea of their donations staying local."

"I certainly do. Put me down for twenty," Liam said.

"Cents?"

"Dollars."

"Oh, you are the sweetest thing."

Matthew beamed at her. "Innovators deserve reward. I think we need to discuss a raise. Why don't you close out your till and come see me in my office before you head out."

Wide-eyed, Sharilyn just nodded and watched him walk away.

"Congratulations," Liam told her.

"It's so unexpected."

"Why? You've been working hard, clearly doing a good job. And in light of that, there's something I wanted to mention to you."

"Oh?"

Liam told her about the apartment. "I wasn't sure if you were to a point you could be thinking about that, but it seemed pretty ideal, and since they lost their last tenant unexpectedly, they're eager to fill it."

Sharilyn gnawed on her lip. "I'll have to do some number crunching, see if I can swing it."

"You just let me know, and I'll go look over it with you." He didn't know why he said it other than she was the kind of woman who seemed like she'd be more comfortable making a decision with a man around to approve. And he could make sure she didn't get herself into trouble.

"I'll do that."

He picked up the flowers.

"And Liam? Thank you for wanting to take care of Riley."

His lips curved as he imagined Riley's reaction to such a statement. "I'm not sure she'd say the same."

"Probably not," Sharilyn acknowledged. "But whether she'll admit it or not, she wants someone to care. And you're headstrong enough to do it for her own good."

That was the absolute truth. He just hoped she ultimately thanked him for it.

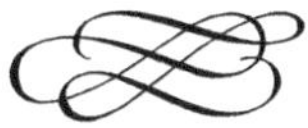

CHAPTER 12

IT WAS SEVEN FIFTEEN by the time Liam rolled up at Riley's place, face freshly-shaved and hair still damp from his shower. He grabbed the envelope from the seat and stuffed it into his back pocket, then scooped up the flowers. He'd planned to wait until dinner to tell her, but as it was too damned hot for a coat, he had nowhere to put the thing and didn't want to get distracted and leave it on the table at Tosca. If Riley was wearing The Dress, that was a distinct possibility.

She opened the door as he was climbing the steps. "Hey, Boy Scout." The sultry smile softened as she took in the bouquet he carried. "You brought me flowers."

"I did." He passed them over, and she buried her face in the blooms with a distinctly feminine purr.

She *was* wearing The Dress. And those shoes that made her legs look long and luxurious. He got a good view of what those heels did for her backside as he followed her into the kitchen and waited while she put the flowers into water. Her makeup was a bit more subdued than the first time he'd seen her in this outfit and her hair was a bit less vintage, but she was no less a knockout. And this time he had the right to touch her. It was too damned bad they didn't have the privacy for that.

"You're stunning." He lifted her hand to his lips, shifting at the last moment to press a kiss to her palm.

"You're a charmer. I like it." A faint blush

streaked across Riley's cheeks and down the column of her throat.

Liam wanted to follow that trail into the bodice of her dress to see if the rest of her flushed that gorgeous rosy color. "I aim to please." And he really had to stop thinking about pleasuring her. They were about to be out in public and her mom could get home any minute. "You ready?"

"About that, is there a time attached to this surprise of yours? Reservations or anything?"

"No. Why?"

She stepped away and headed back to the front door. "Because we're going to be late to dinner."

"We are?" Were they about to have some serious Talk?

"See, I have a surprise for you, too, and you're going to want to unwrap it here." Her expression was very serious, but Liam could see the sparkle in her eyes and he relaxed.

"I am?" He made a show of looking around for a box. "Where is it?"

"Right here." She locked the door and stepped into him, sliding her hands up his chest and around his neck. "My mother is out of town. For the *entire weekend.* We are finally, blessedly *alone.*"

In a second, Liam's plans for the evening shifted and his body stirred. "There is a God."

"There's an Autumn, and I can't even get annoyed at her interference. She's Mom's ride to Lawley, so there will be no interruptions."

"Remind me to send her flowers next week." He gripped her generous hips and pulled her closer to his growing arousal. "Is tomorrow Mom's Saturday to work?"

With a hum of pleasure, she rubbed against him. "It is."

"Better and better. How do you feel about an entire weekend of debauchery and delivery food?"

Delight lit her face. "I love that idea almost as much as I love the fact that you just used the word debauchery."

"Seems the appropriate term for what I have

in mind." He skimmed his hands over her curves. "I've given it a lot of thought since December."

"Have you now?"

"Thorough, detailed thought."

"Then you'd better come to bed and show me." She rose to her toes and rubbed her lips over his—an invitation, a promise—before she took his hand and led him upstairs.

The bedroom was larger than he'd have expected, given the size of the other rooms in the duplex. It was a mishmash of furnishings, dominated by a queen-size bed and an assortment of wood pieces that matched only insofar as the distressed pale green paint. Mosquito netting was draped artfully around the head of the iron bed, which was already turned down, waiting. Liam sniffed, accustomed by now to the fact that she'd have some essential oil diffusing wherever she was. This one smelled sweet and exotic with an undertone of something woody.

"Ylang ylang and sandalwood," she explained.

"You're you, so I know they're not just for atmosphere. What do they do?"

"They're aphrodisiacs."

"You are all the aphrodisiac I need." He slipped his arms around her waist.

She sighed. "You're really good for my ego."

Despite the pounding in his blood, Liam dipped his head to take her mouth in a languid kiss. He'd dreamed of being with her for so long, he wanted to relish it.

"Liam," she said, against his lips.

"Mmm?"

"You should unwrap your present." She turned in his arms and presented her back.

With slow, deliberate hands, he slipped the zipper down. Through the narrow gap where he expected skin, he saw a row of laces. Intrigued, he spread the back of the dress and felt his mouth go dry. They were corset laces. Black satin ribbons running the length of her spine, from beneath her shoulder blades to her waist. The corset itself was cream-colored, with some kind of elegant black pattern woven in the fabric.

"This is the sexiest goddamned thing I've ever seen," he said, aware that his voice had gone to gravel.

She looked at him over her shoulder, her eyes heavy lidded and hot. "Don't stop there, Boy Scout. You gotta get the full effect."

Liam ran a knuckle down her bare shoulder. "I was never a rip the paper off my presents kind of guy. I like to savor." He dropped his head to the juncture of her shoulder and drew in her scent, something subtly floral and lemony. "Anticipate."

Riley made a small, sexy whimper and melted back against him, sliding her hand around his nape, skimming her nails down the back of his neck in a move that made him want to growl. Her eyes drifted shut as she tipped her head to the side, a surrender that had his willpower fraying. He closed his own eyes and dug deep, looking for patience. They had time and he wanted to take it.

❧

RILEY'S SKIN came alive as Liam slid his work-roughened hands over her shoulders, pushing the dress down her arms, easing it past her hips to reveal the wisp of black satin that was her underwear.

He swore reverently and helped her step out of the dress. "Okay, I have to know. Were you wearing this when we went to Magnolia Heights?"

"I was."

He knelt and unfastened her shoes. "If I'd known…"

"If you'd known?"

"I spent half that night mentally reciting weapons components to keep from being a giant walking hard-on."

"Really?" Delighted, she turned to face him. "I spent the whole night thinking you weren't affected at all."

"If I'd known this was underneath, I don't

think I could've stopped myself from trying to seduce you."

"I'd have probably let you."

"I'm glad I didn't know."

Riley pouted a little. "Why?"

"Because that would've just been lust." Liam cupped her face, stroking a thumb along her cheek. "This is more."

Her heart trembled at the look in his eyes. Their relationship was so new, she'd meant this to be simple, fun. But it wasn't new. Not really. And it wasn't simple. In truth, it had never been simple.

Before she could reply, he kissed her again. She could feel him working at the knot in her laces, feel the whisper of satin against her legs as he began slowly unlacing the corset. For a moment she thought to stop him, explain how to loosen the lacing to unlatch the front because it would take forever to relace the thing correctly. But he'd said he wanted to take his time, so instead she reached between them to tug his shirt free from his pants. By the time she'd bared his glorious shoulders, he'd only made it about a third of the way up the lacings.

"Okay, seriously, how the hell did you even get in this thing?"

Riley chuckled softly. "Normally it stays laced. Just loosened." She reached back, made a few tugs to ease the upper laces, then unlatched the steel busks.

Liam's eyes went all but black as she shrugged out of it, standing before him in nothing but the panties. "Let me just say, that's a glorious little piece of engineering. I'll remember it for next time."

It was a thrill to know there would be a next time.

"At the moment, I'm mostly concerned with this time." She tugged him toward the dresser, until he stood behind her at the mirror.

His hungry gaze met hers. "One of your fantasies?"

Dropping her hands to his, she drew them up her bare torso. "I want to see you touch me."

"Your wish," he murmured, getting with the

program and cupping her breasts in his big, broad palms.

She loved the feel of his hands, bold and possessive. Loved, too, the sight of his darker skin against hers. His calloused thumbs brushed her peaked nipples, and Riley went wet. With a hum, she pressed back against him, glorying in the heat of his chest against her back and the evidence of his desire.

Liam stroked his hand over the soft curve of her belly, down to cover the scrap of satin between her thighs. She gasped at the touch, part shock, part pleasure. Her body flushed and she rocked into his hand, wanting, needing more.

"Have you ever watched yourself come, Riley?"

Speechless, she managed to shake her head once. If he kept talking to her in that voice and looking at her with that unwavering, laser-point focus, she was going to find out in a hurry.

Liam lifted her hands to loop around his neck. "Hold on to me."

She did as ordered, fingers gripping the taut muscles of his neck as he slid the satin aside and went to work. The sight and feel of him stroking, possessing her, had her knees melting, her body going pliant. And when she shattered, the only thing holding her up was the grip she had on him and the arm he banded around her waist.

"So goddamned beautiful." Liam spun her, taking her mouth, even as she still quaked from pleasure.

When her legs tried to give out, he lifted her up, resting her butt on the dresser as he took her nipple into his mouth. Feeling an answering tug much lower, Riley wrapped her legs around his waist, settling against the bulge behind his fly.

"Too. Many. Clothes."

He turned toward the bed, blindly lowering her, letting her go only long enough to strip out the rest of his clothes with a speed and efficiency she admired almost as much as his beautiful body. Then the mattress sank as he joined her, slowly crawling up her body, lips and hands igniting every inch.

Restless, aching, she reached for him. "Now, Liam."

He started to pull away from her.

"What—?"

"Condom," he muttered, pressing a kiss to the inside of her thigh.

Riley took a firmer grip. "Birth control."

He shifted up, settling himself in the cradle of her hips. "I'm clean. You sure?"

She wanted him, all of him, with no barriers, no more walls. "Yes. God yes!" Her answer shifted into a shout as he slid inside. "More."

"I like the sound of that."

He draped one of her legs over his shoulder and thrust forward until she could feel every hard, hot inch of him buried deep.

"Okay?"

"Perfect," she managed.

Dipping his head, he made love to her mouth as he withdrew and thrust in again, an achingly slow rhythm that kept her deliriously on the brink. She lost track of everything but the flex and play of muscle and the glorious friction of his body moving in hers.

Riley nipped his lip. "Harder."

"Hang on."

She curled her hands around the spindles of the headboard. He drove deeper, harder, pausing just a moment at the end of each stroke, so her body clung to his. She matched him beat for beat, feeling the wave begin deep in her core. He cried out as she crested, clenching around him, and they rocked into each other, chasing the last delicious streaks of pleasure.

Riley lay boneless beneath him, flushed and sated. Liam's face was pressed against her throat, his breathing hard.

"I'm crushing you."

As he started to move, she groaned in protest, sliding her leg from his shoulder to wrap around his waist to keep him buried inside her. "Not yet. I love the aftershocks."

Liam propped himself on his forearms and

gave a slow swivel of his hips that had her body quivering.

"Mmm. You feel wonderful." Riley dragged her hands down the muscles of his back.

"You are a constant surprise to me."

She tucked a pillow beneath her head. "Why?"

"You've got this incredibly wholesome, girl-next-door vibe, so the fact that you know what you want from a lover and aren't afraid to ask for it is this amazing turn on."

"Well, it's not like people are psychic. If you don't ask, it's not likely to happen just by accident."

"True enough. I guess I just didn't expect you to be so comfortable with your sexuality." There was just a hint of worry in his eyes.

Riley traced patterns over his chest. "I think what almost happened to me colored your perceptions more than they did mine. At least for the long-term. If you hadn't been there, things probably would've turned out much different. But you were, so I never had to deal with that beyond the realm of what if. You made sure of it."

His arms tightened around her and he rolled so she straddled him. "I worried about you when I left."

Not so long ago, Riley wouldn't have believed him. But she understood him better now. Somewhere in the past few weeks, she'd let go of her anger and dropped the walls she'd built all those years before. So she let the thought of him worrying about her slide through her, warm and sweet, like sun-warmed honey.

She pressed a kiss to the hollow of his throat. "It's nice to be at a place where we don't have to worry about each other anymore."

Liam brushed a kiss over her brow. "Nice, too, to be in your bed rather than under it."

"Good surprise?"

"Superior surprise. Mine's going to pale in comparison."

She folded her hands over his chest and rested her chin. "What is it?"

"Where are my pants?"

Riley grinned and wiggled. "I'm pretty sure I already got the surprise in your pants."

"And it's yours any time you want it. But no, that's not the surprise." He shimmied across the bed, one hand possessively on her butt, until he could stretch his arm to the floor to grab something.

She loved that he wanted to keep touching her and stay close.

A moment later he came back up with an envelope. "Open it."

Riley sat up and took it, wondering if he'd gotten tickets to something. But whatever was inside was several pieces of folded paper. The envelope wasn't sealed, so she slid the contents out and unfolded them.

Mississippi State Board of Contractors

Liam's name and contact information was filled out on the front page. She flipped through skimming the rest.

Riley frowned, not really making the connection. "You're applying for your contractor's license?"

He stroked her thighs. "I told you that night at dinner that I wasn't sure I was cut out for civilian life. That I didn't know my place anymore. You told me to build my own."

She went still, watching him.

"I've spent seven months trying to figure out how the hell I fit here, and it wasn't until you that I felt like I did. I hate that you've been slapped with all this pain in the ass need for repairs, but it's helped me figure things out. *You* helped me figure things out. I *like* building stuff. I like seeing measurable progress to the work I'm doing instead of a big ass pile of rubble and destruction."

Riley smiled at him. "That's perfect! You weren't made for life behind a desk. And I see why we're celebrating, but how exactly is this a surprise for me? Or did you already know about that fantasy I have about you and your tool belt?"

Liam's lips curved, but his expression remained serious. "I wanted to give this to you as proof that I'm serious and I'm committed. I didn't want you to worry that I'd leave again."

What began as a tremble shifted to a quake as her heart cracked wide open, all the adolescent hero worship, all the lust and affection gave way to a love that warmed her down to her toes. That he'd think of that… Her throat went tight, and for a moment, Riley was terrified she'd cry. She swallowed the lump and cradled his face. "Thank you." Then she kissed him, pouring out everything she wasn't yet ready to say.

His arms wrapped around her, his hand snaking into her hair as he answered with equal passion. He stirred inside her, and she murmured against his lips, "You promised me celebration, Boy Scout."

He took a firm grip on her butt as he thrust up "Let it never be said that I don't give my girl what she needs."

Liam woke Sunday morning with regret. Not that he'd been with Riley—if there was a better way to spend a weekend than making love to a beautiful woman, watching classic movies, and noshing on Chinese and pizza, he didn't know what it was—but because their alone time was almost over. Who knew when the next opportunity would present itself? Determined to make the most of what time they had left, he slipped out of bed and headed downstairs.

Riley was not a morning person. He'd known this about her in an abstract sense, but seeing the truth in action was a whole different thing. She was so adorably befuddled in the morning until she'd had her coffee. Granted, she'd gotten very little actual sleep, but Liam had a feeling that didn't matter much, so he went ahead and started the coffee. As the Columbian brew began to drip, her cat wandered into the kitchen and began to meow pitifully. Valium had finally deigned to show himself during their movie marathon yesterday.

Or maybe it was just that they'd finally surfaced long enough to notice him.

While he searched out the cat food, Liam thought back to the problem of their lack of privacy. There were only two possible solutions he could see. Either he went ahead and got his own place or Riley's mom moved out. Getting himself a place would be simple enough; though, time was an issue until he finished renovations on the pharmacy. He didn't want to wait that long. He wanted her beside him when he went to sleep, in his arms when he woke. The truth was, he didn't want his own place. He wanted a place with Riley.

That realization slammed into him, leaving him stunned.

And he'd thought his *mom* would push once he got serious about a woman?

Valium sank claws into Liam's leg, reminding him to actually put the kibble in the bowl. Shaking off the cat, Liam finished feeding him and poured coffee before heading back upstairs. Riley was still sleeping. Not wanting to disturb her, he sat on the chair in the corner to drink his coffee and think.

That night they'd had dinner at Magnolia Heights, she'd told him to build his own place. Liam wondered what she'd say if she realized he'd been building that place around her? He wasn't entirely sure how he felt about that himself. It was way too damned soon to talk about moving in together. Which meant the easier solution was helping Sharilyn get her own place. That would alleviate Riley's burden of taking care of her financially and give them the option for privacy when they wanted it. Win-win, really.

Riley stirred, reaching across to his side of the bed. "Liam?"

"Morning beautiful."

She propped herself up on one elbow, expression faintly confused as if wondering why he was all the way across the room.

"I made some coffee." He nodded toward the travel mug on the bedside table.

Sleepy blue eyes blinked, shifting between

him and the coffee. Something in her face softened. "Come here."

Liam crossed to the bed, bending close at the crook of her finger.

She brushed her lips over his. "I got to sleep in and a sexy man brought me coffee in bed. I had to make sure I wasn't dreaming."

"That enough proof for you?"

"Mmm, I think I could go for some more convincing."

"What about your coffee?"

"The sexy man was smart enough to put it in a travel mug to keep it warm. Because he's a Boy Scout like that."

When she tugged, he tumbled back into bed.

As it turned out, the coffee was cold by the time they got to it.

They stumbled into the kitchen, stomachs growling. She was wearing his shirt from Friday night. Damn if he didn't like that.

"You gonna give me my shirt back?"

"Oh no, you have forfeited all rights to this shirt. I'm keeping it." She leaned back, propping her elbow on the peninsula and striking a provocative pose. "If you want it back, you'll have to peel me out of it again."

Liam grinned. "That can be arranged."

"There's just one thing you should know first."

"What's that?"

She straightened and turned her back to him, looking over one shoulder and arching a suggestive brow. "Pharmacists do it over the counter."

"Have I mentioned I like the way you think?" He trapped her against the cabinets and ran his hands up her legs to find nothing but her perfect, round ass. "Why Miss Gower, what do we have here?"

"Underwear is more like a suggestion than a rule during a weekend of debauchery."

Yeah, okay, maybe breakfast could wait.

He tugged the shirt back to bare one of her shoulders.

"I thought you were hungry."

"I'm starving." He bent his head to nibble.

Someone knocked on the kitchen door. Riley shrieked and dropped down behind the counter.

Laughing, Liam looked down at her crouched on the floor. "What are you doing?"

"It's *your mother.*"

His gaze shot to the door. His mom wiggled her fingers in a cheerful wave. "Oh my God."

"I'm not wearing *pants.*"

Liam's lips twitched. He must've made some sound because Riley looked up at him with narrowed eyes.

"Don't you *dare* laugh at me."

"You have to admit, it's kinda funny." Though, thank God *he* was wearing pants already.

"It isn't funny at all, and so help me, if you laugh, you will never be welcome in my bed again. Don't just stand there. *Do something.*"

"And what precisely am I supposed to do?"

"You're a Marine, for God's sake. Create a diversion." She began to crawl toward the hall

Liam looked toward the door, where his

mother was patiently waiting. He held up a finger in the universal *just a minute* signal, then scooped Riley up and sprinted for the hall as if a bomb was set to detonate behind them.

"*That* was a diversion?"

He set her on the stairs. "You're out of sight, aren't you?"

She covered her face with both hands. "Jesus, I haven't even had coffee."

"Get dressed. I'll take care of it."

Liam detoured back through the living room to snag his t-shirt from the floor—it'd been abandoned there sometime yesterday after a screening of *From Here To Eternity* inspired a little naked reenactment of the beach scene—and went to let his mother inside. He'd braced himself for a tongue lashing of epic proportions, so when she stepped inside, stood on tiptoe to kiss his cheek and said, "Hey, baby," he didn't know what to think.

"Um, morning, Mom."

"It's after twelve."

Did that mean they were going to Hell for

staying in bed all morning instead of getting out to church?

"So I guess you don't want coffee, then?"

"No, but you go ahead. I'm sure Riley will want some."

Molly crossed to the kitchen table and sat, as if she dropped by all the time. And what did he know? Maybe she did. Valium wandered in from the living room, twining around her legs and meowing pitifully until she picked him up to snuggle. Other than cooing to the cat, she didn't say a word.

Molly Montgomery was a master interrogator.

Not wanting to incriminate himself any further than being caught all but *in flagrante,* and knowing she'd get to her point in her own time, Liam made more coffee, pulling the creamer and prepping a mug with sugar exactly how Riley liked it. When she walked in a few minutes later, her hair tidied into a neat pony tail and dressed all the way down to her shoes, he handed her the coffee.

His mother beamed.

Riley held the mug like a shield, every line of her body tense. He reached out automatically and began to knead at her neck muscles. She flinched, her expression freezing like a deer in the headlights.

"Oh relax, honey. It's just me," Molly said. "You're practically part of the family."

It was Liam's turn to freeze. *Please, dear God, don't let her start talking about weddings and babies.*

"I'm sorry to just drop by like this, but I just couldn't wait. It's too good an opportunity."

"What is?" Riley asked.

"Norah snagged me after church to tell me about the latest project Peyton Consolidated has planned, and it's *big*. There's going to be a ton of construction going on downtown for the next several months, and that means lots of workers. You need to go for the treatment and vaccine contracts. Exclusivity on a project that size would be a real boon to the business."

"It would be. But don't you think it might be more sensible to wait until the repairs are finished, in case the man in charge wants to come visit the pharmacy to check it out? We're not exactly giving our best impression just now."

"This is true. But I wouldn't wait too long."

Liam dragged out a kitchen chair and sat. "When is the project announcement going public?"

"In a couple of weeks. The details of *what* they're building are being kept under wraps, but the general announcement will still go out. Nobody's going to be giving Walgreens a heads up. You stand a good shot. From everything Norah's said, Gerald Peyton believes in local business. This kind of agreement would be right up his alley."

"I'll start putting together a pitch."

"And I'll dive into demolition tomorrow," Liam said. "Have y'all decided on flooring?"

They discussed details of the renovation for a few more minutes before Molly put Valium down and rose. "I apologize again for barging in. I just wanted to let you know ASAP so you can move on it."

"I appreciate it Really." Riley's smile was still a little stiff around the edges. "I'll, um, see you at work."

"Sure thing. And if you need to take some more personal time, please don't hesitate to let me know." She winked. "I really want grand-children."

Liam covered his face. "Oh my God."

"Ta!"

The door shut behind her.

Riley's face was frozen in a mask of mortification. "I can't ever go back to work."

"I'm sorry. I should've expected that."

"It's not that she knows we have a physical relationship. It's that we know that she knows, and she knows that we know that she knows, so nobody can just politely look the other way and pretend this isn't the twenty-first century."

"Could be worse," Liam suggested. "The Casserole Patrol could be stopping by with a covered dish and an already started baby blanket. I heard Miss Maudie Bell totally did that after Cam and Norah got engaged a couple months ago."

"She wanted to give Norah her choice of the yarn color."

"How do you even know that?"

"Autumn. She volunteers at the senior center twice a week. Speaking of, she texted while I was upstairs. She's picking my mom up in an hour."

Liam rocked back on his heels. "So that's it, then."

"We've got maybe two hours?"

"Well, since *my* mom effectively killed the mood, let's go hit the gym. I've got some weapons disarms I want to teach you."

Riley pouted.

"It's practical and you promised. Besides," Liam curved his hands around her hips, "up close and personal work like that can be…stimulating."

"You make a compelling argument. I'll go change."

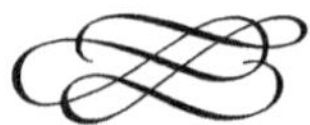

RILEY STARED IN DISBELIEF at the empty storage unit. Well, empty but for the roach carcasses, spider webs, and other things best not to contemplate. Years of her family history had collected dust in there, and Liam and Judd had emptied all of it in half an hour.

Liam circled around the little U-haul to join her. "Did we miss something?"

"No. Y'all got everything."

"You seem to be not entirely happy about that," he observed.

"I'm fine. I just keep expecting to wake up and find out this was all a dream." Because she just couldn't quite wrap her mind around a reality in which her mom was about to be completely self-sufficient.

"No dream. A fact which I intend to prove to you beyond a shadow of a doubt later tonight."

Judd stuck his head out from the cab of the U-haul. "Quit talkin' sexy to your woman, man. It's too damned hot to wait around for that."

Liam cheerfully flipped him off. "If we're good to roll, then Judd and I are gonna head on over to the apartment."

"I'll be right behind you. Autumn and I are going to sweep this thing out, then go close my account."

"I'd kiss you, but I'm disgusting."

"We're both disgusting." Riley ignored the sweat to take the kiss she wanted.

"We can get clean together later," he murmured.

With the image of a naked, sweaty Liam and

a bar of soap in her brain, Riley watched them pull away. "Too hot, indeed."

"Come on, lover girl. This storage unit is a sauna. Let's get this done."

They set to work, falling into an easy rhythm.

"So has it been weird, having Molly know that you and Liam are *together* together?"

"More for us than her, I think. She actually said if I needed to take some personal time, to just let her know because she wants grand-children."

"Seriously?" Autumn laughed. "Man, I knew Molly dug the idea of you two together, but I had no idea she'd go *that* far. Make sure she doesn't know where your condoms are kept."

"Why?"

"I heard somewhere about a woman who wanted grandchildren so badly, she took a needle with her when she had dinner at all of her children's homes and poked holes in all the condoms. She wound up with a whole brood."

"Oh, Jesus. Thank God for pharmaceutical birth control."

"Watch her. She could get around that, too. Who better to give you a placebo than a pharmacist who works in your pharmacy."

"She wouldn't."

"I don't know…" Autumn drawled.

"Hush your mouth. Don't even suggest that."

"You and Liam would make pretty babies."

For just a moment, Riley softened at the thought. A little boy with her dark hair and his big gray eyes and impish smile. "Of course we would, but not the point and all kinds of ahead of where we are. Whose side are you on?"

"Yours. Always yours, girl. So your mom seems super pumped."

"We're both pumped. It's just a little studio apartment, but it's within walking distance of everything downtown, so the fact that she doesn't have a car right now won't be a big deal. She's looking forward to having a proper bed to sleep on instead of the fold out sofa in my living room." And Riley was looking forward to the ability to have a cup of morning coffee in silence.

"Has she ever had a place all on her own?"

"Nope. She married Daddy before she graduated college, and after I left for school, I was still managing the finances. This will be her first ever truly solo mission." And that worried Riley as much as it relieved her.

Sharilyn had been trying so hard since she got back to Wishful. Riley desperately wanted her to succeed, not only for her own self-confidence but so that Riley herself would finally be free of that life-long burden. But what were the odds of that actually happening? Riley couldn't generate a proper level of enthusiasm because she was waiting for the other shoe to drop and wondering what she'd have to do to pick up the pieces.

"Stop waiting for her to fail, Riley."

Riley sighed. "I can't help it. Old habits die hard. But she's doing really well. For once, she's not doing this for some guy and there's no guy doing it for her. That's a huge step in the right direction."

"Have some faith, hon. She might surprise you."

"God, I hope so."

Riley took care of business in the mini storage office, and they headed downtown to the apartment. The U-haul was already half-empty. She picked up the nearest box. Might as well contribute to the cause. As she turned toward the apartment, she almost plowed into someone.

With a yelp, she bobbled the box.

"Whoa there. I've got it." Capable hands righted the load to reveal Matthew McSweeny, dressed for labor, sweat glistening at his silver-shot temples.

"Mr. McSweeney? I'm sorry, I didn't see you there." Which she hadn't, but what she really wanted to say was *What are you doing here?*

As if she'd asked the question anyway, he said, "No problem. I came to help. It's a full house up there."

"It's a tiny place. That doesn't take much." Because her arms were starting to burn and because she didn't have a clue what she thought about him being here, Riley went on into the apartment.

He hadn't exaggerated. Between Liam and Judd moving furniture at her mother's direction, Molly unpacking kitchen stuff, and Autumn stacking boxes near the bathroom, there wasn't a lot of room to move, let alone stack more boxes. Riley hadn't realized she was looking for someone else from the market until she didn't see anybody. Which meant Matthew McSweeney was here on his own, not as part of some Help-A-Coworker-Move gesture.

"We have an extra set of hands." Molly nodded as Matthew came in with more boxes.

"So I see."

"Shari, where do you want these?" he asked.

Shari?

"What are they labeled?"

"The ever so informative 'Miscellaneous.'"

Her mother waved a hand. "Oh, just find a

corner. I can't remember what's in most of these boxes."

That was because Riley had been the one to pack the majority of them back when they'd sold the house.

"Randy always was the organized one," Matthew remarked.

"Of course he was. Until he set foot in a kitchen. Then don't you dare ask him the difference between a whisk and a colander."

"How did you and Randy meet?" Autumn asked.

Riley watched Sharilyn's face soften in that way it only ever did when she talked about her father.

"It was our own little fairy tale."

Autumn perched on a barstool and propped her chin on her hands. "Ooo, tell. I love fairy tales."

Sharilyn smiled over at Riley. "This used to be one of Riley's favorites."

Feeling a bit of a pang at the thought, Riley smiled back at her. "Still is."

"We met at a wedding. My college roommate got married on the beach down in Gulfport. Randy was already in the Air Force at that point, and he was on leave. Just wandered right on into the reception looking for a party."

Riley laughed a little, as she thought of her rakish, reckless father crashing a strange couple's wedding reception.

"I didn't even realize he wasn't a guest when he started talking to me. We talked and danced all night, saw the bride and groom off, and talked some more. And we were still talking and walking on the beach when the sun came up. He walked me back to my hotel and told me he had to be getting on back to base. Then he thanked me for an amazing night, and he kissed me. One of those knock-your-socks-off, toe-curling kisses."

"Best kind," Autumn agreed.

"Anyway, he told me to think of him and then left me standing there, completely senseless. It wasn't until I'd showered and fallen into bed that I realized we'd never even exchanged last names. Of course, he was long gone by then, and I had no way of tracking him down on base, so I went home the next day just heartbroken."

"Obviously that's not how the story ends."

"I thought it was. Didn't hear a thing from him for six months. Then one day he was just waiting for me outside my English lit class, leaning against a tree in his dress uniform. There is nothing so breathtaking as a man in military dress uniform."

Riley looked over at Liam. "True thing."

"I'll keep that in mind."

"And what did he say?" Autumn asked.

"That he was sorry he was late. He'd gotten called overseas and it took him a mite longer to track me down than he'd originally planned. I told him as far as excuses went, that one was pretty good. And he asked if I'd thought of him. Well, of course, I *had.* All the time, even though my girlfriends told me I ought to forget about him. His buddies all had pictures of their sweethearts tucked into the cockpits of their planes, so they'd always be with them when they flew. He said he had a picture of me. Here." Sharilyn tapped her heart. "And he'd carried it with him wherever the road had taken him since we'd parted."

"Damn, that's romantic," Autumn sighed.

"Right? I certainly thought so. And when he held out his hand in that 'Do you trust me' kind of way and said, 'Are you up for an adventure?' I took it. Forty-eight hours later, I was Mrs. Randall Gower."

Autumn went brows up. "You eloped with a guy you'd known for like two days?"

Sharilyn shrugged. "When you know, you know."

"Randy knew. Talked about you the whole time we were deployed," Matthew said. "Kept saying how he was gonna track you down when we got back and marry you. We thought he was nuts. Then he came back with you in tow. Gotta say, we were pretty jealous of his good fortune."

Her mother grinned. "I remember he used to say if you wanted something good out of life, you had to stop waiting around for it to fall in your lap and go after it with everything you had."

Because she felt odd hearing her mom reminisce about her dad with someone else, Riley headed on outside.

Autumn followed her back out to the truck, grinning. "I think I smell a romance."

"You do not," Riley snapped.

"Oh, come on. Mr. McSweeney's not part of the beer and pizza brigade like the rest of us. Why else would he be here?"

"He's an old friend of my dad's. He just wants to help." But that excuse sounded weak even to her own ears.

God, it would be just like her to have wrapped him around her little finger. Sharilyn was good at doing that. Was Matthew bankrolling this apartment?

No. Riley had forced her mom to go through the finances and prove she could afford it before agreeing to help with the move. Sharilyn had a budget. This little place was within her means. And surely if there were something going on, they wouldn't have chosen this tiny studio apartment. Matthew wasn't married. He had a house of his own and plenty of room.

By her own admission, Sharilyn was turning over a new leaf. She was moving out on her own, not in with a guy. And she was so excited about this. The least Riley could do was have the same faith in her mother that Sharilyn had had in her all these years.

But as she watched her mom and Matthew laughing together, she couldn't help but wonder.

"THE KITCHEN IS OFFICIALLY *DONE*," Molly announced.

"I'm pretty sure it's a rule that the kitchen isn't done until it has food," Autumn said.

Liam's stomach chose that moment to let

out a growl that rivaled a grizzly. "Case in point."

Sharilyn collapsed onto the sofa. "The market is closed. Best I can do is PB and J and tap water."

"You've got an in with the owner," Matthew teased. "I bet he'd open after hours for you."

From his position kneeling by the entertainment center, Liam watched Riley pointedly not react to the flirting as she began to break down the boxes they'd just emptied.

"I promised you all pizza. I'll call it in as soon as I get these hauled to the trash." Riley began to gather up the stack of boxes.

"Here, I'll help you with that," Liam said.

She angled her head in question but didn't argue. Between the two of them, they hauled the flattened boxes to the dumpster around the corner of the building. Liam waited while she'd called in the order for pizza, thankful that the brutal heat of the day had finally broken and a breeze kicked up enough to ease the humidity.

She hung up and started back toward the apartment, "They said twenty-five minutes."

"Good, I'm starved. Hold up a sec." Liam snagged her hand, towed her to a stop before she rounded to the stairs.

"What?"

"You okay?"

"Why wouldn't I be okay? I'm just tired. It's been hella hot today."

"I just thought you might be a little…sensitive," he decided, "about Matthew flirting with your mom."

Riley shrugged. "She's a single, unattached woman in her own place. Whether I think she should be chasing after another relationship is neither here nor there. As long as he's not bankrolling this apartment, and I know he's not, then there's no objection I can raise that would be valid."

"That's a real pretty speech. You keep saying it long enough, you might start to believe it."

She huffed out a breath. "I'm being stupid. I want her to be happy. She deserves to be happy.

I just worry. We've been down this path in one form or another many, many times before, and in the end, it always comes down to me having to save her from herself."

Liam couldn't blame her for being braced for that. That kind of pattern was hard to break. "You want my take?"

Riley shot him a suspicious look, clearly not sure if she'd like what he had to say. "I suspect you're going to give it either way, so go ahead."

"I think your mama regrets all those years she's had to depend on you." She'd told him so herself. "You've been doing the adulting in your family since you were a little thing. That wasn't fair to you, and she knows it. She wants to make this work on her own."

"And Matthew?"

"Your mama is a fun, flirty woman. There's no crime in that. I don't know if they're more than friends or not, but he's a good guy. Steady. Responsible. A fixture of the community. He's not some fly-by-night cowboy type who'd use her and lose her. And I think he respects what she's trying to do."

Riley was silent for a few moments. "I think…I think it's good for her to have someone to talk to about my dad, someone who knew him well. With Matthew, the fact that she still misses him every day isn't going to be some secret she tries to hide. He was there. He knows. Whatever else happens with them, I think there's probably some healing in that. I don't know if she ever really dealt with those feelings before because she was, on some level, looking for a substitute all these years. So, I guess I'm glad she has his friendship, if nothing else."

Liam kissed her brow. "It'll get easier. Let's go finish helping her unpack."

Inside, the AC was finally starting to make a dent since the door had been shut for longer than five minutes at a time.

"What took y'all so long?" Judd asked.

"Were you canoodling in the alley?" Autumn teased.

"It's too damned hot for canoodling any-where," Riley said. "If you leave now, our order at Speakeasy should be ready by the time you get there. And by the time you get back, I might've decided to pretend you never said that."

"Then I guess I'm on pick up duty." Autumn grabbed her purse. "I shall return with suste-nance post haste."

"And beer!" Judd added.

"And beer," she acknowledged, and shut the door. She was back in a matter of minutes. "So my car's dead."

"Is there something in the gas around here?" Liam asked.

"No. I didn't get the door shut when I came up to start with the unpacking. It's been sitting there for hours."

"I told you you needed to get that battery replaced," Judd said. "I had to jump it twice last winter."

"I know, I know. I just haven't gotten around to it."

"We'll take care of it," Liam promised.

"Oh, I can help with that," Riley told her. "I actually have jumper cables in my trunk."

The last thing he needed was Riley snooping under her own hood. She didn't know cars, but even she would be able to tell something wasn't right. "You keep your hands off that engine," he ordered. "You can't be trusted not to put the positive on the negative and the negative on the positive. I spent too many hours fixing Jo to have you blow something up."

Riley stuck her tongue out at him.

"Just let us finish with this, and we'll be out to deal with it in a few minutes," Judd added.

Both women rolled their eyes.

"You forgot to do the King Kong beating of your chest and pronounce yourselves Tarzan to our Janes," Autumn said.

Judd shook his head. "I tell you, we get no respect."

"None at all," Liam agreed, and bent back to the task at hand.

A few minutes later Judd looked past him.

"What do you want to bet they've gone to go take care of it themselves?"

"Huh?" Liam cranked his head around. But Autumn and Riley were out of sight. "Shit."

"Eh, let 'em. It's probably a statement about feminism or something."

"No, it's not that. I don't want Riley to—"

"Liam Montgomery!" Her shout carried from the sidewalk outside.

"—look at her engine," he finished.

Judd went brows up. "What did you do?"

"What had to be done." And now it was time to face the music.

Rising to his feet, he headed outside, where Riley had moved Jo nose to nose with Autumn's Altima. Jo's hood was up, and Riley stood beside her, hands on hips, glaring as Liam came out. She pointed to her engine. "I may not know a carburetor from an alternator, but I know what the whole thing looks like. That is not my engine."

"Of course it's your engine. It's in your car." Not that he really thought that would work.

"Don't play dumb with me. I helped your daddy rebuild my engine the first time. I know what a rebuilt one looks like. Even freshly done, it doesn't look that clean. What did you do?"

"What had to be done," he repeated. "Your engine was shot. I put in a new one."

"Well, I can see that. And what the hell was that bill for parts and fluids you gave me?"

"The rest of what I did to it."

"Liam, you can't just buy me an engine. That's not like a gift of chocolates or flowers. We weren't even together when you did this."

"I didn't buy you an engine."

She flailed a hand in its general direction again, color rising. "Then what the hell is that?"

Oh hell, he knew that look. There was only one thing that would disarm the fit of stubborn she was about to unleash.

"I didn't buy it. Dad did."

Riley blinked. "What?"

"The last time he worked on your car, he saw this coming. It's in the service records at the garage. He picked up a replacement engine at auction. It was just sitting in the warehouse collecting dust."

She softened. "Your daddy…" One hand rubbed over her heart, as if to soothe an ache.

Liam knew the feeling.

"Then I need to pay back the garage. Or your mother. Or somebody."

"No, you don't," Molly swung an arm around her shoulders. "He loved you like a daughter, and he wanted to take care of you or he wouldn't have bought it. The business accounts for the garage have long been settled. There's nothing for you to pay."

"But—"

"No 'buts,' Riley. Take this as a last gift from Dad." *Even if you won't take it from me.*

She closed her eyes. "God, I wish he were here so I could hug him around the neck."

"You and me both, sugar," Molly said.

Riley gave her a squeeze, then stepped to Liam. "Since you were the one who were kind enough to do all the work, I'll hug you instead."

"Now that I can get behind."

Her grip was tight as she tucked her head against his chest. "Thank you."

It was a little thing that she'd let his late father do something to take care of her, however indirectly. But it was a step in the right direction. One of these days, maybe she'd actively let him do the same.

CHAPTER 14

"To TWO WEEKS OF an empty house." Riley raised her wine glass to Autumn's.

"It's hardly been empty. Liam's stayed over every night." She waggled her eyebrows and smirked.

Riley's cheeks heated. "Fine, to two weeks of a house free of parental units."

"I'll drink to that." Autumn tapped her glass and sipped. "Now, details, woman. I'm living vicariously through you, so hold nothing back."

Riley shot a look around Speakeasy, but nobody in the pizzeria was listening to their conversation over the currently heinous rendition of "The Boys Are Back In Town" screeching out of the karaoke speakers. "I'm not giving you the down and dirty on our love life."

Clapping her hands together, Autumn brightened with interest. "Ooo, so there's dirty? You naughty girl. Dish."

"Not. Happening."

"Oh, come on! You owe me for playing chauffeur to your mom. We are not going to talk about how long it's been for me. Take pity. I need a tale of a good pounding against the wall or the front door because you couldn't wait to make it to the bedroom." Autumn tipped back her glass and drank deep.

Riley lifted a brow. "Have a thing for wall sex, do we?"

"You have no idea. Smutty books and toys can only do so much. I have *needs.*" She tried to make a joke of it, but an innate sadness lurked behind the lust, and the sight of it broke Riley's heart. Autumn polished off her wine. "But we are not here to talk about me and my non-existent love life. We're talking about you and Mr. I'm Too Sexy For My Toolbelt."

Not knowing how to comfort her friend, Riley let the subject drop as their pizza arrived. In silence, they slid steaming slices of the New York-style pie onto their plates.

"We haven't had time to get around to my toolbelt fantasy. While I've been up to my eyeballs in presentation stuff, he's been working his very fine butt off on the repairs at the shop. He'll be starting on the floors tomorrow, so the end is actually nigh. Thank God."

"Hooray for that." Autumn bit into her pizza, chewed. "I guess you're waiting until all the repairs are done before he formally moves in."

Riley stopped with a slice of pizza halfway to her mouth. "Moves in?"

"Yeah, you're right. There's not a lot of room at your place. It'd be better for y'all to find a place together, though I'll miss having you next door. Meanwhile, have you cleared out closet space for him yet?"

"Closet space?"

"Do you need to clean your ears out? You keep repeating me."

"Because you're totally fast forwarding our relationship. We haven't talked about living together. Nobody's moving. In or out."

"Why not? If he's staying over every night anyway, it seems more expedient than having him live out of a bag."

"We're just getting started, Autumn. Just dating."

"Baby, you and Liam aren't *just* anything. That complicated history of yours means you bypassed all that. You may not have talked about it yet, but you've totally fallen into some level of domestic bliss, and I think it's adorable."

"We're not living together." They couldn't be. Not after so short a time.

"Are his toothbrush and razor on the bathroom counter?"

"Well, yeah. He used them this morning."

"Do you keep his favorite snacks and beer on hand?"

"Yes, but I also keep yours and you don't live with me. It's called being a good hostess."

"Point taken, but the emergency chocolate stash doesn't count. Does he have his own key?"

"Yeah, but so do you."

"I don't use it when you're not there unless you need me to do something or I need to raid said emergency chocolate stash. Did he clear it with you before heading off to poker night with the boys tonight?"

Riley frowned. "He didn't ask my permission. He doesn't need to. He just let me know because it was the polite thing to do."

"Because the expectation has become that he'll be spending the night with you."

She resisted the urge to hunch her shoulders. "We've just been spending all our free time together now that we've got some privacy."

Autumn gestured with a garlic knot. "Which is totally code for burning up the sheets."

"Oh for heaven's sake, we don't spend all our time in bed."

"I bet if he wasn't in it, you wouldn't be able to sleep as easily and you've already got sides."

Could she sleep without him? It had been so incredibly easy to get used to having him sprawled beside her or wrapped around her. Who knew her badass Marine would be such a snuggler?

"None of that means we're living together."

"Okay, have you, at any point, called him to get him to pick up something from the grocery on his way home?"

"No."

"Has he called to ask *you* if he can pick up something on his way home?"

"Take out doesn't count."

"No, you're missing the point. Has he used the word 'home' in reference to your place?"

Riley opened her mouth to rebut, then re-membered his parting words as he'd left for Mitch's. *I'll try not to be home too late.*

"Ah *ha!* I can see it on your face. He totally has."

Riley gave up pretending to eat the pizza. "Oh my God."

"From my perspective over here in the cheap seats, he looks happier than I've ever seen him. And so did you until you hit panic mode about sixty seconds ago. What's the matter?"

"I'm not panicking."

"Your face is taking on the same shade as the banana peppers, babe."

"It's just… It's too much too fast. Circumstances have escalated things between us and we've completely bypassed all the normal dating and get to know each other rituals."

"So? You already know each other. I fail to see the problem here."

"Relationships have a proper order for a *reason.* I don't want him to start feeling like I pushed him into something."

"You haven't pushed Liam into a damn

thing. That man is stubborn as a mule. He doesn't do anything he doesn't want to do."

That was true enough, but what if he started feeling caged in? Trapped? Riley had seen that often enough in the men her mother dated, when things moved way too fast.

Autumn laid her hand over Riley's. "He wants to be with you. Don't start borrowing trouble where there is none."

"I just—I don't want to screw this up because we didn't think things through and rushed into something more serious than either of us was ready for."

"You're allowed to rush when you're in love, when it's right. You know that in your gut or you wouldn't be where you are with him."

"I didn't say I was in love with him." She'd kept that to herself.

Autumn arched one brow. "Please. This is me. I have eyes. You're both crazy about each other, and you make each other happy. And you were completely fine with that until I opened my big fat mouth. So I'm going to shut up now, you're going to go back to being happy and making googly eyes when his name is mentioned, and I'm going to sit over here and smile in appreciation that two of my favorite people got over themselves and found each other."

"That easy?"

"That easy," Autumn assured her.

"Why are you so invested in this?"

"Other than the fact that I want my friends happy?"

Riley nodded.

"You two give me hope. And that's a pretty rare commodity these days." As the karaoke announcer called out their names as next on deck, she reached for her refilled glass of wine. "Drink up. There's no way I'm doing 'Love Shack' sober."

"THE PRODIGAL RETURNS!" Mitch crowed as he opened the front door.

"Prodigal my ass." Liam pushed past him

and headed straight for the kitchen to add the six pack he'd brought to the fridge.

Mitch followed him into the massive cook's kitchen, full of gleaming stainless, granite, and high-end appliances that rarely saw use. "We haven't seen hide nor hair of you since the playground was finished."

"In case it's escaped your notice, I've been kinda busy."

"Oh, it's escaped nobody's notice, buddy boy." Judd smirked and handed him a cold Abita. "Not that anybody blames you for spending all your available time with the very fine Miss Gower."

"She's way prettier to look at than all y'all, that's for damned sure."

Mitch punched some buttons on the microwave before turning his attention back to Liam. "She's got you well and truly smitten. Never thought I'd see the day."

Smitten? What the hell was that supposed to mean? Could a guy be smitten? It wasn't like he had little cartoon hearts and birdies circling his head all the time. "Why do I get the sense I should kick your ass on principle?"

Reuben strolled in. "Your pansy ass wouldn't get beaten if you'd get back to hauling it up to the gym and sparring again."

"And risk messing up this pretty face?" Mitch stroked a hand along his smooth-shaven jaw. "I think not. Is Darius coming now he's back from the honeymoon?"

"Not tonight. He and Vivian had a thing."

"Like a *Mama Pearl called a family summit* kinda thing?" Judd asked.

"More like an *I'm married now and my hot wife bought new lingerie* kind of thing," Reuben replied.

Mitch set the freshly nuked bowl of cheese dip on the table, along with a bag of tortilla chips. "See? That just proves my point. You're all dropping like flies. First Darius. Cam's next, if he and Norah can ever set a date."

Reuben took a beer. "If Mama Pearl has her way, I'll be right behind."

"With who?" Judd wanted to know.

"Viv's sister Violet. Mama Pearl made sure we were paired up all through the wedding. Vi was pretty pissed, but I can't say as I minded. She's a firecracker. I like that in a woman."

Liam tried to imagine the ex-Navy SEAL with Vivian Buckley's twin. Both were headstrong and stubborn. They'd either spontaneously combust or kill each other. Either way, it'd be fun to watch.

"Jesus. It's a sickness and it's spreading." Mitch shook his head. "I'm not sure whether it'll be Liam or Judd to succumb next."

"Succumb to what exactly?" Judd asked.

"Marriage fever," Mitch said in funereal tones.

Judd's face went slack with shock. "Marriage?"

"Yeah, you know, that thing you do with the woman you want to spend the rest of your life with," Reuben said.

"Mitch is right. It's a sickness, and I most definitely don't have it." Judd twitched his shoulders as if to shake off the marriage germs.

"You have been dating Mary Alice for going on two years," Liam pointed out.

"So? We're good as we are."

Liam couldn't resist pressing, just a bit. "So you ought to know by now whether you want to marry her."

"Oh, like it's that simple."

"Sure it is. You imagine your life in the future. Five years. Ten. Fifty. Is she in it?"

"Is Riley?" Judd shot back.

Yes. Liam could see the years unfolding, imagine the life, the family they'd make together. He waited but didn't feel a trace of the panic flashing in Judd's eyes. Just rock steady certainty. How about that? But admitting that fact just now would turn attention back to him

"We aren't talking about me and Riley."

"We weren't talking about me and Mary Alice either. Jesus, how the hell did we get off on this shit?"

"Hey now, save it for the ring," Reuben warned.

Mitch whistled. "Touchy. Touchy."

Because he's with the wrong woman. But some things you didn't say, even to your closest friends.

Judd scowled and tipped back his beer. "I'm not touchy. I just came to play poker."

"Don't get your panties in a wad, Hamilton. Come sit down and take your chips. I'm going to get the brats off the grill. Liam, you wanna grab that plate?"

Liam picked up the platter and followed Mitch outside to the one cooking appliance he *did* use.

Mitch lifted the top off the Big Green Egg and nudged the fat, sizzling sausages with his tongs. "You're skating on thin ice in there."

"He's making a mistake."

"It's his mistake to make."

"Even if it hurts more than just him? You and I both know Mary Alice isn't the woman he's built his life around."

Mitch began loading brats on the plate. "Does Riley realize you're building your life around her? Do you?"

Liam kept his face impassive, just lifting a brow in mild interest. "Did you drag me out here to talk about my relationship? Are we gonna braid each other's hair, too? Because Riley and I are good."

His friend studied him. "Yeah, I think you are. You may take forever to make up your mind, but once you've decided, you move quick."

"What's quick?"

"Your poker face isn't that good, Montgomery. You're serious about Riley. Like, long-term, marriage and kids serious."

"That tends to be the ultimate point of relationships."

"Are you sure she wants the same thing out of a relationship as you?"

Liam narrowed his eyes. "What the hell kind of question is that?"

"A rational one. Anybody with eyes can see the two of you have chemistry, but you're really different people. Riley's a single minded, intensely driven woman. She's been on her path for a really long time, and that path didn't include you."

"So? I'm not asking her to change it for me. I'm really fucking proud of what she's accomplished."

"I'm not saying you're not."

"Then what are you saying?" How the hell had this become about him?

"I'm saying you've been looking for something since you came home. And it seems like you think Riley is it. If she is, great. But be sure before you rush too far down that path."

What the fuck? He and Riley were fine. "Are we done with this backyard episode of Dr. Phil?"

"Yep."

"Good. Because I'm in a mood to take all your money."

Mitch's grin spread slow. "You can try, brother. You can try."

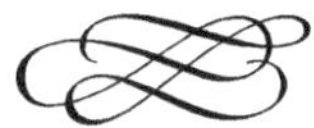

CHAPTER 15

"WELL, THIS IS A surprise." Cassie Callister greeted Riley from her post behind the counter at The Daily Grind. "Not your usual routine."

"I've been kicked out for demolition. We closed for the rest of today, all the way through noon on Monday. Molly's been enduring the noise so I can work on a presentation. I've been up to my eyeballs in that all afternoon, so I figured I'd come here for a bit of pick me up." It felt good to be out of a chair.

"We aim to deliver. What can I get you?"

"A large General Burke for me, a chai tea for Molly with extra cinnamon, and a cold brew with cream and sugar for Liam."

Cassie bustled to put together her order.

It felt patently weird to be not at the pharmacy on a workday. She'd eaten, breathed, and practically slept there since she bought the place last year, worrying, nurturing, and doing everything in her power to make the business thrive. Was this what single parenthood felt like? This was a rough patch, no question. Maybe the business was hitting its terrible twos early. But she'd get through it, somehow. And she'd start by landing Peyton Consolidated as a client.

Cassie slid the drinks into a cardboard caddy. "You look happy."

Riley blinked. "Do I normally look sad?"

"No, not at all. You've just been working so hard since you bought the pharmacy, you've been kind of perpetually on edge." Cassie leaned her hip against the counter. "I know what that's like. The first year after I bought this place, I swear my wares were the only thing keeping me going."

"You've certainly been keeping *me* going."

"And we appreciate your continued patronage." Cassie grinned. "But anyway, I just mean you've got a glow. And I suspect a certain sexy Marine Staff Sergeant has something to do with that."

Riley chuckled. "He's certainly a big part of it. But life in general is pretty great. Liam and I are in a good place right now. My mom's in her *own* place, finally. Things are getting back on track with the pharmacy. The only thing that would make it better would be Wynne coming home. Since she's firmly entrenched in New Orleans, I'll take what I've got and be grateful."

"Good. You deserve it. Which is the only reason I don't hate you on principle for taking one of Wishful's most eligible bachelors off the market." Cassie winked.

"Thanks for that." She laughed. Turning to head for the cream and sugar station, she almost mowed over Babette Wofford. "Whoops, sorry!"

"Not a problem, dearie. I just finished my weekly Skype session with Delilah and was in the mood for a pastry. How's your mama settling in?"

"Just fine. She's all unpacked. The apartment really is perfect for her."

"As soon as he saw it, Liam said it would be."

Riley cocked her head. "Liam?"

"When he heard my tenant had skipped, he wanted to see it."

Liam had been the one to find her mom's apartment?

"I'm just glad it all worked out," Mrs. Wofford continued.

"Oh, did you have a lot of interest in the place?"

"No, it never made it to being formally advertised. With the extra security deposit and the first and last months' rent required up front, I wasn't sure Sharilyn would be able to manage. But that big sweetheart of yours took care of it." She beamed.

Riley felt her jaw tighten and had to fight not to growl. "Did he now?"

"He didn't want to risk the place going to someone else since it was so ideal, so he fronted the money. I like having an older, more responsible tenant there anyway, so it was a win-win for everybody. I tell you, that man's a real keeper."

"He's something." And as soon as she got ahold of him, his ass was grass. That overbearing, meddling… Unless her mother was behind this, which was equally possible. She knew exactly how to play a natural caretaker like Liam.

Mrs. Wofford continued, oblivious to Riley's rising blood pressure. "Listen to me chattering on. You're obviously headed somewhere to deliver those coffees. Give your mama my best."

"I will." Ears ringing and half blind, Riley moved to doctor her coffee.

She'd told him. Explicitly forbade him from

getting involved with this. And he'd gone behind her back.

"Well, if it isn't Riley Gower."

Riley closed her eyes. *Just fucking perfect.* It was beyond her capabilities to manage a polite smile, but she thought she managed not to grimace as she looked up to see Amber Hopper Butts.

"Amber."

"How are things?"

Riley didn't trust that cheerful smile for a moment. This woman was a shark. "Things are great. Couldn't be better." *Go away.*

"No, I don't suppose they could. Taking the old dog's tricks and adding some of your own, I see."

Her hands curled to fists. "I beg your pardon?"

"You've got Liam Montgomery on the hook to pick up the tab for you *and* your mother. That's a pretty trick. But then your mom always excelled at that, so I guess you had a good teacher."

Through a red haze, Riley was dimly aware of the coffee inches from her hands. She imagined grabbing a cup, hurling the scalding contents into Amber's face, listening to her scream. Another more rational part of her mind pointed out that Amber was the type to sue, and Riley really couldn't afford an attorney right now, even if a jury of her actual peers would never convict her.

Amber was still talking. "You may as well enjoy him while you can. He'll tire of you soon enough and walk away, just like all your mother's men. He's far too smart to stand for being used by a needy woman."

Riley opened her mouth, but nothing came out. She tried to reel the humiliation in, to remain impassive, but her face suffused with heat and her hands began to tremble. How could she be just as trapped, just as helpless now as she had been as a child?

Amber's lips curved in satisfaction. "Still tongue-tied? It's no wonder. There's no real defense for being a gold digger." Without another word, Amber strolled away, unhurried, as if she hadn't just shivved Riley between the ribs.

Even knowing Amber's perspective was skewed, Riley couldn't stop herself from seeing the situation through her murk-colored glasses. And she felt dirty. Did people really think it was like that? That she was using Liam for his generosity? That she was stringing him along on her behalf and her mother's? Shame and humiliation washed through her, kerosene to the flame of temper already licking up her spine.

She couldn't do anything about Amber, but she could sure as hell confront the most recent source of the problem.

LIAM'S back ached and his head throbbed after hours of ripping up flooring. Whoever had laid the original planks had never intended them to come up. Ever. An hour in, he'd been forced to call for reinforcements. Mitch had managed to round up a few guys, but Liam had let them go a couple hours ago to get on home to their families. He could finish up the last little bit. And then, God willing, he'd get a nice cold beer and something to fill the gnawing in his belly. Lunch was way too many hours past.

He wondered how Riley was getting on with her presentation and whether she was getting close to a stopping point herself.

As if summoned by his thoughts, she walked through the door. His heart gave a happy little bump.

"Well you're a sight for sore eyes." He started to lean in to kiss her, but she lifted the caddy of coffees she carried.

"I brought drinks. Cold brew?"

He plucked it out of the carrier. "Don't mind if I do. Thanks."

"Chai tea for you, Molly." She set the drinks on the counter, but didn't pick up her own.

Molly grabbed hers. "Mmm, with the cinnamon on top, just like I like it. You're a sweetheart."

Riley folded her arms and surveyed the

progress, her face strangely blank, the way it got when she was trying not to look upset. "You've been very, very busy."

Liam wanted to smooth out those ripples he knew were underneath. "I know it's a mess right now, but once the new floors are in, you won't even be able to tell it happened."

"I've got a long memory. It'll take me a while to get past it."

His mother stroked a hand down Riley's back in the same gesture she used on him. "You okay, honey?"

"Just tired. Been working on the presentation all day." She sounded it. Maybe the work hadn't been going well for her.

"Get it finished?" Molly asked.

"Nearly. I'd like to go over it with you when I do."

"Sure."

Riley worked up a dim smile. "I'm sure you're tired of listening to all the noise. Why don't you head on home. I'll stay 'til Liam's finished."

"You don't have to tell me twice." Molly gathered up her purse. "Don't work too late, baby."

"I'm nearly done for the night."

"See you later then." She paused, grinned. "Or not. Whatever. Bye."

Liam shook his head and took a long swallow of his cold brew. It wasn't the beer he really wanted, but it was damned tasty. "You know, I appreciate that she's supportive of us as an us, but I would really love if she'd stop making suggestive remarks. It's totally weird."

When Riley didn't comment, his internal alarm started to sound. She was well and truly upset about something, and it wasn't the chaos in her pharmacy.

Liam ran a hand down her arm, gave a little tug, but she didn't turn into him and didn't soften. Not good signs.

"What's wrong, Riley Marie?"

"I ran into Babette Wofford at The Grind."

She paused, and he fought not to tense. It could be nothing.

"Is there anything you want to tell me?" Her blue eyes were glacial as they fixed on him.

Shit. He'd hoped she'd never find out. Or that he'd be better prepared when it came to asking forgiveness when he knew she'd expected him to ask for permission. Considering the temperature in her general vicinity had plummeted a good ten degrees, that wasn't happening.

"Your mom didn't have enough for the deposit and both the first and last months' rent on the apartment, so I helped out."

"I see." Her tone that indicated she was seeing a helluva lot more than he did. "Was it your idea or hers?"

"Mine. The apartment was perfect. She wanted out. You *needed* her out for your own sanity. She needed a hand to do it, so I gave it. It's not a big deal, Riley." He shrugged, feeling the pinch of strained muscles as he did so.

"I would have thought that a man who's spent the last twelve years as a Marine would be more capable of following orders."

Was she fucking kidding? "Oh, give me a break."

"A break? A break. I'd like to break your head." Riley unfolded her arms and jabbed a finger into his chest, her voice rising. "I explicitly told you not to get involved in the situation with my mother. Verbatim, point blank. In words you could not *possibly* misunderstand. And you did it anyway."

"Yeah, I crossed that line. Deliberately." Might as well own it.

"Worse, you did it behind my back. She's *my* responsibility. Not yours."

Exasperated and trying desperately to cling to reason, Liam gripped her shoulders, gave them a gentle squeeze. "She doesn't have to be. You don't have to deal with all this alone anymore."

Riley jerked away. "I may have invited you into my bed, but that doesn't give you the right to run my life. You don't get to make decisions for me or my family."

Liam absorbed the slap of that. *Me. My*

family. Because, for her, those had nothing to do with him. Almost his whole life, he'd considered her a part of his family. His to protect. To take care of. It'd been nothing to extend that mantle to cover her mother, to try to ease the burden he saw Riley struggling under.

Pain jabbed at his temple, chiseling away at his hold on a rising anger. "I'm not trying to run your life, I'm trying to *help* you."

"I was just fine on my own before you walked back into my life. I'm not some needy princess with a rescue complex, and I'm not some gold digger in search of a sugar daddy."

There was fury in her eyes, but the faint tremble of her chin told him something else was going on here. That gave him a little more control. "That's not who you are. It's not who your mom is either. Where is this coming from?"

A muscle jerked in her jaw, but she continued as if he hadn't spoken. "I don't need your help. Not with her. Not now, not ever. If that's not a line you can live with, then we're wasting our time here."

Mitch's words from the night before circled back through his brain. *Are you sure she wants the same thing out of a relationship as you?*

This was no line in the sand that could or would erode over time. She was building a goddamned wall and expecting him to stay outside it. That wasn't who he was, wasn't how he operated. And it wasn't what he expected from a relationship.

"This line of yours is more important to you than us?"

Her cheeks were drawn, but her eyes still sparked with temper. "I won't bend on this."

That was where he ranked in her priorities. After some idiotic need to be a goddamned martyr. Or something. His head was throbbing too fucking much to analyze it right now.

"You know what? Fine. I'm done. I'm tired from busting my ass to give you that help you apparently don't want. I'm headed home. I'll be back in the morning with a crew to lay the floors. Sorry to force more help on you, but you don't get a say in that since it's my mother's building. If you decide you're ready to be reasonable, you just let me know."

Because he needed to throw something, he picked up the pry bar he'd been using and hurled it with a satisfying clatter into the toolbox. Riley said nothing. She was still standing there, arms wrapped her middle, as he stalked out.

CHAPTER 16

RILEY FLINCHED AT THE slamming of the door. She hadn't thought she could feel sicker than when Amber had taken her pound of flesh. She'd absolutely been wrong.

He'd walked away.

Not until she watched Liam's retreating back did she realize she hadn't expected he would.

Her eyes flew open, her heart jolting as the door opened again. But it wasn't Liam.

Autumn stepped in. "So I just saw Liam, and

he looked…oh shit." She shut the door and immediately wrapped Riley in a hug. "What happened?"

Her throat felt tight. "We just had our first fight. Or maybe our last. I don't know."

Autumn looked around. "Okay, there's nowhere to sit in here. Let's go for a walk, okay?"

All the fight had bled out of her, so Riley followed without comment, shutting and locking the door behind them. Autumn linked her arm through Riley's, part comfort, part prevention, as if maybe she thought Riley would bolt. They walked up toward Market Street, past Sweet Magnolia's Bakery—sadly closed at this hour. She could really go for one of Carolanne's devil's food cupcakes with chocolate ganache—her ban on sugar be damned.

Autumn gave her until they hit the town green. "Okay, what did he do?"

Riley tipped her head over to the other woman's shoulder in a walking sort of hug. "You're a good friend."

"Why's that?"

"You automatically assume it's his fault."

"Well, even if it's your fault, somehow it's still his fault. So what did he do?"

Riley let the whole thing spill out, from the ultimatum she'd given him about her mother weeks before, to her encounter with Mrs. Wofford.

As she recounted the showdown with Amber Hopper Butts, Autumn scowled. "Leave it to her to turn something kind into something filthy."

"I gather you've had your own run-in with Amber?"

"Not Amber. Her sister. Same kind of thing. I'm white trash from the wrong side of the tracks. And of course, the only reason I have Judd's undying devotion is because I spread my legs for him on a regular basis. Everyone knows I'm his little piece on the side."

Riley felt a fresh bout of rage on her friend's behalf. "That bitch! Nobody thinks that."

"I don't give two shits what anyone thinks about me and Judd," Autumn said mildly.

"Seriously?"

"Seriously. You shouldn't let her phase you. Nobody believes what she said about you and Liam."

"Obviously somebody does."

"Okay, nobody with two brain cells and an opinion that matters worth a damn believes it. Truthfully, I feel sorry for her."

That was the absolute last thing Riley expected. "For *her?* Why?"

"Must be sad to live your life thinking everything is about checks and balances. Not that I'm surprised. That's how her entire family has always worked. None of them could ever fathom why anybody would do anything for someone else without expecting something in return." She tugged Riley to sit down on the edge of the fountain. "Any*way*, you were upset and all your buttons were pushed, so I presume you went to confront Liam?"

Riley finished the story. "He just left. And he

had a right to." Now that her fury had begun to wane, she could see that. He deserved her gratitude, not her defensive bitchiness. "I'm not sure I could've handled it any worse. I sure as hell could've handled it better. As you said, he did a kind thing. A necessary thing, to his mind. I can see that. But however well-intentioned his motives were, he still blatantly disregarded my wishes. Jesus, he could've at least *asked*."

"What would you have done if he had?"

Riley sighed. "I'd have fought him tooth and nail."

"Which he undoubtedly knew. So he pulled his whole alpha male routine and did what he thought was best, which was completely counter to what you wanted, and he didn't apologize for it. Would you have still been pissed if you hadn't run into the thunder cunt?"

That surprised a laugh out of her. "The *what?*"

Autumn shrugged. "Bitch isn't a strong enough word. So would you?"

"I probably would've been more rational

about the whole thing, but yeah, I'd still be angry. He completely doesn't understand my position on this. There's no way he'd see that my stance is meant to protect his reputation as much as mine. God, the last thing I want is to hear anyone smear his good name."

"Did you tell him that?"

"Well…no."

"Why the hell not?"

Riley fisted a hand around the medallion and dropped her gaze. "Because I was embarrassed…and ashamed. And just enough of me wondered if someone who mattered believed any of the horrible things Amber said." And she hated it. Hated that she was still as much a victim to those feelings now as she had been years ago.

"Sweetie, don't you think he'd understand?"

He'd been trying. She knew he had a righteous temper when roused, and instead of fully losing it, he'd tried to be rational and get at what was really going on. He'd known this wasn't just about him paying for her mom's apartment. Beneath the pissed off and the hurt, Liam had still seen that there was something else. Because he knew her. And she'd shut him out.

Damn it.

"I need to apologize."

"Good girl." Autumn gave her a squeeze. "You're too good together to let something like this split you up."

God, she hoped Liam still thought so. "He was really angry." She looked over her shoulder at the fountain's lazy trickle. "Maybe I should wish for some back up."

"Can't hurt."

"Got any change? My purse is back at the pharmacy."

Autumn dug out a nickel. "I feel it's worth mentioning that there is no correlation with the actual monetary value and the importance of the wish."

"Thanks."

Riley rubbed her thumb over the face and considered, for just a moment, making a wish to save her business. She'd spent the last year pouring her heart and soul into the place, and it wasn't out of the woods yet. There were things still to be done to get it back on track, but they were things that would be done either way once the repairs were complete. It was time she spent some heart on something else.

I wish for a second chance with Liam. Please let him leave that door open.

She kissed the coin and tossed it. It seemed to hit with far more gravity than a mere nickel merited, causing a resounding sort of *thunk* before sinking to the bottom, where it glinted faintly in the dying light.

"I guess we'll see."

BACK AT THE PHARMACY, Autumn gave her one last hug. "Now, no matter what happens, if you need to come knock on my door at any hour, you can. I'm available to listen to details of juicy make up sex, or to support a crying jag and bitch fest if he's an idiot. There's an emergency pint of Ben and Jerry's in the freezer with your name on it, either way."

"Thanks."

"He's not going to be an idiot."

No, that role is pretty clearly being played by me.

"I'll see you later, okay?"

After waving Autumn off, Riley went to retrieve her purse.

Christ, she was tired. She'd been running on fumes for weeks, juggling all the responsibilities for work, spending every spare minute with Liam, and then trying to get this presentation put together for Peyton Consolidated. It was no wonder she was ultra susceptible to Amber's particular brand of nasty.

Liam was justifiably angry. She'd give him a little time to cool off, take some time herself to get past the hurt and irritation, then they'd straighten this out. She'd apologize for jumping his case and explain. But later. After she'd had time to think, to find the right words. Rushing in without a plan certainly hadn't gotten her anywhere, and she was hardly in the right frame of mind to clearly explain herself. Besides, shambles that it was, she wanted some quiet time alone in her pharmacy.

There was comfort in the routine of checking the machine, recording the call-in prescriptions, then going about the regimented process of measuring, counting out, compounding. She made notes about inventory, called a client or two, and retreated to the office to start working up an order for Monday. They were down to their last box of Epipens and one of the two inside was damaged. If anything came up with that before the next delivery, she'd have to send her customers over to Walgreens. There'd been too much of that these last few weeks. A lot of balls had been dropped in the wake of the flood.

As she continued to clear off the paperwork that had accumulated, Riley sent up a small prayer of thanks that the Board of Pharmacy hadn't been by for an inspection. She set the records to rights on that front, and went ahead and started on the quarterly estimates for her accountant. Might as well get ahead on something since she was here and had the time. One hour bled into two. By the time she reached the bottom of the pile, it was nearing ten and her back was making its protests known. Time to wrap this up and head home.

She opened the drawer to put her work away. An envelope slipped out, as she slipped the ledgers inside. Old mail. How long had that been in there? Slipping a finger beneath the flap, she opened the envelope and pulled out the contents. And felt the bottom drop out of her stomach.

Oh shit. Shit. Shit. Shit.

Her insurance had lapsed. The renewal should've been sent in two weeks ago. How the hell could she have let this happen? The check covering her stock losses after the flood should've been enough to jog her damned memory. Jesus Christ, this had potential disaster written all over it. And, *of course,* customer service wouldn't be open again until Monday morning.

"It'll be fine," she told herself. The pharmacy was closed until noon on Monday. She'd call first thing and get it taken care of. There was no reason to worry.

At the faint sound of the bell, she startled and reflexively checked the time. After ten now. She grabbed the last Epipen from the desk before she settled.

Liam.

Of course, he'd come back to check on her. Nice to know he wasn't the type to let a good mad fester.

Deep breaths. He'd come to her. Even if it was to finish out their fight, he'd come. That meant he wasn't through with her.

She slipped the Epipen into her coat pocket. "I'm really glad you came—" Riley broke off as she swung out of the office to see two men in masks crossing the room.

They stopped, as shocked to see her as she was to see them.

One beat passed, then two, as Riley tried to fight through stunned disbelief. This was Wishful. Stuff like this wasn't supposed to happen here. She started forward—to do what, she had no idea—but one of them pulled a gun.

"Hands where I can see them!"

His shout kickstarted the heart that had stopped and she jolted. Adrenaline dumped into her system. *Run. Run. RUN.* But there was nowhere to run, no escape with the counter and both robbers between her and the door. Moving slowly, she laid her shaking hands on the edge of the counter.

Keep cool. She slipped her thumb beneath the edge, pressed the panic button as the gunman crossed the room.

His partner backpedaled two steps. "Man, I didn't sign up for this. Nobody was supposed to be here!"

"Shut up and come on. She'll make this quicker."

"You've done nothing yet but pick a lock.

You could walk away right now." Her voice trembled only a little.

"Oh no. We're here. We're not leaving without what we came for."

Did she know that voice? Hard to say. Hard to even hear over the thud of blood in her ears.

"Where's the safe?"

Riley couldn't drag her gaze from the gun.

When she didn't answer fast enough, the gunman took three quick strides and stuck it in her face. "Where is the safe?"

She flinched back, lifting her hands to shield her face. "In…in the office."

"Get moving." He gestured with the gun.

Riley didn't move, her eyes fixed on the weapon. Matte black. Some kind of revolver. In the back of her mind, she could hear Liam drilling her on what to do in exactly this situation. They'd spent hours practicing disarms for various weapons in various positions, but in the end he'd told her, *If somebody comes in with a gun, you give them what they want. Nothing they can steal is worth your life.*

"Woman, I said *move!*" He was behind the counter, shoving the gun into her face before she could blink.

Riley recoiled, stumbled, and crashed to the floor, her head cracking against the wall hard enough she saw white. The gunman swore, grabbing her arm in a bruising grip and hauling her to her feet. He shoved her into the office, calling for his accomplice.

"Unlock it."

She considered, just for a moment, opening the money safe, giving them the cash she had on hand. But no one robbed a pharmacy for cash. So she moved to the controlled substances safe. Her hand shook so badly, she entered the code wrong the first time.

"Hurry up!"

"Just give me a minute! You're making me nervous, and if I get this wrong again, the system will lock me out."

Forcing herself to slow her breathing, Riley started again. She hesitated, considering her options. How much time had passed since she hit the panic button? Probably not nearly as much as it felt like. Locking them out of the safe would likely get her shot. She finished the code, and the door unlatched.

"Out of the way." The gunman didn't wait for her to comply. He snaked an arm around her neck, jerking her back and pressing the gun to her head.

Riley yelped, reflexively grabbing at the arm around her throat and dropping her chin to keep him from cutting off her air. But he didn't seem inclined to choke her.

"Be still, woman!"

There was no standing completely still. She was shaking too badly. But she dropped her hands.

Think. Think, she ordered herself.

His partner was staring, and even through the mask, Riley could tell he was horrified. "Man, don't hurt her."

"Shut up and fill the bag. Everything."

As the other guy emptied the safe of all the class 2 drugs, she could see the insurance bill laying on the desk. With the insurance lapsed, anything they got away with would be forfeit. Even if it was recovered, it would go into evidence. She'd be out the cost of all of it. All her hard work would be for nothing. There'd be no recovering from that loss.

She hadn't worked her ass off only to watch two idiot drug seekers piss it all away.

Anger made her a little bit steadier. Wiping sweating palms on her lab coat, she felt the bump in her pocket. The Epipen. Could she reach it? And what would he do if she did?

Moving slowly, she slipped a hand into the pocket, curling her hand around the injector. Slowly, she fumbled to remove the safety release. Her captor's grip was firm, but didn't obstruct her airway, and the gun seemed to be more about making a point than about really hurting her. Surely, if he was going to kill her, he'd have done it once the safe was open?

The other guy was more than half through dumping the contents into a duffel bag. "I don't even recognize half these drug names."

"So what? If it's in the safe, it's valuable."

The cap popped off. She didn't dare try anything while the gun was pressed to her head. Her assailant's body was long and wiry and acrid with sweat. He was nervous, too. She felt it in his posture. A shot of epinephrine to a system already flooded with adrenaline might just give him a heart attack. It might kill him. Riley waffled at that. She didn't want to kill anyone.

In the back of her mind, she could hear Liam. *If you get into a situation where your safety is threatened, remember, it's you or them. No holding back. No doubts.*

Steadied by the thought of him, Riley fisted her hand around the pitiful weapon. If she made it through this, she owed him so much more than an apology.

"What about this stuff in vials?"

"I said everything."

"We're running out of room."

"We do not have time for you to be reading

labels. Hurry the fuck up so we can get out of here."

He waved the gun for emphasis, and Riley moved, hooking one arm around his gun arm and yanking, even as she stabbed down and back with the Epipen. Her assailant roared. Riley stepped back, struck with her elbow, but she caught his ribs rather than his gut. Pain burst along her arm as they fought for control of the gun. He struck her hard across the cheek with his free hand. She felt herself start to fall, her hands still around the wrist of his gun hand, griping like a vise. Her momentum tipped them both. In horror, unable to make her fingers release, she watched his aim come down, down toward the floor, as if in slow motion. His hand clenched, his finger squeezed the trigger.

And the gun fired.

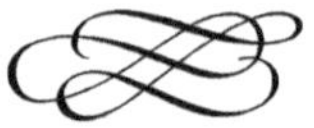

CHAPTER 17

"OKAY, YOU'VE HAD A good three hours to sulk. Tell me what's wrong."

Liam scowled at his mother. "I'm not sulking."

"Brooding then." She sat down beside him on the porch swing. "Did you and Riley have a fight? I could tell something was off with her when I left."

"The only thing wrong is that she's the most stubborn woman on the goddamned planet."

Molly nodded. "A fight then. It was bound to

happen sometime. You're both strong-willed people."

"Remind me why I thought that was an attractive trait in a woman?"

She laughed. "Because a pushover would be boring. What did you fight about?"

"She found out I helped her mom out with the up-front costs to lease the apartment and got pissed."

"Found out? As in, you didn't tell her you were going to do this?" Her tone said everything he needed to know about what she thought about that plan.

Liam hunched his shoulders. "No. She'd have said no, her mom would still be under her roof, and her stress level would be somewhere around the stratosphere. If she was gonna be mad either way, it seemed like they'd both be happier in their own places. Riley's been so much less stressed the last couple of weeks. At least until Mrs. Wofford spilled the beans. Now she's furious. I don't get it. What the hell is wrong with me taking care of her?"

"Oh, my sweet boy. Nothing is wrong with the desire. But Riley has taken care of herself and her mom for a long, long time."

"Shouldn't she be grateful for some help with that?"

"It's not that simple." Molly toed the swing into motion. "You already know Riley took a lot of flack from others about her mother's bad decisions and the help they needed because of it. That night they came for dinner, Riley didn't repeat any of the kinds of rumors that spread about Sharilyn out of respect for her mother, but she was on the receiving end of plenty."

Liam sighed. "Gold digger looking for a sugar daddy?"

"Among others. You've met her mother, so you know that's not really how she is, but people rarely care about the truth. Riley has always hated that Sharilyn looked to anyone else to fix things, hated that she didn't or couldn't deal with it herself. Sharilyn always expected to find that stability elsewhere. My point is, Riley's not going to naturally do that. She's been the anchor in that family since she was a child. She doesn't know *how* to let anyone take care of her because no one ever really has. Your father and I have done our best, but you know we've been subtle about it. What you did wasn't subtle."

"Subtlety is overrated."

"No. Subtlety allowed your dad and I to give Riley help, while actually staying in a position to keep providing it. Your way backfired. This isn't something you're going to be able to blast through with a brick of C4."

"There's no room for these kinds of walls in a relationship."

"Long term, no." Molly paused. "Is that what you want? Long term?"

He hadn't come home looking for long term. A part of him never thought he'd get past the hypothetical of a lifetime commitment to a woman. But Riley had worked her way under his skin—her strength, her determination, and that icing of sweetness that came out when she felt safe and happy. He wanted to give that to her, wanted to make a life where safe and happy were the norm instead of fleeting bursts. He wanted to give her the life she deserved, one where she didn't have to fight and claw and struggle. And, damn it, he wanted her to let him.

"She's it for me, Mom."

His mother smiled. "I know."

Liam looked at her, then shook his head. "Of course, you did."

"I'm just glad you've figured it out for yourself." She leaned over, kissed his cheek. "Give her time, baby. And try to see it from her perspective."

"Am I wrong?"

"Well, to keep to your analogy, you see these walls of hers as something to breach. That's what you've spent the last twelve years doing, so I understand the impulse, but that's not how things work with emotional walls. They get built for a reason, to protect somebody. You don't just come in and rip away someone's shield because you think it's time for them to give it up. You're upset because you feel like that wall is standing between the two of you, but you have to remember, she didn't build it to keep you out. She built it to keep *everyone* out. For you, it shouldn't be about breaking through the wall but about scaling it to get behind it with her, making her feel safe enough to dismantle it when she's ready. That's how long-term relationships work."

He loosed a long sigh. "And I went all bull in a china shop about it."

"Now you know better. I'm sure you'll get past it."

Liam sure as hell hoped so.

Inside, the phone rang.

"Awfully late for calls." Molly rose and went to answer it.

He checked his watch. Just a little after ten. Not *so* late. It might be Wynne coming in after an evening event. Or Norah calling over some detail or other to do with coalition business. But he went inside anyway.

At the kitchen counter, his mother's face went ashen.

Liam crossed to her in two strides, slipping an arm around her. "Mom?" The bottom dropped out of his stomach as he waited interminable seconds to hear whether it was news about Jack or Cruz.

A voice on the other end continued to speak as she tipped the phone away. "The panic button."

He felt his world stop. Not his brothers. "Riley."

Liam tore out of the kitchen, taking the stairs three at a time, sprinting to his room to grab his keys and the Ruger in his nightstand. In less than a minute, he was squealing out of the driveway, demanding every ounce of speed from the 351 Cleveland engine. Being after ten, nobody was on the road, and he was grateful as he drifted around corners and blew through stop signs.

Three minutes.

Please. The word repeated in his head. A litany. A prayer.

He'd trained Riley for this. She'd said he was paranoid, pushing her through scenarios, making her practice how to handle them. But she'd humored him, done the work. Learned. She wouldn't do anything foolish. She'd be okay. She had to be. But a part of him wondered how well his teaching would translate into the moment. A real, live threat was a whole lot different from practice in a gym.

He couldn't think about what was happening. Didn't dare imagine it. He needed a cool head to do whatever needed doing, so he shifted into combat mode as he flew into downtown Wishful. The clock ticked over to five minutes as he hit Pitts Street and saw the lights of the pharmacy glowing in the distance.

Please.

The pharmacy door opened. He screeched to a halt, bumping one wheel up on the sidewalk, as he caught sight of Riley stumbling out. His vision constricted to one pinpoint view of her. Nothing in his training, nothing in his experience had prepared him for the sight of the woman he loved, covered in blood.

Liam all but fell from the car, scrambling to catch her as she hit her knees on the sidewalk. He hit his own, holding her up, fighting the urge to crush her to him. "Riley, baby, where are you hit? How bad is it?" Bad. It had to be. God, her clothes were soaked, her hands covered.

Those hands fell to his chest. Her eyes were glassy with shock. "You came."

"Yeah." He swallowed, chanced touching her face. A bruise already bloomed on one cheek, but he couldn't see any wounds at her throat. "Where are you hurt? We need to stop the bleeding."

In the distance, sirens screamed.

"Not mine."

"What?"

"Not my blood. I'm okay. Maybe concussed."

Liam did crush her to him then. "Oh God,

oh God, I thought I'd lost you. You shaved at least ten years off my life."

Riley wrapped her arms around him as the police arrived, spilling out of their cars. "You came." She was shaking. Or maybe he was. Liam didn't know.

"Christ Riley, how bad are you hurt?" Judd was already radioing for an ambulance before she could answer.

Riley eased away a bit, making a visible effort to pull herself back together. "Not bad. One of the robbers got shot. Bullet nicked the femoral artery. I've got a tourniquet on him, but he lost a lot of blood."

"How many were there?" Judd asked.

"Two. After his partner got shot, he took the bag of drugs and ran. I don't know which way. Um, white male. His shoulder came to the top of my neck, so, maybe 5'10" or so. Dark clothes. Ski mask."

Judd radioed dispatch.

Two assailants. At least one gun. A dozen scenarios unfolded in Liam's mind, none of them good. And yet Riley wasn't the one who got shot. "He shot his partner, not you?"

"My fault. I stabbed him with an Epipen in the process of trying to disarm him."

"You—" He felt another five years shaved off his life as he imagined how that went down.

"I got the gun. Just like you taught me. Well, almost. I went down in the process and the other guy got away."

"I'll be proud of you when my heart starts beating again."

"Oh, speaking of—Judd, the other guy won't make it far. You should be looking for somebody sweating profusely, having massive heart palpitations. If he hasn't had a straight up heart attack by now. He might show up at the ER, if he can get there."

The police sprang into action around them.

Riley straightened. "You should probably let me go. I'm disgusting."

Liam cupped her uninjured cheek. "Not a chance. I'm hanging on, and I'm taking care of you. And you can hate it as much as you want, but you're going to have to learn to get over it." Probably an ultimatum wasn't the best tactic with a traumatized woman, but his own heart hadn't slowed to anything resembling normal yet.

She let out a noise somewhere between a laugh and a sob. "Liam, I—"

"I need to do this, okay?"

Her lip wobbled but she held the tears back and nodded. "I'm sorry for the things I said."

Liam shook his head. "None of it matters. You're okay. That's all I care about. Everything else can wait."

As his mother's car, the ambulance, and more police cars arrived, he thought it might have to wait quite a while.

THE DOOR SLAMMED and Riley flinched, hearing again the shot that had so very nearly hit her. The shot that could've ended everything.

Liam pulled her closer, pressing a kiss to her

brow. He'd stayed by her side, a rock, through the whole thing.

"We'll need you to stay on-site, while we finish collecting evidence." The agent from the Mississippi Bureau of Narcotics offered her an apologetic smile. "And I'm sure we'll have more questions."

Of course you will.

"Fine." She might have to bust out the No Doze to make it, but she'd do what had to be done and fall apart later. She was good at that. But she wished, oh how she wished, she could do more than wash the blood from her hands. Her clothes were stiff with it and the faint smell of copper coated the back of her throat, making her gag. She just wanted to go home.

"Have you cleared the apartment upstairs?" Liam asked.

"It was still locked, and a sweep didn't turn anything up," Judd said. "So yeah, it's clear."

"Then you can be done with her for long enough to shower." Liam's tone brooked no argument.

The agent nodded.

Molly appeared from somewhere, a bag in her hand. "Towels, toiletries. Change of clothes for you both."

Riley stared at her. "When did you…?"

"Liam sent me."

A wet fist of tears squeezed in her chest.

Molly squeezed her arm. "Go on. Get cleaned up, sweetheart."

Liam took the bag and led her upstairs. "There's nowhere for you to lay down, but at least you can get clean."

Riley couldn't speak around the fist, so she just nodded and followed him into the bathroom. He emptied the bag, neatly laying out towels and clothes on the counter, putting soap, shampoo, and conditioner on the edge of the tub. Quick, efficient, he turned on the water, adjusted the temperature.

"Arms up." With minimal help from her, he stripped off her bloody clothes with equal efficiency. "In you go." He handed her into the tub, waiting until he was satisfied she had her legs before letting go of her hand. "I'll be right outside."

"Thanks."

He pulled the curtain to. She heard the quiet close of the door. He wouldn't go far. There was extraordinary comfort in that. In knowing that, when it mattered, he stuck, whether she was being difficult or not.

She stepped beneath the spray, wanting at once to shrink back and lose herself in the steady fall of water. Her body shook, cold down to the bone. Even knowing it was shock, she dialed the temperature almost to scalding. Water sluiced down her body, pooling pink at her feet before circling down the drain. That had so very nearly been her blood. And for what? The thief had gotten away. He'd be caught—the epinephrine should've messed him up enough. But the drugs were gone. With everything else—her business wouldn't be far behind. And then what?

She'd spent her life scrimping, saving, and clawing her way out of the debt incurred after her father's death. The thought of having to start over, of having to do that again, without a job, without prospects, had the fist in her chest clamping down to the point of pain, squeezing her heart, closing her throat. What pharmacy would hire a pharmacist who ran her own pharmacy into the ground? What was she going to do?

A sob wrenched free of her constricted throat. Bracing her hands against the wall, she fought to hold back the panic bubbling up in her chest as the brutally hot water beat down on her. Instead, another wounded animal sound spilled out.

The curtain was ripped back.

Before she could get a scream out, Liam was stepping into the shower, clothes and all, pulling her into his arms, tucking her against chest. "I've got you."

He was strong, capable, and in control. Everything she hadn't been since her world started spinning off its axis. He was her port in the storm, and she was tired, so goddamned tired, of rejecting that gift on the grounds of some stupid personal principle. She needed him. As the shower continued to pound on her back and steam rose around them, Riley pressed her face into his throat and let herself fall to pieces.

The water had gone to lukewarm by the time she quieted. Without letting her go, Liam reached past her to grab the soap. Throat raw, feeling weak as a newborn kitten, she stood as he gently scrubbed away the last signs of violence. It was an intimacy so different from being lovers. In bed, she felt they were on even ground—giving, taking. But this, this, for her, was a deeper trust.

Liam helped her out of the shower, wrapping her in one of the big fluffy towels. She drew the line at letting him dress her again, and took over the drying herself.

He stripped out of his own wet clothes, reaching for the other towel.

She squeezed the towel tight beneath her chin. "I'm sorry."

Irritation flashed in his eyes. "You don't have to apologize."

"No, I do. I over-reacted."

"We don't have to talk about this now."

"I need to get this out. I need to, at least, explain *why* this is important to me."

"Okay. But I have an apology of my own. I'm sorry I went behind your back on the apartment for your mom. She and I made arrangements for her to pay me back, and to my mind that made it okay. It wasn't meant to subvert you, and it wasn't her manipulating me. I saw a chance to do something that would make life easier on you. Getting your own space back, seeing her out on her own lessened some of your stress. I couldn't *not* do that when it was within my means. But I should've told you."

The dry clothes she slipped on were some of his. "I understand why you didn't. You knew I'd fight you about it."

"Yeah."

"I hurt you today, and I never wanted that.

You've given me so much, and I've been so ungrateful."

"I'm not keeping a balance sheet, Riley."

"No, you wouldn't. That's not part of who you are." Autumn had seen that before she had.

She sat on the closed lid of the toilet and tried to find the words. "I don't know how to accept help with her. For so long, it's just been us, Mom and me. And our roles got reversed so long ago, I don't even remember what it was like to be the child instead of the one in control. It's like...when you carry an exceptionally heavy load, and it's something really important that you can't drop. And it's more than you can reasonably bear for a long period of time, but you don't have a choice, so you just dig in and hang on."

She curled her hands into tight fists in her lap, stared at them. "After a while, the muscles in your hands begin to cramp, until it's nothing but the cramp keeping you from dropping things. And then somebody comes along to help lift the burden, except your hands have been cramped so damned long around that rope, you can't actually let go and it *hurts* as much to release as to hang on. And on top of that…you don't trust that whoever this person is will really hold up their end—because nobody else has, And why would they? It's not their job. What if they drop it? And worse, what if you let go and then you can't pick it up again?"

Riley raised her gaze to Liam's, searching for understanding. "That's what this is like for me. Holding the line, holding that load, keeping things together and trying not to drown—that's been my life for as long as I can remember. And I hate it as much as I'm proud that I've managed it. I resent the hell out of the fact that I had to do it, but I don't know how to stop, either. Because, for me, letting go, letting you or anyone else take some of that off me, is admitting I can't do it all. And that makes me weak."

"There's nothing weak about you."

"No, you never thought so. I couldn't ever understand that."

He knelt in front of her, taking her fists in his big, strong hands. "I've always seen your strength. That quiet endurance is something I recognize and respect the hell out of." With unhurried motions, he uncurled her clamped fingers, stroking the tension out before pressing a kiss to each palm. "But you aren't alone anymore, and you don't have to hold that line by yourself. I won't let you drop it. And I won't let you drown."

God, what did she do to deserve this man?

"I know. Deep down, I really do know that. I don't know how long it will take me to be easy with that." She took a breath, took the leap. "The fact is, loving you is the easy part. I've been in love with you most of my life. But I need you, and I don't know how to deal with that. I've never known how to deal with that."

Liam circled his thumbs on her palms. "Needing somebody isn't something you're supposed to have to deal with." He gave a half laugh. "It's not like having a root canal. Especially when the one you need needs you back."

He needed her? The idea of that was as ludicrous as it was appealing.

"I have a hard time imagining the big badass Marine needing anyone."

"Clearly we need to work on your imagination. I'm in love with you, Riley. Down-to-the-bone crazy about you. Maybe not for as long as you, but I'm there. We've got time to figure out the rest. I'd just ask one thing of you."

Riley swallowed against the burn in her throat. "What's that?"

"Don't shut me out. I want to be there for you. All the way, not just in whatever areas you feel comfortable."

"You're the only one who's ever gotten this far. I can't promise I won't fight about it. But swear I'll work on it."

"That's good enough for now."

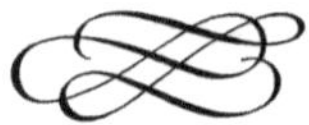

AT THE SOUND OF the shot, Liam rocketed awake, the Ruger in his hand before his eyes had even fully opened. But no one stood in his room. Beside him, Riley still slept, whole and unharmed, other than the bruise that shadowed her cheek in the pale dawn light.

Shouldn't have watched the surveillance video.

The only reason Judd had showed him at all was because Riley had kicked ass. But Liam's brain had spent the night playing the footage on repeat, with every possible way the situation could've gone wrong. Easing back, he replaced the pistol on the nightstand and scrubbed a hand over his face, as if that would erase the images still bright in his mind.

Thunder rolled, no doubt the sound that woke him. Rain began to ping against the window and lash against the roof in gusts. He loved a good thunderstorm. He wished it were a normal day after a normal night, when he could sweet talk Riley into playing hooky and staying in bed, cocooned from the world.

But it wasn't a normal day, and it sure as hell hadn't been a normal night.

A full twenty-one hours had passed before they'd released her to come home. Despite the fact that the pharmacy was closed, pretty much all of Wishful had come by—a combination of concerned customers and general Lookie Lous, not to mention all the friends and family. Sharilyn had been near hysterical. Molly had intercepted her, calling Matthew McSweeney to take her home, once she'd been assured Riley was okay. Mitch and Reuben had helped maintain the perimeter, and Autumn had made sure they'd been fed and that someone had checked on the cat. Wynne was stuck in New Orleans for work, but she'd called almost once an hour to check in. Everybody had been waiting for Riley to drop.

But she'd held up through all the questioning, the waiting, the inventory. As soon as the police were through, Liam had brought her to his mother's house, wanting them both under one roof so he could keep an eye on them until the second thief was caught. Molly had given Riley something to help her sleep. She'd been so exhausted, she'd already been out by the time Liam got her upstairs and tucked into his bed.

With the gray from the rain, it was later than he'd realized. Careful not to disturb her, he pressed a kiss to Riley's brow and slipped from bed. She needed the sleep. He'd just go down, start coffee, text Judd to see if there was an update.

As soon as he hit the hall, he realized someone had already started coffee. The rich scent of French roast perfumed the air and drew him to the kitchen.

Molly looked up from where she whipped something at the counter. "How is she?"

He thought of Riley falling apart in the shower. A purge long overdue. "Still tender yet. The robbery was pretty much the icing on the shit cake she's been eating all summer."

His mom gave him a long look. "How are you?"

Liam considered playing it off and opted for the truth instead. "I'd rather go up against insurgents again than face another phone call like that."

She rubbed a hand down his arm. "There's not much harder on a man of action than not getting the chance to act."

"It was all over by the time I got there, and I couldn't do a goddamned thing."

"You did plenty. You taught her how to handle herself. The situation might've been a helluva lot worse than some stolen inventory if you hadn't."

"You're up next." He poured himself coffee. "And neither one of you is to be up there alone again. Ever." He'd have a hard enough time letting them go anywhere alone for a while. "I want to do a full evaluation of the security system. When will we be allowed back in to work on the place?"

"Not sure yet." She poured batter over thick sliced sourdough bread. "The Bureau of Narcotics is done with us for now. Riley and I got through the full inventory of controlled substances before we left. Hopefully, we'll be back in later today or tomorrow."

"I'll get on the phone later and start rounding up additional crew as soon as we know. This whole mess is throwing the renovation schedule off, and Riley needs things to get back to normal as soon as possible."

"Issuing orders already, Boy Scout?" Riley's voice was rough with sleep. She shuffled into the kitchen, eyes at half mast, one of his button-down shirts hanging almost to her knees, a pair of his sweatpants puddling around her feet.

"Hey. What are you doing up already?"

"What? Thirteen hours isn't enough sleep?" Yawning, she crossed to him, sliding an arm around his waist and reaching up to cup his face. "You had a nightmare."

All freaking night. "I didn't mean to wake you."

"You didn't. I'd been working on convincing myself to move for about an hour, but I kept losing the battle. Ambien is a great will-sucker. You'd already gotten up by the time I got my eyes to open. I wanted to check on you."

After everything she'd been through, she was checking on him? Who was caretaking who here? "That's my line. I'm fine."

"Fine is sleeping with a pistol under your pillow?"

No reason to mention the rest of the arsenal under the bed. "Until the one who escaped is caught, yes."

"It wasn't personal, Liam. He wasn't after me."

His eyes tracked over to the bruise on her

cheek and he had to fight back the impotent rage that he hadn't been there to stop it. "He hurt you."

Her eyes narrowed. "And I gave as good as I got, exactly like you taught me."

"Sorry. It's going to take me a year or ten to forget the sight of a gun pressed to your head."

"You're not going to let me out of your sight without an armed escort, are you?"

"Not for a while, no." Liam waited for her to argue.

Instead, she heaved a sigh, brushed her lips over his. "Judd should never have showed you that surveillance footage."

The doorbell rang.

"I'll get it." Molly was out of the kitchen in a flash.

"You know," Riley walked her fingers down the center of his chest, "if you're going to be on guard duty anyway, can you do it in your dress blues? Maybe pull an *Officer and a Gentleman* and whisk me off to somewhere tropical, where they serve drinks with little paper umbrellas and have people standing by to fan us with giant palm fronds? Because that would really work for me."

Liam arched a brow and tried to keep his twitching lips serious. "You've given this some thought."

"When you don't have time to actually *take* a vacation, you spend a lot of time dreaming about them. Plus, the last time I saw you in your dress blues was when I was still trying to be mad at you, so I didn't properly appreciate the view. And it's a really excellent view."

"Maybe if you're a really good girl—"

"Even if she's not, I think she's demonstrated she could kick your ass, so I'd do whatever she wants."

Liam shot Judd a Look. "Don't encourage her."

"Too soon," Judd decided.

Never would be too soon to joke about that.

"Can I get you a cup of coffee?" Molly lifted the half-full pot.

"Don't mind if I do." He hitched himself up

on one of the barstools. "I just came by to give y'all the update. Most importantly, we found the son of a bitch."

Liam felt the tension drain from his shoulders. "Where?"

"Got picked up at the hospital in Lawley. He'd been admitted for a heart attack, just like Riley said. Thanks, Molly." He took the coffee, blew on it. "Also, the assailant who was shot made it out of surgery. He's gonna be fine thanks to Riley's quick action."

To keep his hands busy, Liam poured coffee for Riley, began to doctor it. "He better be thanking God she's got a humanitarian streak."

"I wasn't going to let him die. He didn't want to involve me from the get-go and kept insisting that they not hurt me."

"If that really mattered to him, he would've intervened to stop the robbery from going down as soon as they realized you were there."

"He wasn't the one with the gun and was clearly not the brains of the operation. Thanks,

Boy Scout." Riley sipped at the coffee, made a low hum of appreciation.

"That might mitigate his sentence some, but it'll be up to the judge. Both are going to make full recoveries in time for prosecution."

"What about the drugs?" Molly asked.

"Shooter stashed them before he went to the hospital. There's a team of deputies searching now, but it shouldn't take long to unearth them."

"Good. That's good." Liam rubbed the back of his neck. "Does that mean y'all are done with the pharmacy?"

"We are. Gotta check with the Bureau of Narcotics, but I don't expect they'll be far behind. I'll confirm and let you know. Thanks for the coffee."

"I'm about to make French toast. You're welcome to join."

Judd rinsed his mug out and set it in the sink. "Thanks, but I'm about to head home and crash. I'm officially off-shift and I have a date with my pillow for at least the next eight straight."

"Thanks for coming by to give us the update, man." Liam bumped fists with Judd, then pulled him in for a thumping hug.

He shot Liam a knowing look. "Figured you'd rest easier knowing the threat is contained."

"He will." Riley gave her own hug. "So will I. Thanks, Judd."

After he'd left, Molly cranked up the heat under the griddle. "Well, I'd say this is excellent news. Things are moving apace. And crime scene or not, we've got the controlled substances inventory, and we can go ahead and get in touch with the insurance company, get the ball rolling there."

Riley froze with the mug halfway to her lips, all the blood draining out of her cheeks.

Liam automatically braced a hand at her back, ready to catch her. "What's wrong?"

"I forgot," she whispered. "How the hell did I forget?"

He eased the coffee out of her hands and set it on the counter, turning her to face him. "Forget what?"

"The insurance." She pressed her face into his throat and whimpered.

A flood, a theft, and a near hostage situation, and it was the insurance that was sending her over the edge? Liam stroked her back and met his mother's baffled gaze over the counter.

"I know it's a pain in the ass after the flood already, but it will be fine," Molly said.

"No, it won't." Liam felt Riley brace herself, and when she lifted her head, tears glimmered. "There is no insurance."

THE ADMISSION WAS like lancing an infection. A quick, sharp pain, and then the words spilled out in a flood, with barely a pause for breath. "I screwed up and missed the renewal payment, and it's lapsed. I found the bill right before the robbery. I guess it got lost in all the shuffle and chaos from the flood and my mom coming back and...I know it's no excuse. It's a titanic screw up, especially when people are depending on me for their livelihood. Jessie and Ruby have been all worried since Walgreens opened, and I've been telling them everything will be fine, but it's not fine. I barely made payroll last month. And I kept thinking things would turn around, that I'd find a way to fix it, but it just got worse and worse, and then the flood, and then I couldn't tell you because you trusted me not to run the business you spent over thirty years building into the ground, and now I've destroyed everything." Riley sucked in a shuddering breath, and felt the hot burn of tears spilling over. "I'm so sorry, Molly."

On the opposite side of the counter, Molly looked heart-broken and horrified. And it felt every bit as horrible as Riley had known it would to have let her down.

"That's why you went for the gun. Because you were trying to keep them from getting away with the stock."

Shoulders hunched, Riley nodded once before dropping her eyes.

"Are you fucking kidding me? You risked your life because of some damned insurance?"

Riley's head snapped up and she glared at Liam. "I risked my life to save my business. That was thirty or forty grand they walked out with—and whether the police find it or not, it's evidence. I can't recover from that with all the other debt I took on trying to stay afloat, so yes, goddamn it, I took a risk."

"A risk that could've gotten you killed!" Breathing hard, he made a visible effort to reel himself in. In softer tones, he said, "Do you have any idea what that would do to me?"

"Yes. Yes, I know exactly, because I felt the weight of that possibility every single day you were deployed. And I spent twelve years being furious that you put yourself in harm's way. So if you need to be mad about this, be mad. I absolutely understand that. But maybe you could save it for later, when my professional life isn't falling apart, because I'm pretty much at my limit."

Liam let out a long, slow exhale. "Sorry. Not dealing too well. My issue. I shouldn't be taking it out on you."

When he reached for her, Riley didn't hesitate. She snuggled into him. "I'll train harder if it'll make you feel better."

"We'll talk about that later." He brushed the hair back from her face, used his thumbs to wipe away the tears. "Other problems to fix right now. I made you a promise the other night, and I intend to keep it. How bad is it?"

"Not sure it could be much worse. Strangely, it's not even the money I'm most upset about." She turned her head to look at Molly. "It's that I disappointed you."

"Okay just...wait a minute." Molly took a few deep breaths before coming around the counter and taking Riley by the shoulders. "Honey, you haven't disappointed me. And you haven't screwed anything up. I took care of the insurance bill weeks ago."

Riley blinked. "You—what?"

"You had a lot on your plate with the flood, and Liam was doing his level best to distract you, which I fully supported, so when I found the bill, I went ahead and paid it. I couldn't find the line of credit info, so I just paid it out of pocket. Business as usual. I didn't see any reason to bother you with it. But God, I wish I had."

"There are no lines of credit," Riley murmured. Her heart thrummed a desperate tattoo against her breast. "The policy hasn't lapsed?"

"No, it hasn't. What do you mean there are no lines of credit?"

"I'm not ruined." Riley's knees went to Jello, and she had to grab hold of the barstool. "Oh, thank God. Thank *you*." She launched herself at Molly, wrapping her in a tight hug. "Thank you, thank you."

"I'm just glad you're okay." Molly framed her face with both hands. "I'd never forgive myself if something had happened to you. What do you mean there are no lines of credit, honey?"

Riley scrubbed the tears from her cheeks.

"I don't use them. After all the debt I clawed my way out of with my mom, I don't use it unless I absolutely have to. So I never opened any for the business."

Molly stared at her. "You've been running the pharmacy for *over a year* without a revolving line of credit? And actually keeping it in the black?"

"Barely. But yeah. The thing is, I've been stubborn and proud and really, really foolish. Things are bad. I've been hanging on by a thread. And things would be so much worse, if y'all hadn't been looking out for me despite myself. I've joked in the past that you have to hold a gun to my head to get me to ask for help—not something I'll be kidding about in the future, by the way—but it seems like that's true. Because this is me doing what I should've done months ago." She took a bracing breath. "I'm asking for your help. Because I'm in way over my head, going under for the third time, and I don't know what to do."

Molly wrapped an arm around her in another hug. "Whatever it is, we'll figure it out together."

Together.

She'd spent most of her life believing that together was something to avoid, that depending on someone else made her weak. And her way had almost lost her everything.

Definitely time for a change.

"That sounds amazing."

Molly made French toast, as she'd done for family breakfasts countless times before. Judd texted the all clear to let them back in the pharmacy. While his mother manned the griddle, Liam made calls to organize a work force to deal with the cleaning and last of the renovations. And Riley sat at the table, drinking her coffee, feeling more positive than she had in months. She didn't know how they were going to fix things, but she was so grateful not to be in it alone.

Molly heaped French toast onto Riley's plate. "I have something I've been wanting to talk to you about for a while now that will, I think, alleviate a lot of the strain you've been under."

Riley braced herself. If Molly was about to suggest buying the business entirely back, it wasn't like she was in a position to argue. Clearly, she hadn't been ready for the full responsibility of owning the pharmacy.

"I want to buy back part of the business. Come back as a full partner."

Partners? Not something she'd considered. But surely if Molly was interested in doing something like that, it would've come up before Riley bought her out last year.

"I hate for you to have to break your retirement because of me."

"Don't you dare look at this as some reflection of you or some sign of failure. The fact is, I didn't really want to fully retire."

That was news to Riley. "Why didn't you say something?"

"Because you buying me out was what we'd agreed to when you came to work for me after college. You'd been working toward it for years, and when we came up with that plan, the idea was that I'd retire, and John and I would go take some of those trips we always talked about. When he died, you picked up all the slack, while I grieved. You'd made it yours, and you wanted so much to spread your wings, so it didn't seem fair to go back on my word. And I thought I'd go ahead and make the most of it. To a certain extent I have. I've loved the work I've done with Norah and the coalition, helping breathe life back into this town. But truthfully, I am so bored with retirement, I can't even tell you. You'd be doing me a favor for my sanity by letting me come back."

"Letting you? Please, Molly, it's still your business. And God, I would love to have you come back as a full partner. I'm beyond grateful that you're willing."

"Good. I'll talk to Vivian, get the paperwork drawn up."

"We should probably go over the books." A necessary but painful evil.

"That can wait a bit. Insurance and distributors first."

The sound of a car door slamming pulled their attention to the door.

"Looks like we've got more company." Liam waved in Norah when she appeared at the kitchen door.

As Norah stepped inside, dressed with her usual big city flair, Riley looked down at the clothes she'd robbed from Liam's closet. She hadn't expected to be seeing anyone but family until she had a chance to go by her own place to change.

"Sorry it's so early." Norah held up a covered dish. "Spicy cheese grits. I'd hoped to get here in time for your breakfast. Consider me the first wave of food. The Casserole Patrol is already active and cooking. I saw Miss Maudie Bell at church early, so I expect you'll have a flood after the late service."

"Nobody died or had a baby. Why has the Casserole Patrol been activated?" Riley wanted to know.

Norah set the dish on the counter and came to squeeze Riley's shoulder. "Because cooking is what we can do to show we care about you. You shouldn't have to cook a thing for at least two weeks."

Riley's throat went tight. "Thanks."

"Pour yourself a cup of coffee and join us," Molly invited.

At home, Norah hit up the coffee pot. "I'm actually here for another reason. Y'all are going for exclusivity contracts for Peyton Consolidated. Gerald is going to be here at the end of the week to check the progress on his latest baby, so you've got the perfect shot to hit him up. I've already penciled you into the schedule for Friday."

"Friday?" Riley's heart bucked. "But with all the…I couldn't possibly…I don't—"

Molly laid a hand over hers, stemming the babble. "Together, remember."

"You can and you will. Because you have me to help you tailor everything to hit all of Gerald's soft spots. I landed contracts with Peyton

Consolidated for the entire town. This will be cake."

Together.

Riley took a breath. "Okay, when do we start?"

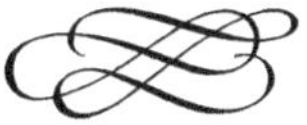

NORAH CLAPPED HER HANDS together. "What a fabulous idea!" She whipped out one of her ever-present notebooks and began scribbling things down, with a backdrop of hammering, the whine of saws, the thunk of nail guns. "I will make this happen. How quickly do you think the space will be ready?"

Liam surveyed the six men rounded up for the job, based on recommendations from both Mitch and Tyler Edison at the hardware store. All were fairly seasoned and had been out of steady local work for some time, due to the economy. This job would be a good trial run. If any of them worked out, it'd be a great start to forming his own crew.

"Obviously, our focus is on getting the main pharmacy back to normal. But given the group we've got out there right now, I think that's going to happen within a week. The goal is to get all the flooring installed and vacuumed today. I'm planning on staining and sealing tomorrow. The longest part there will be waiting on the stain and sealant on the new floors to dry. Three days for that. Mitch and I already finalized the designs, so I can get the rest started while that's going on. So…maybe two weeks?"

"Good. Keep me posted on timeline. I'll handle my end. I want to talk to Riley about setting up an open house to show off the new space anyway, and that would be a great means of launching this as well."

"You really think you can pull it together that fast?"

Norah gave him a pitying look. "Please. Have you met me?"

Liam laughed. "Fair point. I want you to keep this under your hat, at least until we're finished. I want to surprise Riley."

Norah crossed her heart. "Discretion is my middle name." She checked her watch. "With that in mind, I'm going to get out of here. Your lady fair will probably be finishing her presentation soon, and I want to be back to talk to Gerald when it's through."

"How did she look?" Liam asked.

"Like a million bucks. Maybe a little bit nervous, but she'd already gotten off on a tangent about essential oils when she busted Gerald's headache in thirty seconds, so I think she's going to be fine. She nailed all the practice runs of the presentation. I'm betting a celebration will be in order later."

"Good. She needs a win in her column. It's been a rough summer for her."

"Not all bad." Norah stroked a hand down his arm. "She got you."

"True enough." But Liam wasn't sure Riley was as comfortable with that as he was.

"I'll be in touch. Bye, Molly!" She sent a sunny wave to his mother, who perched on a stool behind the counter.

As the door jangled, Molly pinned him with a Look. "You're up to something."

"I am." He was, in fact, up to several some-things. "Working on a surprise for Riley."

"Is this the kind of surprise that's going to make her angry? Because that didn't work out well for you before."

"No. It was her idea, actually. I'm just bringing it to fruition. And in keeping with that, I need to go."

"You're leaving in the middle of all this work?"

"Gotta pick up more supplies at the hard-ware store. I've had a few things on special or-der, and Tyler texted earlier to say they were in."

She smiled at him. "You like it. Building things."

"I like seeing the possibilities and maximizing potential. And yeah, it's good seeing solid results of the work. Having a real finished product that will last."

"It suits you. And, with that in mind, perhaps it's time to start talking about turning the garage into a proper wood shop for you. Unless you plan to get your own place sooner rather than later."

Liam thought about the other plans kicking around in his brain. "That depends."

"Well, I'm not trying to rush you out. You know I love having you home. But if your plans change, I completely understand."

She knew. She was standing there looking all innocent and casual, but she knew. Who knew how. Her Mom-dar put military intelligence to shame. Time for a tactical retreat.

"There's plenty of other stuff to worry about for now. You okay holding down the fort until I get back?"

"You go ahead. I've got this."

As the weather was gorgeous and unseasonably cool for this close to August, Liam rolled the windows down on his truck and took the long way, weaving through the shady streets of town. The parking lot at Waldrop Park was half full as he drove by. On impulse, he swung into the lot and got out to inspect the new fence. He'd been on deck to help assemble it, but with everything that had happened, he hadn't been able to make it to the work day.

Norah had wanted whitewashed pickets, but Mitch convinced her to go with a better quality stain and sealant. The final result wrapped the perimeter of the property. Liam walked the length of it, reading names of the individuals and businesses that had donated. Children's laughter split the air and drew his attention to the playground proper.

A trio of boys pounded across the new bridge.

"Get to higher ground! The dragon's almost on us!"

The one bringing up the rear dove off the side with a fairly impressive roll, coming up to face his imaginary foe with a sword branch in his hand.

Liam grinned, thinking of his brothers. They'd fought their fair share of dragons back in the day.

The banks of swings were full. Young mothers pushed toddlers and chatted. At the other end, a dark-haired little girl kicked her legs hard, her pink bow slipping down her curls as she rose higher. He remembered Riley at that age and Wynne, though neither of them would've been caught dead wearing a bow. They usually had scraped knees and grass stains on their clothes, so determined to keep up with the boys.

"Again!" At one of the lower slides, a little boy, maybe three years old, ran from the foot of the slide to the ladder. His dad lifted him up and set him at the top, where he slid into the arms of his waiting mother with a delighted giggle. Then he raced around to do it all over again. The parents looked at each other with a shared smile that shot a sharp pang of yearning through Liam's chest.

He wanted that. Wanted that foundation of family, that new beginning. For all the fumbling he'd done in his first months back, he was ready for the next chapter of his life. He'd been heading there the moment he got involved with Riley.

"You look like you're thinking deep thoughts."

Liam jolted, wondering how long Autumn had been standing there. "I suppose I am. What are you doing here?"

She held up a book. "Just got off work and thought I'd enjoy the pretty day by reading in the park. What's your excuse? I know you're doing floors at the pharmacy today."

"Detour on my way to the hardware store."

"Odd place to detour to for you. What's on your mind?"

"Do you think I'm impulsive?"

"No. You're one of the most decisive people I know. You don't make decisions without considering all the angles. That being said, you don't lollygag around once you've made up your mind. You're a man of action."

"I think that's the problem. I'm ready to act on something, and I'm not sure it's the smart thing to do."

"With the exception of a few select adventures back in high school, I can't ever recall you doing anything stupid."

Because he needed something to do with his hands, Liam gripped the top of the fence. "Well, it's less that what I want is stupid and more that I'm not sure how it would be received, at this point."

"Okay let's just drop the oblique speak. Riley loves you."

He huffed out a laugh. "I know. But even so, I'm not entirely sure we're on the same page."

"And you think what you want is rushing things."

"My gut says no. More practical people would say yes."

"Screw practicality."

Liam arched a brow at her vehemence.

"I mean it. Nobody's in this relationship but the two of you and nobody else's timeline applies. Love isn't supposed to be *practical.* You love her; she loves you. Period. End of story. And if you want to do something that's an expression of that, I say go for it."

Autumn Buchanan, always a champion of love.

"I'd need some help to pull it off."

"Lay it on me."

She was all but dancing by the time he finished explaining what he wanted to do. "Oh my God, Liam! That's just—"

Smiling, he waved his hands in a tone-it-down motion. "I'm glad you approve."

"I approve this so hard, I just can't even." She did some kind of celebratory booty shake, ending with a double fist pump.

"So you'll help?"

Autumn swatted his arm. "Of course, I'll help. I'll even offer a few suggestions for how you can take an already awesome concept and elevate it to stupendous."

"I'm open to suggestions." He pointed a finger at her. "But you tell no one. I don't want one whiff of this getting back to Riley."

She offered a smart salute and clicked her heels together. "You can count on me, sir!"

"Here's to Peyton Consolidated. May they be the first of many lucrative contracts. Well done, Riley." Molly tapped her glass to Riley's and grinned.

"Couldn't have done it without your help and Norah's. I don't know how she does it, getting up in front of people and talking all the time. Give me one-on-one any day." Riley sipped the champagne. *Now this is a celebration.*

The white tablecloths and fine china of Tosca were a far cry from the emergency bar of Toblerone at the beginning of the summer. And, at last, she wasn't alone. Liam and Molly sat on either side of her, and Sharilyn and Matthew McSweeney rounded out the party. Riley wasn't quite sure how to feel about that, but she was feeling far too mellow and pleased about her success with Gerald Peyton to let it spoil the evening.

"I have a toast, too." Riley lifted her glass to Liam. "Here's to finished floors and my own personal Superman, who's busting his chops getting things back to normal."

"Hear, hear!"

Liam tapped his glass to hers and leaned in for a follow-up kiss.

"While we're in a celebrating mood, I've got something else to toast." Across the table, Matthew took Sharilyn's hand.

Riley tensed. *Oh God, not again.*

Her mother glanced up at him, then across the table. Riley didn't miss the quick flash of hurt.

Damn it. She liked Matthew. She really did. But she wasn't ready for her mother to dive headlong into another too serious, too soon relationship.

Beneath the table, Liam curled his fingers around hers and squeezed.

"Back in the beginning of July, this sweet lady here came to me with the idea for the Good Food For Good Neighbors program, as a way the store could give back to the community and help those in need."

Riley blinked. She'd heard about the program, of course. But being wrapped up in her own troubles, she'd given no thought to it past the round up donations she'd made doing her grocery shopping since then. It'd been her mom's idea? She thought back to that family dinner and to Tara Honeycutt. Clearly, she hadn't been the only one to feel a need to take action.

"I'm pleased to report the program has been a raging success, and we've already been able to help fifty families."

Fifty families. So much good. Pride swelled in Riley's chest. "That's amazing, Mom. Truly."

"It was an inspired idea." Molly lifted her glass.

Sharilyn's cheeks pinked. "I just wanted to do something to give back. So many people helped me when I needed it. It's my turn to help now."

"Well, I'm glad you said that, Shari, because we're getting more and more applicants every day, and somebody has to go through and determine eligibility. I want to promote you to full-time head of the program, along with a commensurate raise in pay to go along with the responsibility."

Sharilyn gaped at him. "Are you serious?"

"I told you we had something else to celebrate. To your success." Matthew clinked her glass with his.

Riley raised her glass. "Congratulations. You've earned it."

As additional congratulations swept the table, she thought back to that quick flash of hurt and felt the sandpaper rasp of guilt along her conscience. Her mom didn't deserve that knee-jerk response of dread. She'd well and truly lived up to her promise and turned over a new leaf.

Riley continued to mull it over as their meal was served and conversation flowed around her. And she watched Matthew and Sharilyn, noting the casual way they swapped half their entrees for a surf and turf, seeing the attentive way he leaned toward her when she spoke, and a half dozen other tiny intimacies that said more than words ever could. Sharilyn herself smiled often, but it was a different smile than Riley was used to seeing when she was with a beau—and Matthew was most definitely a beau. She seemed...relaxed and confident. No trace of that sense of trying too hard, as if by will alone she could make him into what she wanted, what she needed. Because maybe Matthew McSweeney *was* what she needed.

When Sharilyn excused herself to go to the ladies' room, Riley rose too. "I'll go with you."

The restroom, a fancy one with a little sitting room, was blessedly empty. She waited until her mom was washing her hands, meeting Sharilyn's soft brown eyes in the vanity mirror. "I owe you an apology."

"For what, baby?"

"For being so hard on you. For always expecting the worst and not really giving you a chance. You're not me, and I shouldn't expect you to behave like me. What you've done is wonderful. And I just wanted to say that I'm really, really proud of you. You've worked so hard since you came home, and it's finally paying off."

"I owe it to you."

"Me?"

Sharilyn dried her hands and turned to face her. "You finally made me stand on my own two feet. You've been doing that yourself since you were a little thing. Even before your daddy died. Always so independent. Randy used to say you were his little carbon copy, and in a lot of ways you are. He took care of me. After he was gone, you stepped into that role far too early. I shouldn't have let you do it. But I've never been as strong as you."

"Mom—"

"No, let me finish. I'm grateful you were strong, that you have that much of your father in you. It helped. It helped that you're so like him. Because as long as you took care of me, it was a little like having a piece of him back." She stroked Riley's hair back.

Riley swallowed past the tightness in her throat.

"I let that go on way too long. I'm under no delusions about where we'd have ended up without you. But I'm glad you finally broke the pattern and made me break it, too."

It hadn't been for her mother to break. Riley had played her father's role for far too long, trying to take over and do everything. Enabling and perpetuating the cycle they'd been stuck in. And that hadn't been what Sharilyn needed.

"I think, maybe, it's helped me stop looking for your daddy in other men. Randy was one of a kind. I was so, so lucky to have found him.

But it feels *good* to take care of myself. Good to contribute to something. So, thank you."

"Seems like Matthew's helped with that, too," Riley conceded.

"He has. That man has the patience of Job and a heart bigger than the ocean. He understands where I came from and seems to know exactly how to support me without taking over. Your daddy never had the patience for that, God love him."

That was what Sharilyn had needed.

Liam instinctively understood that kind of support. He was strong enough to help, strong enough to stand back. And maybe it was exactly what Riley needed, too.

As if she knew where Riley's thoughts had turned, Sharilyn linked her arm through Riley's. "We Gower women seem to be doing pretty well for ourselves in the man department lately.

"You two seem good together."

"He's good for me. And I hope I'm good for him. But we're taking things slow." Sharilyn dimpled. "A novel concept for me."

"Slow is good."

"It can be. But there's nothing wrong with fast either. Not when it's right." She shot Riley a meaningful look.

"Don't get ahead of yourself, Mom. Liam and I are fine exactly as we are."

"If I were you, I'd grab on to that man with both hands and never let go."

"For once, Mom, I'm inclined to agree with you."

"He's got a very nice behind for grabbing."

"Mom!" Riley laughed.

"No harm in appreciating God's artwork, honey. Now come on I want to get some tiramisu."

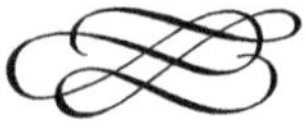

CHAPTER 20

"I DON'T UNDERSTAND WHY I have to wear a blindfold." Riley started to reach up and remove it, but Liam stopped her.

"You have to wear a blindfold because it's a surprise."

"Nobody else is wearing a blindfold."

"It's not a surprise for *them*. Now come on." He took both her hands and led her through the doors into the newly renovated pharmacy.

Molly, Jessie, and Ruby followed them inside, trailed by Norah and Mitch, who'd joined the back of the group without Riley noticing. They'd all already seen it when the group convened late the night before to set all the displays and stock back up, so they kept silent as ordered. Riley had been kept out of the loop, under the impression that the floors needed a couple of days longer to cure than they really did.

Liam led her down the center aisle, to the front counter, then turned her to face the finished space. "Ready?"

"So ready."

Strangely nervous, he slid the bandanna off.

Other than a sharp intake of breath, Riley didn't make a sound. She scanned the completely stocked aisles, the reclaimed wood floors, the freshly painted walls with their new wainscoting, past the new shelving displaying her entire collection of antique pharmacy memorabilia, all the way up to the ceiling, which had not only been repaired, but had been covered in vintage tin. The whole place fit neatly in with Norah's historic restoration concept, the building having been dialed back as much as possible to the original early 20th century architecture from the Woolworth's it had once been.

"It's finished." Riley's voice was barely audible.

For a moment, Liam wondered if he and his mother had miscalculated, if Riley wanted to do that part herself. But she turned into his arms and buried her face against his chest, squeezing tight.

"It's beautiful." Her eyes were suspiciously glassy as she looked up.

Liam felt a trace of panic. "No crying." She'd done far too much of that this summer.

Riley laughed a little "They're happy tears." She rose to her toes and kissed him. "Thank you."

"Hey, I helped too," Mitch protested.

"Get your own woman, Campbell."

"I keep telling him he should do that," Norah said.

Mitch clapped a hand to his heart. "The good ones keep getting snapped up."

Riley kissed Mitch's cheek. "You will find someone when you're least expecting it. Autumn swears that's how this works."

Liam snorted. "Give her the least bit of encouragement and she'll start matchmaking you."

Riley arched a brow. "Oh, you mean unlike all the female members of *your* family?"

He tucked an arm around her. "I'd have gotten here on my own eventually." Sensing his mother was about to speak, Liam pegged her with a look. "Not one word."

Molly pressed her lips together, but he could see the laughter in her eyes.

"Now come see the rest." He pulled Riley over to the wide, cased opening into what had been the storage room and turned on the light. The new displays lit—carousels, shelving, freestanding units that could be converted to shelves or hanging space, as needed. All were currently empty.

"You built my artisan marketplace!" She ran her hand along the smooth wood of a tall unit serving as a partial room divider. "Oh, it's wonderful! Where's my actual storeroom now?"

"Back here." Liam opened the double doors. "You've got stainless steel racks around the perimeter. It's a smaller space than you had before, but it's actually organized. With all the junk that was in here tossed, you don't actually need more than this. Which left plenty of room to maximize your consignment space out here."

"Do you think we can find enough people to use all this?" Riley asked.

"Already on it." Norah stepped forward. "I've put together a list of artisans who are interested in leasing booth space from you, along with a couple of example contracts for how the terms can be laid out. All you need do is pick your poison and call them, and you'll have the whole place full up by the open house. Oh, and the draft marketing plan is also in the folder."

Riley accepted the folder and stared at her. "You never just sit on things, do you?"

Norah grinned. "Now, where would be the fun in that?"

"Thank you."

"You're welcome. Although, I should warn you, it's not entirely altruistic on my part. I've got this whole big Master Plan to highlight local artisans and bring more out-of-towners to Wishful for our rural tourism campaign. This is just a cog in that whole big machine."

Mitch wrapped an arm around Norah and covered her mouth. "Do *not* let her get started on her Master Plan. We'll be here all night. She's secretly planning on taking over the world."

Norah tugged his hand away. "Shhh. It's not a secret if you *tell people.*"

"C'mon, General Burke." Mitch tugged her toward the door. "We're due at Grammy's for peach pie."

"I should be getting on, too," Jessie said. "There's a new episode of *Game of Thrones* and a pint of Ben and Jerry's with my name on it."

Everyone made their excuses and headed for the door.

"See you at the open house!" Norah called. "Liam, I'll be in touch about the rest of my plans."

And then they were alone. Alone was good. They hadn't had much opportunity for that recently, and he hoped to sweet talk her into creative expression of her gratitude back at her place. But there were a few more things to show her here first.

Riley turned another circle. "I just can't get over how good it looks. All the little historic touches are wonderful! But how on earth did you get this done on the original budget?"

"Also part of Norah's Master Plan is the historic restoration of downtown. Mom's into that, too, so she upped the budget. That, combined with the insurance payout, made this more than possible. This was, essentially, my audition. Norah pitched me as the contractor for the job, and the City Council accepted."

"Liam, that's amazing!"

Her obvious pride in what he'd accomplished had something warm sliding through him.

"There are a few more things I want to show you. C'mon." He led her behind the counter. "I've added electronic locks to the doors. So if you're here at night by yourself and realize you've forgotten to lock the doors, you can do it from the computer here at the counter or back in the office, wherever you're working." He demonstrated and heard the *whine snick* of the lock out front. "And you can unlock it from here, too. The security system has been updated, so it can be set not only to the typical away, but also to stay. If you're here by yourself after hours, you can set the alarm to stay, and it'll be armed, but the motion sensors inside will be off while you're working. If somebody messes with any of the doors or windows, the alarm will trigger and the call will go out automatically. That way if you can't get to the panic button for some reason, the alarm still sounds. And unlike the panic button, it's actually audible and *loud,* so it would hopefully deter anyone from actually coming on inside."

"That's good. Although, I expect it'll be a long time before I actually stick around to use it." Her eyes flickered to the door of the office.

"Nothing wrong with that. But maybe this will help." He opened the door and tugged her inside.

Riley's mouth fell open. "Holy crap. You gutted it."

"Not completely, but close. You've got a built-in desk here and custom cabinetry throughout."

"Where did you move the safes?"

"I didn't. Just covered them up." Liam opened the cabinet doors masking both.

"It's beautiful. And had to be so much extra work on top of everything else you did."

Liam jerked a shoulder. He hadn't gotten more than nine hours of sleep over the past three days. Totally worth it. "I wanted to do whatever I could to keep it from reminding you of bad memories when you had to come in here."

She turned another slow circle. "I keep saying thank you but that doesn't seem like enough."

"Well, if you're looking for other ways to show your appreciation, I have a few ideas."

Her eyes took on a wicked gleam. "So do I." She shut the office door and turned to the computer terminal. A few mouse clicks and she'd relocked the front door of the pharmacy, setting the alarm as he'd showed her.

Liam arched a brow. "I'm thinking your ideas just got more interesting than mine."

"Well, it was a good notion to change what it looks like in here so that I don't have all the visual cues. But it seems like we should take it one step further and just replace those memories with new ones entirely." She stripped off her shirt and tossed it to the side, revealing a silky bra of midnight blue lace. "I'd much rather not want to walk in here because it gets me all hot and bothered thinking of you."

The shorts dropped next, and Liam's mouth went dry as he saw the matching panties.

"What do you say, Boy Scout?"

What kind of man would he be if he didn't answer such a call?

Sliding his hands around her generous hips, he bent his head. "I live to serve."

THE PHARMACY open house was in full swing. Displays were moved again, this time to make room for the band of pickers and fiddlers, who currently rocked out "The Battle of New Orleans" as patrons circulated. Tables of food and drink were set up near the front counter, heavily weighed down with fresh watermelon, pimento cheese sandwiches, sausage balls, pinwheels, and other classic Southern party food. Wearing a swingy, A-line sundress in a bold cherry print, Riley was enjoying every minute.

The place was hopping. Part of that was due strictly to word-of-mouth and part to the front page article run in this morning's newspaper. And part, her cynical side reminded her, was probably due to the free food. But the important thing was that people were here. Patrons she knew had moved over to Walgreens were back in her store. That didn't guarantee they'd be moving their business back, but it was a good start. And absolutely everyone loved the Artisan Market. Zach Warren was snapping photos to document the event, and Norah's intern, Cecily Dixon was chatting folks up, getting quotes for the town blog.

Ginny Honeycutt bounced up, a broad grin stretching across her cheeks. "Hi, Ms. Riley!"

"Hey there, sweetie. Where's your sister?"

Tara brought up the rear, balancing two paper plates. "We just wanted to thank you again for recommending that tea tree oil. It worked wonders."

The little girl beamed. "No more creepy feet!" And she bounced off again to join some friends.

Tara shook her head. "Someday we'll learn about appropriate things to say in public."

Riley laughed. "Honey, if you could hear some of the things people tell me in here. That was nothing. How's your booth doing?"

"Already half sold out of stock. I can't believe my jewelry's been so popular!"

Riley tapped at the earrings she wore and grinned. "I can."

"The market was a great idea."

"I'm just the idea woman. Liam's the one who made it happen."

"Well, thanks to you both. I'd best go keep track to make sure Austin doesn't eat you out of house and home."

As Tara headed off, the band transitioned into a waltz. Across the room, Howard Tolleson began to circle his wife, Winnie, his cane hooked on the crook of his arm, his wrinkled cheek pressed to the top of her cloud of snowy hair.

With a happy sigh, Autumn linked her arm

through Riley's. "They are the cutest thing ever."

"True thing." The sight of them made her heart go gooey.

"I want that someday."

"Don't we all?" With a smile, Riley saw Matthew pull her mother into a dance, too.

"Well, these days, you're closer to it than I am. Where is your other half, anyway?"

"I don't know. Actually, now that I think about it, I haven't seen him in a while." Riley craned her neck, scanning the crowd for Liam. At his height, he was generally easy to spot, but she didn't see him anywhere. "I don't see Judd or Mitch either. Maybe somebody should go check upstairs to see if they snuck away for a six pack."

Autumn tugged at her elbow. "I don't think he snuck away for a six pack."

Riley followed her gaze to the front door, where Liam stood decked out in his dress blues. "Oh my."

Tall, straight, and gorgeously built, he commandeered the attention of everyone in the room as he made his way through, shaking hands, answering questions. And that smile…

Autumn tapped Riley's chin. "Pick your jaw up, honey, you're drooling."

"Well, my God, he's totally worth it." He looked even better than she remembered from the one time she'd actually seen him in dress blues.

"Can't argue that."

He finally reached them, grinning from ear to ear.

"To what do I owe the glorious eye candy?" Riley asked.

Liam removed his hat and sketched a bow. "You, my lady, made a request for sandy beaches and palm fans, complete with a heroic, movie-worthy exit. I'm here to deliver. So start saying your goodbyes. We've got a plane to catch in—" He checked his watch "—three hours, and we've got to get to Jackson."

Riley gaped at him. "You're serious?"

"As a heart attack. Seven full days of sun and tropical breezes."

Vacation lust hit her square in the chest, followed immediately by doubts. "But I can't go anywhere. We just got the pharmacy back open, and I'm not even packed."

"Mom's got the pharmacy, and sure you are. Autumn packed for you."

Riley turned to look at her friend.

"It's true. I did. I was all up in your closet, double-oh-seven style." Autumn mimed sneaking like a spy.

"When?"

"I have a key. It's not like it was *hard.* Liam's got the bag in his car."

"But how do I even know you got everything?"

"I have a list." Liam pulled a folded paper from a pocket.

Riley waved a hand. "Of course, you do."

"Boy Scout. Always prepared." He began to read down the list. "Bikini."

Autumn nodded. "Check."

"Shorts."

"For both beach and hiking, check."

Riley felt like she was watching a tennis match as her gaze bounced from one to the other during the exchange.

"Shirts."

"Check."

"Couple of dresses."

"Check."

"Underwear for a week."

Riley immediately sent Autumn a warning glare. She could just imagine what her friend had deemed the thing to pack on a tropical vacation with Liam. She wouldn't put it past her to see that Riley went commando the whole week. Or wore nothing but skimpy lingerie. With Autumn it could go either way.

Autumn didn't bother to hide her grin. "Check."

"Toiletries."

"Double check. I probably had a better list than you did for that."

"True thing. Passport."

"Check."

"You actually found my passport? *I* didn't even remember where I put it."

"Took a while. I thought for sure you'd cop to the fact that your drawers had been rifled."

"Somebody made sure I didn't notice." It hadn't occurred to Riley that Liam had been trying to distract her on purpose.

He just winked at her, unrepentant, before turning back to the list.

"Shoes?"

"Tennies, two pair of sandals, and some really excellent heels. Check."

"Chargers for various devices."

"Check."

"Engagement ring."

Riley's head snapped toward Liam—

"No, that was for you to pack."

—then back to Autumn—

"Oh right."

—and back to Liam.

He reached into his pocket. Pulled out a box. "Check."

Riley couldn't breathe.

Liam started to slip the box back into his pocket, then shook his head. "On second thought, you should probably hang on to this, for a year or sixty. Gotta give the Tollesons a run for their money." He flipped it open, took out the diamond solitaire inside.

"Liam," she croaked.

"Not done yet. You're one of the strongest, most independent, most stubborn women I've ever had the privilege to know. I know you're not looking for somebody to come rescue you or expecting the fairy tale ending, and somewhere in there you stopped believing in those things. But I want to give them to you, on whatever terms you want. And if that means you want your own sword and horse, by damn, we'll make it happen. You told me months ago that I should build my own place, and you were absolutely right. But you can't build something without a good, solid foundation. You're mine. So—" He sank down to one knee "— how 'bout it, Riley Marie. Are you up for an adventure?"

Any minute now, her knees were going to buckle and she was just going to keel over in shock.

Autumn elbowed her. "Breathe."

Riley sucked in a breath. Her head was spinning like a top and her heart was about to pound right out of her chest. She reached out to frame his face. "The answer's been yes since I was fifteen."

Liam grinned. "And here I thought I was moving fast." He slid the ring on her finger and pulled her in for a long, slow kiss, while the room erupted in cheers and applause.

The band launched into a snappy rendition of "Here Comes The Bride" and the party *really* got started as Riley and Liam were pulled away for a long string of hugs, kisses, and congratulations from everyone present. It made her delirious and dizzy, until her fiancé —*her fiancé!*—pried her away from Babette Wofford, who already had ideas about the dress. "Okay, now seriously, we have a plane to catch."

"Just let me get my purse."

"Autumn will bring it."

"I can carry my own purse."

"This last part works better if you don't."

"What last part?" She burst into delighted laughter as he lifted her into his arms. "*An Officer and a Gentleman?*"

"You did make a request."

Riley plucked the hat off his head and perched it on her own. "Think you can kiss me and walk out the door without running into it?"

"I'm a Marine. I can do anything."

And he proved it as he carried her across the threshold to start their own happily ever after.

Choose Your Next Romance!

Who do you want to see next in Wishful?

Are you just *dying* to see whether Autumn finally gets up the nerve to change things with Judd? *Make You Feel My Love,* Book 1 in my light romantic suspense spin-off Wishing For A Hero series, is friends-to-lovers crack. Seriously, you're gonna love it. It's my favorite epilogue I've ever written. This series is the same Wishful you know and love, with a little bit more of an edge.

Do you want to know all about the guy who broke Tyler's heart? Then you'll want to nab Book 3, *Be Careful, It's My Heart.* This second chance romance capitalizes on my absolute love of the movie *White Christmas,* as some of our favorite Wishful citizens band together to save the old Madrigal theater by putting on a community theater production of the story. Piper pulls some shenanigans in the name of matchmaking that you won't want to miss!

Can't make up your mind? Keep turning the pages for previews of them both!

- *Those Sweet Words* (Pru and Flynn)
- *Stay A Little Longer* (Athena and Logan)
- *Bring It On Home* (Maggie and Porter)

RESCUE MY HEART SERIES
SMALL TOWN MILITARY ROMANCE

- *Baby It's Cold Outside* (Ivy and Harrison)
- *What I Like About You* (Laurel and Sebastian)
- *Bad Case of Loving You* (Paisley and Ty prequel)
- *Made For Loving You* (Paisley and Ty)

MEN OF THE MISFIT INN
SMALL TOWN SOUTHERN ROMANCE

- *Let It Be Me* (Emerson and Caleb)
- *Our Kind of Love* (Abbey and Kyle)

WISHFUL SERIES

SMALL TOWN SOUTHERN ROMANCE

- *Once Upon A Coffee* (Avery and Dillon)
- *To Get Me To You* (Cam and Norah)
- *Know Me Well* (Liam and Riley)
- *Be Careful, It's My Heart* (Brody and Tyler)
- *Just For This Moment* (Myles and Piper)
- *Wish I Might* (Reed and Cecily)
- *Turn My World Around* (Tucker and Corinne)
- *Dance Me A Dream* (Jace and Tara)
- *See You Again* (Trey and Sandy)
- *The Christmas Fountain* (Chad and Mary Alice)
- *You Were Meant For Me* (Mitch and Tess)
- *A Lot Like Christmas* (Ryan and Hannah)
- *Dancing Away With My Heart* (Zach and Lexi)

WISHING FOR A HERO SERIES (A WISHFUL SPINOFF SERIES)
SMALL TOWN ROMANTIC SUSPENSE

- *Make You Feel My Love* (Judd and Autumn)
- *Watch Over Me* (Nash and Rowan)
- *Can't Take My Eyes Off You* (Ethan and Miranda)
- *Burn For You* (Sean and Delaney)

MEET CUTE ROMANCE
SMALL TOWN SHORT ROMANCE

- *Once Upon A Snow Day*
- *Once Upon A New Year's Eve*
- *Once Upon An Heirloom*
- *Once Upon A Coffee*
- *Once Upon A Campfire*
- *Once Upon A Rescue*

SUMMER CAMP
CONTEMPORARY ROMANCE

- *Once Upon A Campfire*
- *Second Chance Summer*

ACKNOWLEDGMENTS

THIS BOOK WOULD not have been possible without the unwavering support of my critique partners/editors, Susan Bischoff and Jessica Fritsche; my extremely tolerant husband; or the unflagging cheerleading of my girls of The Pie Society.

I love you all!

Kait is a Mississippi native, who often swears like a sailor, calls everyone sugar, honey, or darlin', and can wield a bless your heart like a saber or a Snuggie, depending on requirements.

You can find more information on this

RITA ® Award-winning author and her books on her website http://kaitnolan.com. While you're there, sign up for her newsletter so you don't miss out on news about new releases!